FAITH MARTIN has been writing for nearly thirty years, under four different pen names, and has published over fifty novels. She began writing romantic thrillers as Maxine Barry, but quickly turned to crime! As Joyce Cato she wrote classic-style whodunits, since she's always admired the golden-age crime novelists. But it was when she created her fictional DI Hillary Greene, and began writing under the name of Faith Martin, that she finally began to become more widely known. Her latest literary characters WPC Trudy Loveday, and city coroner Dr Clement Ryder, take readers back to the 1960s, and the city of Oxford. Having lived within a few miles of the city's dreaming spires for all her life (she worked for six years as a secretary at Somerville College), both the city and the countryside/wildlife often feature in her novels. Although she has never lived on a narrowboat (unlike DI Hillary Greene!) the Oxford canal, the river Cherwell, and the flora and fauna of a farming landscape have always played a big part in her life – and often sneak their way onto the pages of her books.

Also by Faith Martin

A Fatal Obsession
A Fatal Mistake
A Fatal Flaw

A Fatal Secret

FAITH MARTIN

HQ
An imprint of HarperCollins*Publishers* Ltd
1 London Bridge Street
London SE1 9GF

This paperback edition 2019

First published in Great Britain by
HQ, an imprint of HarperCollins*Publishers* Ltd 2019

ISBN: 9780008348670

MIX
Paper from
responsible sources
FSC **FSC® C007454**
www.fsc.org

This book is produced from independently certified FSC™ paper to ensure responsible forest management.

For more information visit: www.harpercollins.co.uk/green

Printed and bound in Great Britain by
CPI Group (UK) Ltd, Melksham, SN12 6TR

For my sister Marion, with many thanks for helping me out with the research!

Prologue

It was a lovely Saturday morning, and less than three miles away as the crow flies from the city of dreaming spires, someone was contemplating how ironical it was that it should be April Fool's Day.

The daffodils were just beginning to bud in the small woods surrounding Briar's Hall. Birds were busy building their nests, and a weak and watery sun was promising that spring really was on its way.

But the person leaning against a still-bare ash tree, moodily observing the fine Georgian building below, cared little for the promise of bluebells to come.

That person was thinking of only one thing: death, and how best to bring it about.

Perhaps, not surprisingly, that person was feeling not at all happy. Not only was death on its own something that you would never consider in detail unless given absolutely no choice, contemplating cold-blooded murder was even more unpleasant.

Not least, of course, because if you were caught at it, you'd be hanged. Which was terrifying.

1

And yet death – and murder – there would have to be. The person in the woods could see no other way out.

Which instilled in that person's heart yet another, stronger emotion. Rage.

It was simply not fair!

But then, as the person in the woods had already learned very well indeed, life had no interest in being fair.

A woodpecker struck up its rat-a-tat-tat drumming on an old dead horse chestnut tree deeper in the woods, its resonance vibrating through the air. But the human occupant of the wood barely noticed it.

Tomorrow, the silent watcher in the woods thought, *would be a good day for it.* With so much happening, there was bound to be confusion, which would almost certainly provide the best opportunity for action.

Yes. Tomorrow someone would have to die.

2

Chapter 1

Easter Sunday morning saw probationary WPC Trudy Loveday going in to work as usual.

DI Jennings, true to form, saw no reason why she should be exempt from working through the holiday. Even though, before the week was out, she was due to attend a sumptuous lunch at the very swanky Randolph Hotel, where she would be the 'star' guest and feted as something of a heroine by members of the local press – as well as a certain Earl of the realm.

After being angry with her for initially keeping the serious-ness of the event from them, her parents were now, naturally enough, as proud as punch about it all. But whilst they were eagerly looking forward to the event, Trudy herself was not so sanguine.

Although it was true that some months ago she *had* tackled and arrested a murder suspect all on her own, at the same time preventing the suspect from murdering the son of the Earl, she did not feel particularly heroic. Worse still, when the news had broken that the Earl intended to set up the dinner and have her presented with a formal letter of gratitude in front of the city's press and various high-up members of the constabulary, she'd been ragged about it constantly by her peers.

3

And to no one's surprise (least of all hers!), her immediate superior had made it very plain what he thought about it all. Which was not much. In Inspector Jennings' opinion, the only woman police officer under his command was in danger of getting above herself. And it was his job to make sure her head was not allowed to swell! But no amount of protestations on her part that she had known nothing about it had convinced him that she wasn't secretly thrilled with the attention.

So it was that she found herself at work during the Easter break, which in truth she didn't really mind much at all. After all, others had to do it and lowly probationary constables (as the inspector had told her with a hard gleam in his eye) were very low down the pecking order when it came to being given prime time off.

Even so, it was a skeleton staff in the police station that morning, as the city's many bells rang out for Easter. Not that Trudy minded that. At least DI Jennings wasn't there to keep on giving her sharp, annoyed looks, and Sergeant O'Grady, as the senior officer present, was in a mellow mood. Some kind soul had brought in a huge chocolate Easter egg, which was very quickly being consumed by the few officers minding the store and, all in all, a holiday air prevailed.

Even the telephones were mostly silent, as if the city's thieves and lawbreakers, too, were all sitting at home, presumably eating chocolate eggs of their own. But at just gone three-thirty, the phone rang, and from the look on Sergeant O'Grady's face, it was clear that their quiet day had just been cancelled.

A slightly chubby man, with a big quiff of sandy-coloured hair and pale-blue eyes, he began scribbling furiously, then glanced up at the station clock. 'Right. Yes, it's a little early maybe to fear the worst just yet, but it doesn't sound good. And the parents are sure he wouldn't miss his dinner? Oh, right, I see. And the address is…' He scribbled quickly, then nodded. 'OK, I'll help organise the search from this end. I dare say you already have some volunteers out and about? Right. And the local constable's already there? Fine, we'll have our own officers at the grounds within half an hour. Bye.'

When he hung up, Trudy, PC Rodney Broadstairs and Walter Swinburne – the oldest constable at the station – were all looking at him expectantly.

'Right, everyone,' the sergeant began briskly. 'We have a missing child, I'm afraid.' The words were guaranteed to make everyone's heart sink, and Trudy felt her breath catch. She knew that the majority of missing children were found within the first few hours of them being reported missing, of course, but still. They were words you never wanted to hear.

'His name is Eddie Proctor, and he's 11 years old,' Sergeant O'Grady swept on. 'This morning he attended – along with nearly twenty or so other youngsters from the local primary school – an Easter egg hunt in the grounds of Briar's Hall.'

Trudy vaguely recognised the name. Briar's Hall was located in Briar's-in-the-Wold, a village just on the outskirts of north-west Oxford. It consisted, if she remembered rightly, of a pub, a church, a handful of mostly farmworkers' cottages, and a modest but pretty, classically Georgian square-shaped house made out of local Cotswold stone. The big house itself, she felt sure, was surrounded by a small patch of woodland, and boasted reduced but still admirable gardens, which is where, presumably, the Easter egg hunt had been arranged.

'Kiddie's probably just wandered off to eat his eggs without having to share them with his friends,' PC Rodney Broadstairs said hopefully. He was a tall, blond, good-looking young lad, who thought far too much of himself, in Trudy's opinion, but she could only hope that, in this case, he was right.

'Be that as it may, he should have returned home at one o'clock for his Sunday lunch. And didn't,' the sergeant said crisply. 'Since it's Easter, the family were going to have roast chicken with all the trimmings, and the boy's favourite pudding – a chocolate

5

sponge pudding with custard. And the boy's mother is adamant he wouldn't miss it for all the tea in China. So…'

For the next few minutes the sergeant was busy ringing around the division's other stations, which were also short-staffed, rounding up as many volunteers as he could find. Meanwhile, Trudy, old Walter and Rodney Broadstairs were dispatched in one of the police cars to make the short journey to Briar's-in-the-Wold. Walter drove, since Rodney was still on the police-sponsored driving course and didn't have his licence yet. Naturally, Trudy's name had never been put forward.

Not that such a minor detail like that was going to stop her. Her friend, Dr Clement Ryder, had offered to teach her how to drive on their own time, and she was going to take him up on it!

But thinking of her friend, the city's coroner, made her feel suddenly pensive. Their last case together hadn't ended exactly how he'd thought it had, and she felt uneasy about keeping secrets from him. Oh, they'd found the killer all right, a very vindictive killer who had chosen to end their own life rather than face justice. But true to form, they hadn't done so before leaving behind a very curious letter about the coroner, designed to do as much harm to him as possible.

A letter that Trudy had been the first to read, and – given no chance or time to consider what to do about it – she had then been forced to make a split-second decision on what to do about her unwanted knowledge. And giving in to her instinctive impulse to conceal it from her superior officers had left her feeling in something of a quandary ever since.

Withholding evidence was such a taboo that she still couldn't quite believe she'd actually done it. But what other choice, really, had she had?

As she sat in the car, vaguely watching the scenery go by, Trudy still wondered if she could have – should have – done things differently.

Although, after much soul-searching, she had burned the letter, all she had to do was close her eyes and she could read it as if it still existed on actual paper.

To whom it may concern

I feel it my duty to inform the Oxford City Police that I have, on a number of occasions, observed Dr Clement Ryder, a coroner of the city, to show symptoms of what I firmly believe to be some kind of morbid disease.

I have noticed him to suffer from hand tremors on several occasions, and also a dragging of his feet, leading him to almost stumble.

Since a coroner is an officer of the law and holds a position of great responsibility, I feel it incumbent on me to point out that, very unfortunately, it may be possible that he is unfit to continue to serve in his present position.

I therefore advise, very strongly, that he be assessed by one of his fellow medical practitioners as soon as possible.

Faithfully—

Of course, she knew that the killer had written the letter out of sheer spite, intending to make as much trouble and inconvenience for the coroner as possible. But it had been a very clever letter, making no outright or unbelievable accusations, merely stating that Dr Clement Ryder was ill, and should thus be removed from his office as medically unfit.

On the face of it, it was a ludicrous claim. And now that she'd had ample time and space to think about it, she wondered if she shouldn't have just left the letter where she'd found it, for wouldn't her superiors have simply scoffed at it? Surely they would have regarded it as sour grapes on the part of a double killer, filed it away and forgotten about it.

Or would they?

Her immediate superior, DI Harry Jennings for one, was no fan of the coroner, since Dr Ryder would insist on sticking his nose into what the DI considered to be strictly police business. So he would have been very interested in pursuing anything that might help rid him of his troublesome nemesis.

And what if it turned out that there was some basis to the accusations? Trudy shifted uncomfortably on the back seat and suppressed a small sigh.

Yes, if she was going to be truly honest with herself, that was what *really* worried her. It wasn't so much whether or not her chickens might come home to roost and one day blight her career. After all, nobody had seen her take the letter or even suspected its existence. No, she felt safe enough from the prospect of having to face any disciplinary proceedings.

But her suspicion that what the letter had alleged might just be true wouldn't go away.

Because, for as long as she'd known him, she'd noticed a few odd things about her friend. The way Dr Ryder's hands would tremble every now and then. She'd tried to put that down to age – after all, old men sometimes did have the shakes, right?

Then there was the way he would sometimes stumble slightly, as though he'd tripped over an obstacle that wasn't there. Again, she'd put that down to him shuffling his feet. She'd noticed that sometimes he didn't pick his feet up properly – ironically a failing that her father had often scolded her for as a child!

Of course, she'd half-suspected that he might drink a little more than he probably should, which would account for most of the things she'd noticed. A colleague had once told her that secret tipplers often kept popping breath mints to disguise the smell of booze on their breath, and it was true that, just lately, the coroner had started chewing on strong mints.

But what if he didn't have a fondness for too much drink after all? What if the trembling hands and unsteady gait meant something else? Because if he really was ill…

Yet the only way she could know that for sure would be to ask him about it. It *sounded* simple enough, but Trudy had a feeling

8

that it was going to be nothing of the kind. The coroner was a private and sometimes intimidating man, and she doubted he would take kindly to her dabbling in what he was certain to feel was none of her business.

But that was a problem for another day. Right now, Trudy thought anxiously, they had a missing child to find.

Chapter 2

It was apparent from the moment they arrived at Briar's Hall, and reported to the officer in charge, that the boy had not yet been found.

The village Bobby wasn't quite as old as Walter, and introduced himself as Constable Watkins.

'Right. At the moment, we're concentrating on the area around the lake, for obvious reasons,' Watkins began grimly. 'You two men make your way to the south side.' He pointed across a small paddock. 'You'll see where the others are. Follow the path, but don't bother searching the reeds where someone's already left markers. Here…' He handed Rodney and Walter a bunch of small wooden sticks, with red and white tapes dangling loosely from their ends. 'Stick them in the ground at more or less twenty-yard intervals.'

Trudy glanced around, trying to get the lie of the land. They'd travelled through the length of the small village, which now sat in a shallow valley to the east of her. They were at the bottom of a slight rise, and surrounded on three sides by woodland. Presumably, the rise and the trees were keeping Briar's Hall itself from view.

'You, WPC…?'

'Probationary WPC Loveday, sir,' Trudy said smartly, earning her a sharp, beady-eyed look.

'Oh yes? You're the one who's got herself in some bigwig's good books eh?'

Trudy flushed painfully. 'I didn't do anything that anyone else wouldn't do, sir,' she began defensively, wondering how long she'd be forced to eat humble pie with her fellow officers. 'It was the Earl who insisted on all this fuss.'

The now infamous letter of thanks, due to be doled out to her by the Earl's secretary during the upcoming bash, would no doubt be instantly snaffled by her mother. Much to her daughter's horror, Barbara Loveday had insisted that she was going to get it framed so that it could hang in pride of place over the front-room mantelpiece. Next thing she knew, her father would be charging the neighbours sixpence to come and admire it!

'Huh. Well, I suppose he would, considering it was his son's neck you saved,' Watkins conceded, obviously willing to give her the benefit of the doubt. 'All right, you can take the far edge of those woods.' He pointed directly north and behind him. 'I haven't allocated anyone there yet. You'll see the woods there come almost right up to the outer walls of the gardens of the Hall in places. But there's a bit of an orchard area between, where formal gardens meet the farmland. Take these with you' – he handed her a pile of the sticks – 'and place them wherever you search. You've got your whistle?' he asked abruptly.

Trudy obviously had, and lifted it from where it was hanging around her neck.

'All right then. If you find the boy, give three short blasts. If you find anything you think needs further investigation and you need help, give two long blasts. Clear?'

'Yes, sir,' Trudy said smartly, and set off briskly with her pile of markers.

It was a cool but pleasant day, with the April sun playing tag with the clouds. She walked through the woods, as instructed. They felt, as most woods do, slightly damp. She kept walking uphill and through growing clumps of wild garlic and jack-by-the-hedge, carefully avoiding the freshly growing and vicious stinging nettles, until she came to the edge of the treeline.

There, below her, as she had suspected, was Briar's Hall. She set off towards it quickly, aware of movement all around her. In one field off to her left, she could see several of her colleagues checking out a hay barn. Below, two more volunteers (villagers she presumed, as they weren't in uniform) were tracking the line of a hawthorn hedge that separated two fields, which were both already showing green with barley shoots. If the boy had fallen in the ditch that usually accompanied a hedge, he would soon be found.

She barely paused to assess this however, instead marching quickly downhill, where she spotted the acreage of smaller, bent fruit trees that Constable Watkins had allocated her.

She could see it was surrounded by an old and mostly broken-down dry-stone wall, which would present no barrier to inquisitive children, and the ground between the trees was high with thistles, sedge grass, dock and various other weeds. No doubt, in the autumn, the estate manager let pigs from the farm estates in here to graze on the fallen or rotten fruit. As it was, she could see she had her work cut out for her avoiding the thistles – although in a few weeks' time they'd be even higher than they already were.

With a sigh for her stockings, which she knew stood no chance of surviving this search unladdered, she set off carefully to place the first stick.

'Eddie! Eddie Proctor? Can you hear me?' she called, but after the first, initial moment of hope, which insisted there had to be a chance that a high, fluting child's voice might answer, there was only silence.

Grimly, Trudy began to circumnavigate the orchard, hoping

against hope that they would not find the boy's drowned body in the lake.

*

It was nearly five o'clock when Trudy's ever-decreasing circle of investigations had brought her almost to the middle of the orchard. Despite the cool April clouds, she was feeling warm in her uniform after so much walking and swishing of the sticks, hoping to catch a glimpse of a sleeping child in the grass.

She spotted a low, round circular wall of red bricks in some surprise, then, after a moment's thought, realised that it could only be an old well. Indeed, the T-shaped thick wooden bracket that would have covered the top of the circle, and from which a bucket would have dangled, allowing water to be drawn, was still lying in the grass beside one edge of it. Over the years, it had been almost covered by a vicious-looking wild bramble and a particularly dense patch of dock, and she surmised that the big house probably hadn't had need of the water supply since before the war.

She sat down gingerly on the outer wall to take a breather, glad to feel that the old red bricks still felt pretty stable beneath her. At some point, she noted with relief, the old well had been safely covered by a lid of thick, roughly nailed-together wooden planks, shaped into a circle and then placed on top – probably to stop wildlife from falling inside.

But as she looked down at it, she realised that it wasn't fitting properly. Or, more likely, had it just eroded away at one edge? For as she looked more closely, she could see that there was now a small gap, perhaps a foot and a half wide, at one side.

Feeling her heartbeat rise a notch, she walked around until she was level with the crescent-shaped gap and without taking the time to think about it, bent down and peered into the Stygian darkness inside.

Instantly the smell of damp, stale water and algae assailed her nostrils. But the well was obviously deep, and she couldn't really see to the bottom of its depths.

'Eddie! Are you down there?' she called.

Silence.

Trudy stood back. She would have to take a proper look, of course, so there was nothing for it but to pull the rest of the lid away – allowing more light to filter inside, giving her a better view. But she quickly found, much to her annoyance and chagrin, that tug and pull and heave as she might, she simply couldn't shift it. It didn't help that, over the years, the wood had warped and sunk into the outer rim of the well, making it hard to get a proper grip on it.

Grimly, she realised she was going to have to get some help. Which would just give her colleagues something else to crow about! A poor little girlie who needed a big strong man to help her. She could already hear them sniggering. As if she hadn't already been the butt of enough jokes all day, thanks to a grateful peer of the realm!

Grunting and groaning, and almost wrenching her shoulder out of its socket, she finally admitted defeat and stood panting for a moment.

Of course, it was unlikely that the boy had climbed through the gap and gone into the well. But you never knew. A boy eagerly on the hunt for chocolate might not have stopped to consider that the people in charge of hiding the Easter eggs might have considered the inside of a disused well an unfit hiding place!

So she took a breath then blew two long blasts on her whistle. It rent the quiet air, and sent a flock of peewits in the nearest field shooting up into the sky, giving their iconic call of alarm.

After a minute had gone by, she repeated the process, and soon

14

heard a voice hail her from the edge of the woods. Her heart fell when she recognised Rodney Broadstairs' figure moving quickly down the hill towards her.

It had to be him, didn't it, Trudy thought mutinously. The golden, blue-eyed boy of the station. As she'd known he would, he started to grin at her the moment he saw her predicament. 'Hello, what have you found then, gorgeous?'

Trudy nodded at the well. 'I can't get the lid off – I think it's stuck. But there's a gap at the side, big enough for a boy to get through. It needs to be checked out,' she said, feeling annoyed that she sounded as if she needed to justify herself to him.

'Yeah, I suppose. Hey, you down there Eddie?' he bellowed, leaning over and peering into the darkness. Trudy had already done the same, without any result. And once again, the silence remained stubbornly unbroken.

'Right then – let's get this lid off,' Rodney said, rolling up his sleeves a little and taking an awkward grip on the edge nearest the middle of the well. Since he had a longer reach than she did, he did eventually manage to lift and drag the cover to one side, but Trudy wouldn't have been human if she hadn't smiled at how hard he found it. The language he used was colourful enough to make her mother blush.

Sweating and red-faced, he finally let the heavy wooden circle fall onto the ground. And as one, Trudy and Broadstairs leaned over the edge of the circular red bricks and peered inside.

Trudy hadn't really expected to find the boy in there. So the sight of a dank circle of unbroken water didn't surprise her. But then she saw what looked like hair, floating just below the top of the water surface. And below that, a slightly lighter shade of something submerged showed through under the dark, stagnant water.

'Eddie was wearing a white shirt, wasn't he?' she heard Rodney say gruffly beside her. His voice was hoarse and dry, not at all like his usual, confident, cocky tone. And when she dragged her eyes away from the sight of that small patch of floating hair, she saw that he looked pale and slightly sick.

'Yes,' she agreed, her own voice wobbling precariously. Before they'd left, Sergeant O'Grady had given them a brief description of the boy, and what he'd last been seen wearing when he'd set off with his pals to hunt for the eggs.

Forcing back the tears from her eyes, Trudy lifted her whistle to give three sharp, quick blows.

As she did so, Rodney Broadstairs climbed onto the edge of the well and started to lower himself gingerly down. There would be a bit of a drop, even for him, for the well looked to be over six feet deep.

She hoped he wouldn't fall on top of the boy and wondered if she should stop him and tell him to wait for somebody to come, perhaps with a rope.

But then she realised they simply couldn't wait. There was just a chance that the boy might still be alive. But with his face fully submerged, and only his hair floating just below the surface, she knew how unlikely that was.

And as she waited for her colleagues to come running, she couldn't stop the tears from falling at last. Because she knew that the poor boy's mother and father, waiting at home for news, would soon have their hearts broken forever.

Chapter 3

'Calling Probationary WPC Gertrude Loveday.'

Trudy, hearing her hated first name called out loudly for all to hear, shot around and rushed forward to the usher, before he could call her for a second time.

'Here, coming!' she said breathlessly, hurrying towards the door being held open for her. She just had time to tug down her tunic top and make sure her cap was straight before entering the room.

It was three days since the death of little Eddie Proctor, and the inquest had been opened first thing that morning.

In a row of benches to one side, the public had filled the seats to overflowing, and in the front row, she recognised many of the immediate Proctor family.

She'd gone with the local police constable that awful day to break the news of Eddie's death to the boy's mother and the rest of his family, and had comforted the poor woman as best she'd could. Now she gave a brief sympathetic nod to Doreen Proctor, a small brunette woman whose brown eyes looked enormous in her pale face.

Forcing herself to keep her mind on the job, she turned her attention to the coroner, Dr Clement Ryder.

Her friend and mentor nodded at her politely but with no signs of open recognition, and looked so much his usual calm and authoritative self, that Trudy felt herself relax.

He also didn't look the least bit ill, she noticed with a distinct sense of relief. It had been some time since she'd last seen him, and she must have been subconsciously dreading doing so, in case she saw any worrying signs of something being wrong with him.

'WPC Loveday, I understand you were the one to find the boy's body?' Clement began professionally.

'Yes, sir,' she said.

'If you will be so kind then as to tell the jury in your own words what happened on the afternoon of Sunday, 2nd of April?'

Trudy turned to face the jury and gave a succinct, accurate report of what had occurred that afternoon. When she was finished, she cleared her throat and glanced questioningly at the coroner, but he had no questions for her. Her account had been full enough that there was nothing that needed clarifying or pursuing.

*

Outside the court, Trudy trudged back a shade despondently to the station. Tomorrow was the day she was to be lauded in front of the press and the city's top dignitaries as the heroine of the hour, but never had she felt less like celebrating anything.

*

After Trudy's departure, Clement called the medical witnesses, who testified that the boy had died of a broken neck, and not due to drowning at all. As Clement had expected, this caused a bit of a sensation in the court.

It was soon explained that the well, being over eight feet deep, also narrowed slightly towards the bottom, so if the boy had been leaning over and had lost his balance, the chances were fairly good that he would have pitched down head first. And the water, which had turned out to be only about two feet deep wouldn't have been enough to have broken his fall much.

Even so, as he listened to the evidence, Clement wasn't totally convinced by this explanation. The lad would only have needed to twist a little to either one side or the other to land on a shoulder. And wouldn't it have been an instinctive thing for him to do so? Wordlessly, he made a brief note on his court papers.

And there was another thing he'd noticed in the preliminary reports that had caught his analytical eye. So after the medical man had finished his piece, he cleared his throat, indicating he had further questions.

'I take it the deceased's hands were examined?' he asked quietly.

The police surgeon confirmed that they had been.

'And did he have any detritus from the sides of the well under his fingernails, indicating that he had tried to scrabble at the sides of the well as he fell? Brick dust, green algae, mould, anything of that kind?' he'd pressed.

The medical man admitted that they'd found no such evidence, but then gave the opinion that that need not be significant. It was quite possible that the boy had been too surprised, and the fall too brief, for him to have had time to try to catch hold of some sort of support to help break his fall.

Clement dismissed the doctor with a courteous nod, but was frowning slightly as he made more notes.

When it was the turn of the boy's family to give evidence, emotions ran high, as they were bound to. But especially so when the boy's mother tearfully insisted that her son was a good lad, and would never have disobeyed the Easter egg hunt organiser's admonitions to stay within the walled garden where all the eggs had been hidden.

Since nothing of further significance was brought to light after all the other witnesses had been called, it surprised no one when an obviously upset and moved jury returned a verdict of accidental death.

All that was left for Clement to do was to censure the organisers of the hunt for not checking the grounds beforehand and spotting the potential perils of the inadequately covered well. No doubt, he added heavily, the de Laceys, owners of Briar's Hall, would be quick to have a new cover made for the well. Or they might even consider filling it in altogether, which meant, at least, that a similar tragedy would be averted in the future.

But for the weary, distraught parents, what could any of that matter now?

Chapter 4

Trudy Loveday took a deep, calming breath as she paused outside the main entrance to the swanky Randolph Hotel.

Behind her on Beaumont Street was the magnificent edifice of the Ashmolean Museum, whilst off to her left was the oft-photographed Martyrs' Memorial. But for all the times she'd passed by this famous building, she'd never imagined she'd ever set foot inside it.

Beside her, she could feel her mother almost vibrating with similar excitement. Like her daughter, Barbara Loveday couldn't really believe that they were about to be treated to lunch by an actual Earl. Well, not the Earl himself, naturally, but his secretary.

Barbara's husband Frank, however, was displaying emotion of a far different kind – that of distinct unease. Not for the first time, his hand crept up to his collar (which clearly felt too tight) to check his tie was straight. It was an article of clothing he only ever wore to weddings, funerals and christenings, and he eyed the passing people warily, as if expecting them to be pointing at him or smiling behind their hands.

But the only people taking notice of him were the members of the local press, who'd been invited by the city of Oxford's top brass to take photographs of the occasion and then interview the heroine of the hour for their various local newspapers.

It had taken some time for this honour to be arranged, as the incident precipitating it had, in fact, happened last summer, but these things, it appeared, took time. Trudy was inclined to wish they hadn't bothered at all. She, like her father, felt distinctly out of place.

'I do look all right, don't I, Mum?' she asked nervously, though, in fact, she hadn't had to make an agonising decision over what to wear.

With nearly all her superior officers in attendance, she was, of course, dressed in her police uniform, the black-and-white suit looking incredibly smart, and cleaned to within an inch of its life. Her cap sat neatly on her severely pinned-down mass of dark brown locks, and her face was totally free of make-up.

'You look lovely, doesn't she, Brian?' her mother said, turning to look at the young man standing beside her.

Barbara Loveday had insisted on including Brian Bayliss as their 'plus-one' to the event, and Trudy looked across at him now with a rueful smile. They had been friends for years, and the occasional trip to the cinema or meal out had somehow led to them being considered 'a couple' by their respective families. Although Trudy wasn't so sure – and she was beginning to suspect that Brian wasn't, either!

'Come on, Mum, don't put Brian on the spot like that!' she admonished gently.

Brian – a tall, handsome rugby-playing lad – coloured softly and mumbled something about her always looking lovely. But he looked even more uncomfortable and out of place here than her father!

His eyes slid over hers and guiltily away again, and in a sudden flash of intuition, she realised that he didn't actually want to be here at all. For just an instant, she felt a flash of anger wash over her. If he felt so miserable about dressing up and coming to a 'fancy do', why hadn't he simply had the gumption to refuse to come? He could always have said he couldn't get the time off from his job at the bus depot.

But as quickly as her irritation came, it went again. She knew for herself just how ruthlessly her mother could steamroller people into doing as she bid them, and Brian had always been the easy-going sort. Anything for a quiet life, that was his motto.

Now she leaned closer to him, and whispered, 'I'm sorry she dragged you into this. I can see you'd rather be somewhere – anywhere – else.'

He shot her a quick look, considered lying about it and then merely shrugged and gave her a sheepish grin. In truth, ever since he'd learned that she was going to get an award for bravery, he'd felt a bit funny about it. It didn't seem… natural, somehow. In a way he couldn't have explained, even if someone offered him a pound note, he felt wrong-footed and uneasy about it all. Apart from anything else, he couldn't quite shake the feeling that it was up to *men* to be brave. Even though it wasn't his fault that he wasn't doing a dangerous job too – like being a fireman or something – he felt as if he was being in some way undermined.

Along with Trudy's parents, he hadn't much liked her joining the police force, and his mates regularly ragged him about it. Now, as he glanced around nervously at the reporters snapping her photograph, and realised that everyone would be reading about her in the papers tomorrow, he felt a sort of squirmy, almost embarrassed feeling, wriggling about inside him. It was bound to make the teasing ten times worse.

Trudy, watching him, frowned slightly, but realised that now was not the time to ask him what was troubling him, and made a mental note to tackle him about it later. Right now, she had more pressing things to worry about.

She had not long turned 20 and was looking forward to the autumn, when her probationary period would be over and she would be a fully fledged woman police constable. Well, she would be, so long as she didn't do anything to seriously blot her copybook, she reminded herself with an inner grimace.

Of course, there were some of her colleagues back at the station who grumbled that, with what amounted to an unofficial award for bravery being meted out to her, she was almost bulletproof in that respect.

But Trudy wasn't so sure. Her immediate superior, DI Jennings, was of the opinion that the only right and true way to acknowledge a police officer's gallantry, was to award them the Queen's Police Medal – which, in his opinion, should never be awarded to women. Also, such medals only tended to be awarded to those with the rank of sergeant and above. And she was sure he was not the only member of the force to think like that.

All of which left her feeling that if she so much as put a foot wrong, they'd be only too happy of any excuse to get rid of her.

Of course, her superiors had to admit that today would provide good publicity for the force – hence their appearance at that morning's luncheon. There would certainly be enough Chief Superintendents and even higher ranks to make Trudy feel like Daniel walking into the lion's den.

But she was thankful that at least DI Jennings wouldn't be present. His glowering presence would almost certainly put her off her soup! Not that she thought, at that moment, that she would be able to swallow a thing.

Her heart was hammering in her chest and her hands felt clammy. She almost wilted with relief when she saw Dr Ryder striding down the pavement towards them, looking debonair and totally unruffled by all the fuss. A quick glance at her watch told her that he was right on time.

At just a touch over six feet in height, and with his shock of silvering white hair, the city coroner cut a fine figure of a man, and dressed in a dark navy suit and his old school tie, he caught many a passing matron's approving eye.

'Trudy, you look splendid,' Clement said. 'And Mr and Mrs Loveday – good to see you again. You must be so proud of your daughter,' he added, turning to address her parents.

'Oh please, call me Barbara,' her mother said at once. 'And yes we are, very proud, aren't we, Frank?'

Her father, who was shaking the coroner by the hand, nodded wordlessly. In truth, he would be glad when the whole thing was over. He'd spent the last week, it seemed, trying to memorise which knife and fork was which, and the difference between a dessert spoon and his soup spoon. (He'd been full of disbelief when his wife had shown him a magazine photograph of a dinner setting at the grand hotel.)

But of course, underneath all that, he felt as if his chest must be thrust out like a pouter pigeon because, of course, he was as proud as punch of his daughter's achievements, as Clement had surmised.

Not that that had been either his or Barbara's first reaction when Trudy had learned of the proposed ceremony, for then she'd had to confess exactly *why* she had been singled out for it. And tackling a killer all on her own – thus saving a Lord of the Realm in the process – was enough to give any parent nightmares.

She was still in the doghouse for not telling them properly all about it at the time, instead, merely passing the incident off as if she'd just made a normal arrest.

Trudy, remembering her manners, introduced Brian to the coroner. True to his usual, tongue-tied form, Brian muttered something indistinct and shook Clement's hand heartily.

'Right, I think we'd best go in,' Clement said briskly.

Trudy, her heart rising to her throat, shot him a dark look. She had her suspicions that Dr Clement Ryder had been one of the driving forces in urging the Earl to instigate this morning's ceremony, and she wasn't sure whether to hug him or kick him.

But right now, she hadn't the energy to do anything except concentrate on not making a fool of herself, for now they were stepping up towards the door, and the liveried doorman was coming to greet them. Behind her, she heard the press photographers snapping away again, and swallowed hard.

Taking a deep breath, she, Brian and her parents followed Clement into the dining room, where the crystal chandeliers alone made her blink in amazement.

Chapter 5

The following Monday morning, Martin de Lacey of Briar's Hall travelled into town and made his way to Floyds Row, where the mortuary and coroner's office was situated.

He wasn't particularly surprised to be regarded with some favour by the secretary who guarded the coroner's inner sanctum.

At six feet tall, with dark, slightly receding hair, a luxuriant moustache and big grey eyes, he was used to women from 20 to 60 regarding him with a certain interest. It helped that he was a well-set-up man, who had a curiously scholarly look about him that gave him a totally spurious air of distinction.

He was not, he knew, particularly clever, but he *was* very comfortably wealthy, and his family had owned land in the north of the county for centuries. And he did wear his country clothes very well indeed.

Widowed, with two children, Martin de Lacey was usually very happy with his lot.

But not recently – no not recently.

'I wondered if I might have a word with Dr Ryder please?' He approached the secretary sitting at her desk and gave his usual smile. It was naturally winsome, and under the dark curl of his moustache, his teeth seemed rather more white and sparkling than they actually were. As a man of some social standing, he was used to getting his own way, and he foresaw no particular difficulties in getting his way this time.

'May I ask your name, please?' The slightly thin woman, who could have been any age between 40 and 60, asked the question with that friendly disinterest cultivated by secretaries who guarded the doors to their boss's kingdom.

'Martin de Lacey. It's about the Edward Proctor case that he heard on Wednesday.'

It was now Monday, and already the papers had moved on to another sensation.

'I'll see if he can spare you a few minutes. Would you take a seat, please?'

Martin nodded, but didn't, in fact, sit down. Instead he wandered over to the nearest window and stared out pensively over the cobbled courtyard and brick buildings of Floyds Row. He was uncomfortably aware of the presence of a mortuary nearby, and wished that he were walking across the fields surrounding his house, instead of feeling cooped up so close to all this death and unpleasantness.

He frowned slightly, wondering if he was doing the right thing in coming here. But damn it, he couldn't just—

'Dr Ryder can see you now.' The secretary was back, holding open the door to the inner sanctum.

He nodded at her and strode in.

The first thing he noticed was the welcome fire, roaring away in the fireplace, and a rather fine landscape painting hanging on one wall. The man, who rose from behind a large and rather fine desk to greet him, seemed vaguely familiar.

Although it had been his land agent who'd testified at the inquest as to the condition of the Hall's grounds – including that damned old well – Martin realised now that he'd seen the coroner around somewhere before. In a social setting.

At the golf club maybe? Or at the lodge? As he shook hands,

he gave the Mason's greeting, and was not surprised to have it reciprocated.

'Thank you for seeing me,' he said gruffly. 'It's a sad business I've come about, but then, I expect in your line of work, you're used to that,' he began pleasantly.

Clement inclined his head. 'I'm afraid so. Please, take a seat.' He indicated one of the padded chintz chairs that faced his desk, curious as to what could have brought the owner of Briar's Hall to his office.

If he wanted to have any guilty feelings assuaged about the safety – or not – of the old wells on his premises, he was going to be out of luck. Clement was in no mood to play nanny to the landed gentry.

'It's about that poor boy, of course. Eddie.'

'Yes?' Clement said, discouragingly.

Martin de Lacey took a long, slow breath. He hadn't mistaken that lack of empathy in the older man's tone, and he knew he'd have to tread carefully now.

'I'm not here to talk about the rights and wrongs of that well not being covered properly.' He decided to take the bull by the horns. He'd always been pretty good at reading other people, and he sensed in the court official a man who wouldn't suffer fools gladly. 'We were at fault, and that's that.' He could see he'd slightly surprised Ryder with his blunt acceptance of responsibility, and felt a brief moment of pleasure. Martin was a man who liked to have the upper hand.

Feeling more intrigued, Clement settled back in his chair. Clearly his surprise visitor had something specific to say, and he rather thought it might prove more interesting than he'd at first thought.

'So I'm not here to make excuses. I just wanted to get that clear.' Martin de Lacey cleared his throat gruffly. 'I'm here, in fact, not on my own behalf at all, but because of Vince. Vincent Proctor, that is, the boy's father.'

'Oh?' Clement said, careful to keep his voice noncommittal. He recalled that the dead boy's father worked as a farm hand on the de Lacey estate. But he wouldn't have thought that that would put the two men on intimate terms – certainly not on the sort of terms that would allow Mr Proctor to think that he could ask favours of the lord of the manor. In the normal course of things, Vincent Proctor probably took his orders from the de Laceys' farm estate manager anyway.

Except, of course, his son had just died, and in most people's eyes, the head of the de Lacey family had to bear some responsibility for that. And that, of course, was enough to change the natural order of things somewhat.

'Yes.' The squire of Briar's-in-the-Wold shifted a little uncomfortably on his seat. 'You see, he came to see me yesterday and asked me to… well… to do something about his boy's death.'

He now sounded as uncomfortable as he looked, and Clement raised one eyebrow in surprise. 'Exactly what does he expect you to do about it? If he wants compensation, I'm afraid I can't advise you…'

'No, no, it's nothing like that,' Martin said, a shade testily now. 'In point of fact, he doesn't hold us responsible for his son's death at all. And by us, I mean either my family, or the school teachers and WI members who organised the Easter egg hunt.'

Clement blinked, regarding his visitor intently. Martin de Lacey was becoming more and more interesting by the minute. 'You mean, he accepts the fact that his son disobeyed the rules by straying outside the limits of the kitchen garden? That he was just doing what little boys did all the time – namely get into all sorts of trouble – when he tried to climb down or fell into that well?'

'Yes. No. I mean…' Martin took a deep breath. 'The fact is, neither Vincent Proctor nor his wife believe that their son's death could have been an accident.'

Clement slowly leaned forward in his chair and thought for a few moments. In the silence, the old clock on the wall ticked ponderously. 'But if it wasn't an accident, that only leaves murder – or manslaughter,' the coroner pointed out.

'Yes. And I know what you're thinking,' Martin de Lacey said heavily. 'It's the first thing I thought too, when he first came to me. I mean, if it is murder we're talking about, who would want to deliberately kill a child?'

Clement blinked thoughtfully as the ugly question hung grimly in the air. There had been no signs of sexual violence on Eddie Proctor's body – which was often the sad, disgusting cause behind the deliberate killing of most children.

The other most frequent cause of child death, as Clement and every police officer knew too well, was domestic abuse. But again, that tended to follow a certain pattern, and there had been no old injuries on Eddie's body flagged up at the post mortem to raise the alarm. No broken bones that had been mended over the years. No faded scars, or more recent bruises.

After a few moments, Clement sighed. 'Of course, it's not unusual for parents to be unable to accept an accident or death due to misadventure,' he said at last. 'It all seems so arbitrary and unfair – they need to believe something more malign is at work. It makes more sense for them if they have somebody to blame.'

Martin de Lacey nodded. He would have to be even more careful now. It wouldn't do to make a mistake at this point in time. 'Yes. It was my first thought too,' he agreed flatly.

Clement watched him carefully. He knew when someone was trying to manipulate him, and he was beginning to sense some other agenda was at work here. But that intrigued as much as it annoyed him.

'Oh? And what was your second thought?' he asked gently.

Martin looked at him, then quickly away again. Once more he shifted uncomfortably in his seat. 'Look, I wish you'd come and talk to Vince yourself. And I might as well come clean straight-away. Er… I've rather taken it on myself to have a word with our Chief Constable.'

Clement went rather still. 'Have you?' he said mildly.

Martin de Lacey flushed slightly. 'Yes. Look, I'm sorry and all that, but one of the chaps at the golf club told me that you… er… well, sometimes look into cases, police cases, I mean, after they'd been closed.'

Clement smiled grimly. 'I've been known to meddle once or twice, yes,' he admitted with a slight smile. He could well imagine the horror stories the Chief Constable could have poured into de Lacey's ear.

As if reading his mind, the squire of Briar's-in-the-Wold shifted uncomfortably in his seat.

'Quite. Yes, so I… well, I took the liberty of asking Sir Penfold if he would mind arranging it with the officer in charge of Eddie's case to, er, let you look into things a little further.'

'Is that so?' Suddenly, Clement's smile grew wider, because he knew that DI Harry Jennings was officially in charge of the Proctor case. And the thought of his reaction on being informed that once again he would have to put up with Dr Ryder's interference was too precious not to savour.

'All right, Mr de Lacey. I'll talk to the boy's parents, and if I think the case warrants further investigation, I'll be happy to oblige you,' Clement said, suddenly tiring of the game. One or two points raised at the inquest had been bothering him, and he wasn't at all averse to being given the opportunity to satisfy his curiosity.

Furthermore, it had been some time since he and Trudy had worked on a case together, and he was looking forward to another break from his usual caseload.

Martin de Lacey looked relieved and then, rather curiously, began to look uncertain. Finally he merely shrugged and smiled, stood up and shook the coroner's hand. 'Thank you, Dr Ryder.'

'Not at all,' the coroner said briskly, rising to see his visitor out.

He walked back to his desk, feeling distinctly rejuvenated. Just what the hell was going on? It was unusual for an influential family like the wealthy de Laceys not to simply sweep unpleasantness under the carpet and forget all about it. Was it possible the dead boy's father had some sort of hold over the family that went beyond their feelings of guilt over an abandoned well? The thought was definitely an intriguing one.

Clement gave a mental shrug. Well, whatever it was, he and Trudy Loveday were going to have an interesting time finding out. For, of course, the first thing he'd demand of DI Harry Jennings was that he release her from her usual duties in order to assist him.

Chapter 6

Trudy's heart lifted as she knocked on the door and then entered the now familiar outer room of the coroner's office, where his secretary smiled up at her and quickly announced her expected arrival.

Needless to say, it had made her day when her sour-faced superior had called her into his office earlier that day and told her that she was being seconded, yet again, to Dr Clement Ryder for a few days. DI Jennings had stressed the 'yet again' with bitter emphasis, but in truth, he hadn't seemed all that unwilling to let her go. In fact, Trudy rather suspected that he was glad to have her out from under his feet.

Trudy, however, wasn't giving her grudging boss much thought as she walked forward and took her usual seat in front of the coroner's desk. She was simply relieved not to have to continue her current task, which was helping the clerk in the records office.

Not that DI Jennings had said much about her latest assignment, only grunting something about it involving the death of the little boy she'd found down the well.

'So,' she said as soon as she'd sat down, 'you really think there's something odd about little Eddie Proctor's death? Did something strike you at the inquest?'

'Yes and no,' Clement surprised her by saying crisply. 'As far as I could tell, all the witnesses called were being honest and truthful – which is not always the same thing, oddly enough – and I have no real or solid reasons as yet to suspect that the verdict was incorrect.'

'Oh,' Trudy said, both stumped and a little dismayed. 'So why am I here then?'

Clement relented slightly and smiled. 'You're here mainly because of Martin de Lacey, head of the family up at Briar's Hall.' He absently reached into his coat pocket, withdrew a roll of mints and popped one into his mouth. 'He came to see me. Apparently, he's not satisfied with the way things stand.'

Trudy blinked, thought about it for a moment or two, then frowned. 'He's feeling guilty about the well not being covered properly and he wants reassurance?' she hazarded. She could understand why that might be so, but she felt rather put out that that was all there was to it.

'You look like a child after someone's just burst their balloon,' Clement commiserated. 'But for what it's worth, I think there might – just *might* – be something more going on here than at first meets the eye.'

'Oh?' This time her tone was more hopeful.

'Yes. Anyway, he went over my head and got the Chief Constable roped in before I knew anything about it. But since, for a change, this time I've actually been *asked* to do a little digging' – his lips twisted in a wry smile – 'I thought you might like to help. But if you'd rather get back to the station…?'

Trudy grinned unrepentantly at him. 'You know I wouldn't,' she said crisply. In truth, she was just glad to see him in such high spirits and looking so undeniably well.

She had not told him about the existence of the letter claiming that he was ill, let alone that she'd read it and destroyed it. Instinct told her that he'd be both angry and indignant about its contents, but more than that, he wouldn't be at all pleased to learn that she'd put her career at risk in order to do him a favour.

Dr Clement Ryder, she was beginning to know, would not take kindly to being in someone's debt.

'So where do we start?' she asked. Forcing herself to concentrate solely on the matter in hand, she gave a slight frown. 'The most obvious place is with Mr de Lacey, I take it? Presumably, he must have had *something* to go on, if he thinks there's more that needs to be investigated?'

But Clement thought about that gentleman – and his very careful way with words, and, after some thought, slowly shook his head. 'No. No, I think we'll leave him for a bit. I have a feeling there might be something odd there…' He paused, tried to put into words the cause of his nebulous misgivings about that gentlemen, and failed. Instead, he shrugged in dissatisfaction. 'I just got the impression that he's keeping something back, or that he's got some sort of agenda of his own,' he finally said. 'And if that's so, then at the moment we won't stand a chance of worming out of him just what it is. No, I want to get a deeper understanding of things before we tackle him again.'

Trudy, recognising the coroner's tone of voice, sat up a little straighter in her chair. Clearly, Dr Ryder meant business. And slowly her heart rate began to accelerate again. Perhaps this wasn't going to be such a dead-end case after all? From very unpromising beginnings, was it possible that they might be on to something again after all?

'All right, sir,' she said. 'Where do we begin?'

Clement smiled. 'I keep telling you, you can call me Clement you know, when we're not in public,' he said, clearly amused by her formality.

'Oh no, sir, I couldn't do that,' Trudy said firmly. Even if, sometimes in her own head, she did indeed think of this man as 'Clement', it would never do to forget herself and refer to him as such in front of her colleagues. Or even her parents! She'd never hear the end of it. 'I don't mind calling you Dr Ryder,' she conceded generously.

'Thank you,' he said, perfectly straight-faced. 'Well, I think the first place we need to start is with the parents. Martin de Lacey would have me believe that he came on their behalf. If that's true, we need to find out why the boy's father in particular is so convinced that the boy's death couldn't have been an accident.'

Trudy nodded grimly, rising from the chair and girding her loins for another heart-breaking encounter with the Proctor family.

Chapter 7

Doreen and Vincent Proctor, along with their remaining three children, lived in one of a row of small terraced cottages leading off from the village green, where the majority of farmworkers for the estate were housed.

As they climbed out of the car and looked around at the rich, arable land, Clement supposed that almost all inhabitants of Briar's-in-the-Wold worked on the de Lacey estate in some form or other. Save for the odd private doctor or professional, of course.

The village boasted the usual square-towered Norman church, a small primary school and a pub called 'The Bell'. A small puddle, probably fondly thought of as a pond by most of the villagers, played host to a few desultory mallards, but it was at least ringed with cheerful just-in-bloom daffodils. Pussy willow shed pale lemon pollen over them as an accent of colour.

A cold wind had the pair of them quickly hurrying up a neatly tended front garden and knocking at the Proctors' front door.

'Eddie's brothers and sister might be back at school by now,' Trudy warned, not sure how long the Easter holidays lasted. 'If they are, do you want me to try and talk to them at some point?'

'We'll see,' Clement said. 'Children sometimes know more than we think they do – but they can also exaggerate, or just make stuff up to try and please you. Besides, it might be a bit too early to talk about their brother just yet. They're probably still in shock.'

Trudy bit her lip, angry with herself for not thinking of that, then stiffened as the door was abruptly opened by the man of the house.

Vincent Proctor was a squat, powerful-looking man, with the hands of a farm labourer, a mop of unruly brown hair, and shaggy brows over large, cow-like eyes.

'You were the coroner for our Eddie,' he said at once, having recognised Clement from giving evidence at the inquest. 'Mr de Lacey said you might call. Come on in out the wind. There's a good fire in the kitchen.'

He led them down a small, dark entranceway to the back of the house, where a large, wood-fired stove gave off some welcome heat.

There was no sign of his wife. Evidence of the remains of a breakfast composed of bread and dripping were still out next to the draining board by the sink, however, and Trudy wondered if it had been the father of the children who'd seen them off to school with something inside their tummies.

'The wife's upstairs,' Vincent Proctor said flatly, as if reading her mind, and Trudy, for some reason, felt herself flush. She had not intended to look in any way disapproving.

'I'm sure she needs to rest,' she said earnestly.

Vincent nodded, saying nothing as he set about putting the kettle on, but silently indicated the wooden, ladder-back chairs that surrounded the well-scrubbed kitchen table. Taking his wordless invitation to be seated, Clement and Trudy took opposite ends of the table and sat quietly as Vincent put a sugar bowl and a bottle of milk on the table, and then, a short while later, three steaming mugs of tea.

'So, I understand you asked Mr de Lacey to come and see me?' Clement began cautiously.

'Yerse. I dunno how to go about these things myself, y'see,'

Vincent confirmed, staring down at his hands, which were wrapped around the mug of his untouched tea. His Oxonian country burr testified to the fact that he'd probably been born in the village and would be happy enough to die in it too. Probably his father before him had worked for the de Laceys, and no doubt he expected his sons to do the same. 'But I knew Mr de Lacey would be able to get things done. Him bein' squire, an' all.'

Clement nodded. 'Mr de Lacey wasn't able to tell me much about what, exactly, you want us to do,' he began tactfully. 'He suggested I talk to you in person about what's on your mind.'

Vincent nodded, but didn't immediately speak. When he did, he was slow and deliberate, but sounded already weary, as if he didn't expect them to take him seriously.

'It's like this, see. There was just no way our Eddie could'a fallen down that well, like you all reckon he did. O'course, you'd have to know him, like, real well, the same as me and his mother do, to understand that. And I know that important people like you' – here he shot a look at both Clement and Trudy – 'ain't likely to just take my word for it. But…'

He shrugged helplessly. He looked so out of his depth, that Trudy felt her heart constrict. She couldn't help it, but reached out to place her hand comfortingly on his.

'Mr Proctor,' she said gently, 'I promise you that both Dr Ryder and I will listen to you. And we will do our very best to understand.'

He nodded, but the poor man looked so defeated already, and clearly didn't believe her, that it made her heart ache. She looked quickly across at Dr Ryder, who gave her an infinitesimal nod to carry on. Almost imperceptibly, he leaned back in his chair, the better to watch and listen as the dead boy's father began to speak.

'See, for a start, our Eddie wasn't really the daredevil sort,' the boy's father began. 'Now if it had been our Bertie… now him I *could* just see taking a tumble down a well. T'would be just the sort'a daft thing he'd go and do. Right from the moment he was born – he's our eldest, y'see – he was into trouble. No sense o' danger, see? But Eddie weren't like that. He wasn't a namby-pamby lad, don't get me wrong,' he said earnestly, looking at Trudy as if it was important that she should understand that he was in no way criticising his dead son. 'He were a proper lad, like. But… If, say, a tree had fallen down over the river, and he was gonna cross it, he would take time first to make sure it was a good strong tree. With lots of good footholds where he could stand without losing his balance, and good strong branches that spread all the way across to the other side. He wouldn't just go at it all 'ell for leather, and then laugh if he was ditched into the water. See what I mean?'

'Yes.' Trudy smiled. 'I see. Whereas his elder brother would have done just that.'

'Oh, ar. But it's not just that. Our Eddie wasn't any too fond of heights, neither. He reckoned he went all dizzy, like, if he got too far off the ground.'

'Some children do,' Clement slipped in helpfully. 'It's called vertigo. It's usually a problem with the inner ear, and nothing to be ashamed of.'

At this, as Clement had rather thought he might, Vincent looked rather relieved. It provided him with further proof that his lad wasn't a namby-pamby.

'Ar… A medical thing then… well, that's different. Yerse. Poor little… But, see, that's just another reason why I know he wouldn't'a gone down that well then, ain't it?' he demanded challengingly. 'Just looking down that far would have made him feel sick like. And another thing…'

He paused to take a sip of tea. 'Eddie weren't all that fond of chocolate. Oh, he'd eat it, but he'd prefer to have humbugs, or bulls eyes, or sherbet dabs. He was more of a sweetie kind of lad.'

He looked anxiously at Trudy, to see if she understood what he was saying.

To oblige him, she nodded quickly. 'So you're saying that the inducement to find chocolate eggs wouldn't have been anywhere near strong enough to make him take chances?' Trudy said.

The boy's father frowned a little, clearly not sure what 'inducement' meant, but relieved to see that she was looking thoughtful. He glanced back at the coroner. Clearly for him, Dr Ryder meant authority and book-learning, and he was the man he needed to convince.

'And that ain't all,' he carried on stubbornly. 'Young Eddie was really pally with little Emily. Thick as thieves, those two.'

'Emily?' Trudy pressed, suddenly not following the conversation at all.

'Emily de Lacey. The squire's little 'un,' Vincent elaborated. 'Ten years old, and going on sixteen, that 'un. Smart as a whip, she is.'

Trudy blinked. 'Really? The squire's daughter and your son were friends?' She glanced curiously at the coroner, who gave her a quick shake of his head, guessing at once the reason behind her scepticism. No doubt she thought it odd that a mere farmworker's son and the little lady of the manor should be such bosom pals, but he knew, from his own childhood experiences, that in small villages, that sort of odd mix wasn't at all unusual. Children from good, bad and indifferent families tended to live cheek by jowl up to the age of 11 or so, sharing the local primary school and all the village's meagre social events.

Of course, it was tacitly understood by all concerned that it wouldn't last into adulthood, and was thus not taken seriously. After the age of 11, they tended to sort themselves out into more familiar roles. No doubt, Emily de Lacey would soon be of age to attend a good girl's grammar – or maybe even boarding school – and would grow up into a proper young lady. Whilst Eddie, had he lived, would have left the nearest secondary school at 14 or so and gone on to work on the land.

Thereafter, if they'd met, they'd probably have nodded and

41

smiled and not given each other a single thought. But at 10 and 11, yes, they could have been very close indeed.

'Is she a nice girl, Emily?' Clement asked mildly.

'Oh yerse,' Vincent said at once, smiling for the first time Trudy had known him. 'She and Eddie ran around the estate like little animals,' he mused. 'Playing cowboys and injuns, and whatnot. I think their latest thing was playing at spies and such stuff. They had a theory that one of the schoolmasters was a German agent, or some such. Emily had been reading that *Thirty-Nine Steps* book to him, and Eddie was all caught up in it…' He trailed off with a gulp perhaps realising that, now, his son would never play at spies again.

'Ah. And why do you think this friendship between them matters?' Trudy asked quickly, to take his mind off his grief. 'What has that to do with Eddie's… what happened to him?' she asked, as delicately as she could.

But instead of answering, the dead boy's father shrugged and took a sip of his tea. Clearly he was feeling more uncomfortable now. It probably didn't do to talk about the family up at the Hall, but Vincent was clearly determined to do right by his son.

'I think them two told each other everythin', he finally said. 'And… I dunno. I think…' He sighed heavily. 'I think you should go and talk to Emmy, that's all. Besides, she was at the Easter egg hunt, and if anyone knows why he went off on his own like that – when he'd been told to stay in the walled garden – she would.'

'Eddie wasn't the sort of boy not to do as he was told?' Clement asked.

'No, he weren't, then,' the boy's father said flatly.

But Trudy knew from bitter experience that it was best to take *that* with a pinch of salt. No boy was an angel, after all. And if Eddie *had* been lured to that well by someone intent on doing him harm – well, it probably wouldn't have been that hard to do. A secret note, promising who knew what, would probably be enough, for a start. To a lad who liked adventure novels, it would be irresistible. Or the promise of a bag of his favourite sweets, if chocolate wasn't his preference.

They talked for a while longer, but nothing more of substance was forthcoming, and they left the house, promising to do all they could to find out what had really happened that Sunday morning.

Trudy waited until the coroner had got behind the wheel, before speaking.

'So what do you make of that? Not much to go on, is it?' she said sadly.

Clement shrugged. 'Maybe yes, maybe no. Some parents *do* have a very strong idea of what their kids are like, and what they're likely to get up to. I thought Mr Proctor was probably one. Didn't you?' he suddenly put her on the spot by asking sharply.

Trudy, caught out, responded instinctively. 'Oh yes. I mean, I think he's genuine in thinking… in believing that Eddie wouldn't have explored that well.'

'So where does that leave us?'

Trudy smiled briefly. 'It leaves us driving up to the Hall to talk to Emily de Lacey. Yes?'

Clement gave her a grin. 'You're learning, WPC Loveday. You're learning!'

Chapter 8

But, as it turned out, Trudy was wrong in her prediction. For at Briar's Hall, they encountered a very formidable obstacle indeed to their plan of action, in the form of one Mrs Cordelia Roper, the de Laceys' housekeeper of many years' standing.

It was this rigid-of-mind and rigid-of-body person who answered the door, surprising Clement slightly since he would have expected a butler. Instead, they found themselves being kept firmly on the outer portico's steps by a woman in her mid-fifties, with a fierce glint in her brown eyes. Her hair, which must once have been a fiery red, had turned mostly to silver, and was held high on her head in a tight bun. She introduced herself, reluctantly, as Mrs Roper, the housekeeper. She wore a plain black dress, which matched the look she gave them, when Clement introduced himself and asked if he might speak to young Miss Emily de Lacey.

'May I ask why you are inquiring after her, sir? Madam?' she added, as a distinct afterthought, and eyed Trudy and her uniform with such a look that it made Trudy want to squirm on the spot. Clearly, her face said, the place for people in uniform was at the side entrance.

Trudy raised her chin and met the dragon's gimlet stare with her best blank expression. It managed to convey a mixture of mutiny and insubordination whilst leaving no room for actual complaint. It was a look she'd learned to cultivate very quickly when dealing with less-than-polite members of the public.

'We're calling at the behest of Mr Martin de Lacey,' Clement responded at once, deciding that, when dealing with one of the housekeeper's ilk, it was best to try to avoid outright battle if at all possible. And the one thing that he thought might earn them entrance was to invoke the squire's name.

'I'm afraid Mr de Lacey hasn't given me instructions on this matter, or informed me of your visit… er…?'

'I'm Dr Clement Ryder, city coroner. And this is WPC Loveday.'

Mrs Roper's eyes widened slightly at Trudy's name, and Trudy fought back a flush, wishing – for about the millionth time in her life – that her parents had possessed a far less memorable surname. As it was, it gave every male colleague she ever met the perfect opportunity for unwanted teasing or fresh remarks.

'I see. Well, I'm afraid, Dr Ryder, that Miss Emily is indisposed at the moment,' she said firmly, thus dashing their hopes of an interview with the little girl that day. 'But I will certainly consult with Mr de Lacey when I see him,' she added reluctantly. 'Good day.' She managed to say the last two words with a semblance of conviviality that, nevertheless, totally bypassed her eyes, and the door was shut firmly in their faces.

Trudy wasn't aware that she was holding her breath until she felt it leave her in a painful whoosh.

'Well, she wasn't very friendly, was she?' Trudy said crossly, not sure whether to laugh or feel insulted.

'No, she wasn't,' Clement agreed, his voice both mild and thoughtful. 'Of course, she's probably just feeling protective of the child. She's only 10 years old and bound to be grieving still for the loss of her friend. The last thing she probably feels like doing is talking to strangers.'

'Oh. Yes, I hadn't really thought of it that way,' Trudy agreed, a bit shame-faced now at her previous anger.

Clement, though, continued to stare at the door thoughtfully for several long seconds. He didn't know that on the other side of the wooden barrier, Cordelia Roper was standing stock-still, listening for the sounds of their retreat. But he wouldn't have been very surprised. In his opinion, the woman's show of recalcitrance had far more to do with fear than innate bloody-mindedness. And he wondered exactly what it was that was worrying her.

*

Behind the door, Cordelia Roper's sharp features remained pinched and white, but eventually she moved away from the front entrance, crossed over the black-and-white tiled floor and made her way back into the sunroom, where she'd been seeing to the flowers. Her hands, however, shook a little, as she carried on arranging the mixed daffodils, forsythia and tulips that she'd brought in from the gardens into three cut-glass vases.

Contrary to what she'd told her unwanted visitors, Mr de Lacey *had* in fact mentioned that someone from the coroner's office might be calling to ask questions, and that she was to give them every courtesy. But she had not approved of this then, and she didn't approve now, and she was determined to do the best she could to make sure that no harm was allowed to come to the de Lacey family name.

It was all very well for Mr de Lacey to be so cavalier when throwing the door open to all sorts, in this new modern way, but in her experience it just didn't do. And it most certainly wouldn't have been allowed had his mother still been alive.

Cordelia Roper snapped some twigs off a bunch of forsythia

branches and jabbed them viciously into the vases. Mrs Vivienne de Lacey had been a proper lady, and she knew how things ought to be done. She also knew how dangerous it could be to let strangers poke their noses into places that didn't concern them.

The housekeeper glanced through the window and paused, one orange-trumpeted jonquil in hand, as she watched the odd pair wander down the drive in the direction of the kitchen gardens. The older man was saying something to that young girl in a police uniform, and for a moment, Cordelia Roper felt her heart flutter.

It had been said in her family that her Scottish grandmother had 'the sight' and in that moment, she felt for the first time as if some of that dubious gift might actually run in her veins also. For as she watched the duo, she felt a distinct shiver of foreboding ripple up her spine. It was as if someone had just said aloud that the old man and pretty young woman were harbingers of disaster to come – disaster for the family, and, therefore, disaster for herself and her own comfortable world.

For a second, she couldn't catch her breath, and she groped for a chair and sat down quickly.

She told herself she was being morbid and silly, and made a concerted effort to pull herself together. As she did so, she couldn't help but glance up, as if she could see right through the ceiling and plaster, past the floor above that, and all the way up to the top of the house, where the nursery was located.

Soon, Emily would be allocated a bedroom of her own on the adult floor. But for now, the child slept in her single bed next to her younger brother's rooms and the old schoolroom. And Cordelia couldn't help but wonder: what was the child thinking right now?

Emily was such a clever little thing, whose quiet manners and innocent smiles could often make you forget just how much it was that she actually heard and understood. Mature for her age though she may be, she was still only a little girl, and she *had* been so very fond of that farmer's lad. And soon her grief would turn to anger. Cordelia Roper's lips thinned. And who knew then what she might let slip if she was ever allowed to talk to outsiders unsupervised? For Cordelia had little doubt that Miss Emily's sharp ears and sharp eyes missed very little. And too much knowledge was not good for anyone, let alone an unpredictable – and unprotected – child.

Although the death of little Eddie Proctor had shocked and distressed her to the core, Cordelia was far more worried about Emily. And she was determined to watch over her, no matter what the squire said.

48

Chapter 9

Unaware of the housekeeper's angst, Trudy and Clement made their way through a sudden spell of welcome sunshine towards a tall, mellowing red-brick wall that Clement guessed might provide the shelter for the kitchen gardens.

Passing through a small archway, upon which climbed a splendid clematis that was just beginning to leaf, he caught sight, off to the left, of the square walls and grey-slated roof of a smaller house. It looked very much like a miniature replica of the Hall itself, and catching sight of it too, Trudy frowned at it thoughtfully.

Seeing her notice it, Clement smiled. 'The dower house, no doubt,' he said.

Trudy frowned. 'What's a dower house?'

'In the old days, the lord of the manor's wife ruled the household,' Clement explained. 'But when their eldest son married, the new lady of the manor and the mother-in-law didn't always hit it off. So it became a tradition, when the old lord of the manor died, that his widow – or dowager – would move out into an establishment of her own. Usually, like the case here' – he nodded towards the house – 'into a smaller version of the big house itself. She'd take her own staff and maids and what have you with her, and still have a home of her own where she could continue to rule the roost, leaving her daughter-in-law – the new lady of the manor – in possession of the main residence.'

'Oh,' Trudy said. Then couldn't help but smile. 'I'll bet that wasn't always done with much grace,' she muttered, making her friend laugh.

'I don't suppose it was,' Clement agreed.

They stepped through into the high-walled kitchen garden and looked around with pleasure. It reminded Trudy a bit of her dad's allotment, only on a much larger and more ornamental scale.

A tall, rather shambling man, with longish brown hair and a weather-beaten face was slowly and carefully training some pear tree saplings to grow along a south-facing wall. He glanced at them with vague curiosity as they stepped through the arch, but it was an older man, almost certainly the head gardener, who approached them first.

He'd been checking under some old galvanised tin tubs to see how the forced rhubarb was getting on, and now he rubbed his hands against the thighs of his not particularly clean trousers as he welcomed them. He had a shock of thick white hair and thick white bushy eyebrows over pale-blue eyes, and was already acquiring a tan, even so early in the season. It had the effect of making the crow's feet wrinkles at the corners of his eyes appear whiter than they should.

'Hello, sir, er… madam,' he said, clearly not sure how to address either one of them. 'Was you wantin' someone from the house?' Clearly strangers in the gardens were not a common occurrence.

'Not really,' Clement said, introducing himself and his companion. 'We're here because Mr Martin de Lacey has asked us to look into the circumstances surrounding Eddie Proctor's accident.'

Instantly, the old man's face fell. 'Ar, that was a bad business, that was. Mr de Lacey is getting workmen in to fill up the old well.'

Clement nodded. 'Perhaps that's a good thing. With the boy's father continuing to work here and all. Do you know Mr Proctor well, Mr… er…?'

'Oh, Cricklade sir, Leonard Cricklade. I'm the head gardener here. But that old well came under the jurisdiction, strictly speaking, of the estate manager…'

Clement held his hands up quickly. 'Oh, we're not here to apportion blame, or cast any stones, Mr Cricklade. I was the coroner at the boy's inquest, and I'm satisfied that the organisers of the event made it clear that the children were to stay within these walls.' As he spoke, he glanced around at the large, walled-in garden with pleasure. 'I've now talked to several of the children who were here that morning, and none of them were aware that Eddie had wandered off.'

'No doubt he'd still be alive now if he'd stayed put,' the old man agreed heavily, and joined Clement in glancing around at his domain.

Among the compost heaps, bean poles, various sheds and rows of well-tended vegetables and odd flowerbeds the coroner could well see that any amount of small eggs could have been hidden in this haven.

'Did you notice the boy leave the garden that morning? And if you did, was he with anyone?' Trudy asked hopefully, but the old man quickly shook his head.

'No, weren't working that day, see, seeing as it was Easter Sunday and all. Me and the missus were in chapel. Methodists, see. We had gone into Oxford.'

'Of course,' Trudy murmured. 'So it was only the organisers of the hunt who were here. None of the family came to watch, for instance?' she probed delicately.

'Don't think so. Well, Miss Emily and Master George would have been here, like, searching for the eggs along with the rest of the village kiddies. But none of the adults from up at the Hall, I shouldn't think. Mr de Lacey, he don't mind doing his bit for the village – letting the fete committee have run of the lower paddock and such. But he's not much of a one for interferin' like. He says he'd only get under people's feet.'

Clement hid a smile. He could well understand why Martin de Lacey would prefer to avoid bucolic village festivities in favour of a drink at his club.

'What about those in the dower house?' Trudy asked. 'Are there any de Laceys currently living there now? Might they have seen anything do you suppose?'

'Mr Oliver de Lacey and his mother live there. Have done many years since. No, they wouldn't have been present. Mr Oliver is a bachelor still, and so a'course don't have no kiddies of his own. His mother is a widow – she was married to Mr Clive, the younger brother of Mr Martin de Lacey's father. I think she was probably in town anyway. She prefers to spend holidays and such in London with friends and her own family.'

'Oh I see,' Trudy said. Well, so much for any potential witnesses within the de Lacey family.

'We will be talking to the members of the WI and the other organisers involved in the Easter egg hunt soon,' Clement said smoothly. 'But can you think of anyone else who might have been here at the time? Maybe one of your gardener's boys for instance,' Clement said, nodding towards the man expertly training the pear trees. Although he was nearing his forties, no doubt the head gardener thought of him as one of his 'boys'.

'Who? Lallie? Oh no, sir. None of the lads were working. They had time off because of the holiday see, like me. Mr de Lacey is good like that. Besides, Lallie doesn't like fuss and rumpus. He's a bit simple-like, sir,' he confessed, lowering his voice a little, lest the man hear them. 'Had a bad war, see. Doesn't like loud noises and lots of people. Mind you, he's fond of young'uns sir, and wouldn't hurt a fly, he wouldn't,' he added anxiously, lest the coroner get the wrong idea.

'I'm sure he wouldn't,' Clement reassured him mildly. 'I suppose he knew the boy though?'

'O yerse, sir, we all did, sir, and right fond of him we were too,' the head gardener said sadly. 'Being such a particular friend of Miss Emily and all, he was always about, the two of 'em running wild. Mind you, they didn't do no damage. We often saw them about the place, playing hide-and-seek and cops and robbers and whatnot. And helping themselves to the fruit and all, when they come into season,' he added, with a wry smile. 'Young Eddie was rather fond of the golden raspberries, as I recall. I used to pretend to try and catch 'em out, but always made enough noise so they heard me coming and took off, gigglin' like.' Suddenly his face fell as he realised that he wouldn't have to do that ever again.

'Well, thank you for your time, Mr Cricklade,' Clement said quickly, before the old man could dwell on it. Then, as a seeming afterthought, he added, 'The family's housekeeper…?'

'Mrs Roper, sir?'

'Yes. She seems rather, er, protective of the family?' He offered the opening gambit gingerly. In his opinion, servants either liked to gossip about each other, or shut up like clams. But he was betting that the housekeeper's prickly personality and obvious sense of entitlement hadn't won her any favour with the rest of the staff.

The old man grinned wryly. 'Oh yes, sir, she be that. Of course, her and the old Lady, Mrs Vivienne – Mr de Lacey's mother – were like this,' he said, holding up his hands and entwining two fingers together. 'So you can understand it, I 'spect.'

'Oh I see. It sounds as if she's been here some years?'

'Oh yes, sir. Not that she's a villager, mind. Born and raised in Brighton she was,' the old man said, shaking his head and making the seaside town sound as if it were on a level standing with Sodom or Gomorrah. 'But she met a lad from the village here when he was billeted near Hove during the war, and he married her and brought her back here to live. The old lady took a shine to her and so she went into service like. At first, it was supposed to be just while her Wilf was off fighting. But he didn't come back from the war, o'course, like a lot of our brave lads didn't, and so she sort of took to devoting herself to her mistress, like, as the ladies sometimes do. Yerse, real devoted to Mrs Vivienne, she was.'

Clement nodded. Yes, that explained quite a lot.

'Well, we shall probably see you around from time to time, Mr Cricklade. If, in the meantime, you can think of anything you think we should know, just say so,' Clement adjured him heartily.

The old man, however, looked slightly puzzled at this. 'Like what, sir?' he asked cautiously.

'Well. Did Eddie ever look worried or scared that you can recall? Did he ever confide in you about anything that troubled him? Did anything you saw him doing strike you as odd? Did you ever see him talking to strangers?'

'Oh right you are, sir. But I can tell you now, there was nothing like that. He was just a happy, normal little kiddie. And as for strangers…' The old man shrugged graphically. 'Round here, everyone knows everyone, if you see what I mean, sir. And like as not, everyone knows everyone's business before you even know it yourself.'

Clement, who'd also grown up in a small village, did.

'Mind you,' the old man said, then hesitated when both Trudy and Clement looked at him keenly.

'Yes?' Clement urged.

'Well, it might mean nothing, sir,' the old man began, clearly reluctant to start what he'd finished. He began to shuffle his feet and looked uncomfortable, glancing up at the big house, then away again.

'It's all right, the squire has given us carte blanche to ask anything we want,' Clement said.

The old man nodded. He might not have understood the fancy French-sounding words, but he got the gist of it all right. He sighed heavily.

'Ar, well... See, sir, it's on account of something sort of odd the boy said to me once.'

'When was this exactly?' Clement asked sharply.

'Oh, a week or so before Easter, I reckon it must have been. I caught him tearing across the kitchen garden, almost trampling some strawberry plants. Told him to keep off. There was no harm in him, sir, but he could run a bit wild and be careless like, like all kiddies when they're playing "chase" and such.'

'I'm sure he was a good lad,' Clement said, trying to keep a check on his impatience. 'But what was it he said that made you worry?'

'Well, not to say I worried, as such,' the gardener said cautiously. 'I just didn't understand what he meant, sir. He asked me if all grown-ups were rich.'

Clement blinked. 'Well, that sounds pretty normal to me. I suppose to most children, grown-ups always seem to have more money than they do!'

'Yes, sir, that's more or less what I told him, an' all.' The old man grinned. 'But then he looked up at me, all serious like, and said something like, "Yes, but are they usually mad when you find out?" Well, sir, that sort of stumped me a bit,' the old gardener admitted.

'So what did you say?' Clement asked, intrigued.

'I asked him if someone was mad at him, and he shrugged, and said he thought they might be.'

'Did he say who?'

'No, sir, he didn't. At that point, young Miss Emily, who he was playing chase with, ran up and "tagged" him and the pair went haring off. 'Course, at the time, I just forgot about it.' The old man scratched his nose and looked uneasily at the coroner. 'But now... well, it just makes me wonder a bit, what he could have meant, like.'

Clement nodded. He could well see how it might. A young boy hints that he's got on the wrong side of somebody, and a week later, he's found dead at the bottom of a well. He would wonder a bit too.

'Well, I'm sure you have nothing to reproach yourself for, Mr Cricklade,' he said heartily. 'Children often say things that don't amount to much.'

'Thank 'ee, sir,' the old man said, feeling at least better for having got things off his chest.

They took their leave of the old man, who set off to check his new potatoes for black fly, and Trudy looked at the coroner sharply.

'Do you really think the poor lad had made an enemy of somebody?' she asked.

'It certainly sounds possible,' Clement agreed. 'But whether or not anybody will actually admit to having had cross words with him is another matter.'

'It's beginning to feel more and more as if the accident might not have been such an accident after all, doesn't it?' she mused tentatively.

Clement nodded. 'It does, rather, doesn't it?' he agreed gravely.

'Something tells me this investigation is going to be difficult though,' she said dryly.

Clement paused to light his pipe, took a few puffs, and then shrugged. 'Well, so what if it is? It's nice to be out and about in the springtime, isn't it, instead of cooped up in our respective offices.'

A blackbird, busy finding nesting material, chose that moment to burst into song, and with a smile, Trudy had to agree with him. Anything that got her out from under the watchful, disapproving eye of DI Jennings was all right in her book.

'So, where next?' she asked more cheerfully.

Clement nodded towards the roof of the dower house. 'Well, why not call in at the dower house and see if anybody there was more observant than our Mr Cricklade?'

Chapter 10

At the dower house they were again out of luck. Neither of the residents, it seemed, were at home.

This time, at Trudy's suggestion, they had gone around to the back and to the kitchen entrance, which meant that a maid admitted them to the house. She appeared to be a village girl born and bred, still feeling happy to have her first job with 'the family'.

Perhaps her relative inexperience led her to rashly inviting them into the kitchen, where the cook – a middle-aged, comfortably padded woman – looked on them with less enthusiasm.

But the coroner soon had her eating out of his hand, and within a few minutes, both he and Trudy were seated at the cook's well-scrubbed kitchen table, eating wonderful, still slightly warm scones with home-made plum jam, and sipping from large mugs of tea.

Mrs Jones, the cook, had nothing but sympathy for the Proctors.

'That poor little lad,' she said, seeming pleased that her jam was going down well with her handsome, silver-haired visitor. 'To think of him falling down that well. It don't bear thinking about.' She shuddered theatrically, and gave a mournful sigh.

'Poor Miss Emily was distraught, I heard Mr Oliver say the other day. And I don't wonder at it.'

'I don't suppose you saw anything odd that morning, Mrs Jones, did you?' Trudy asked, surreptitiously licking her sticky fingers and hoping that nobody else had noticed. Was it only her who couldn't seem to eat jam and scones without making a mess of it?

'No, lovey, I wasn't here,' the cook said quickly. 'On account of Mrs Sylvia being in London with her aunt and uncle, and Mr Oliver insisting I take the Easter weekend off, like.'

'They sound like thoughtful employers,' Trudy encouraged gently.

'Oh they are. Mrs Sylvia's no trouble, and lives real quiet here. Mind you, I suppose she feels it a little bit. Being here at Mr Martin's grace and favour as it were.'

The cook said this blandly enough, but Clement knew when bait was being cast under his nose, and smoothly reached out for another scone. 'Hope you don't mind, but these are really delicious!'

The cook flushed with pleasure, and he said casually, 'I suppose Mrs Sylvia is regarded as being a bit of a poor relation then? Not a very enviable role to have to play, I've always thought,' he said mildly.

'Well, she has her husband's war pension,' the cook said judiciously, 'and her son, Mr Oliver, he's very well thought of in the government. A very clever man, he is,' she said, with obvious pride. 'One of them dons at Oxford. And he has an important job in London, as an Adviser.'

She said the last word with an obvious capital letter, and a slightly hushed tone of reverence.

'Ahh,' Clement said, matching her hushed tone with a conspiratorial smile of his own. 'Well, things don't sound too bad for them then. I suppose the house belongs to the head of the family though?' he added, glancing around casually.

'Oh yes. But the old lady, Vivienne – her what's been dead for the past ten years or so – she insisted Clive have this house when he brought his bride home. And when he died in the war, there was never no question that Mrs Sylvia and Oliver would continue to live on here. Mind you, recently... well, that's nothing and least said, soonest mended,' she suddenly veered off, as if realising that she was on the verge of becoming truly indiscreet.

And Trudy, not wanting her to start feeling uncomfortable, quickly steered the conversation back to the matter in hand.

'It must have come as a terrible shock when you heard about poor Eddie,' she said. 'I take it you know the Proctors well?'

'Oh yes. Well, as well as I know all the farmworkers,' she qualified quickly. 'You see them around, like, and have a nice chat. And come harvest time, when it's all hands on deck, me and Mrs Verney – she's cook up at the Hall – we get our heads together and bake up a storm for harvest festival, and all the workers and their families come to the service and attend the picnic when the gathering's all done.'

'Were you surprised to hear about the accident?' Clement asked curiously. 'I mean, was Eddie the sort of boy you might expect to do something dangerous?'

'I dunno about that, sir,' the cook said uncertainly. 'I'd have said Eddie was a clever boy, rather than a tearaway, like. But then, kiddies do some silly things, don't they. But oh, his poor mother...'

For the next ten minutes they made small talk, but nothing of use was learned, and eventually the young maid, who'd been listening silent but wide-eyed throughout it all, showed them back to the door.

'You know, sir, if you don't mind my saying,' she said tentatively, when she'd opened the kitchen door for them, and had stood to one side for them to pass, 'I couldn't come to think how Eddie fell in that well either. He was friends with my little brother, sir, and he always struck me as a lad with a good head on his shoulders.'

But after this promising opening, they learned little of use from her. It wasn't until they'd all but begun to walk away, that they learned one little titbit of family gossip that, though interesting from a purely prurient point of view, probably wouldn't prove to be relevant.

The coroner had just said that he hoped their visit hadn't disrupted their morning routine, and that he was afraid that some of his questions, especially those concerning the set-up at the dower house, might have upset the cook. 'I rather thought, at one point, that Mrs Jones had been about to say something about the family, before changing her mind. I only hope we didn't come across as being too nosy about family affairs,' Clement finished cannily.

'Oh don't be frettin' yourself about that, sir,' the maid said with a smile. 'Cook be fond enough of Sylvia, ma'am, but she don't like to think that she and Mr Oliver might be running into difficulties with Mr Martin.'

'Oh?' Clement said encouragingly.

The maid shrugged helplessly. 'It's on account of the American lady, sir,' she said, glancing nervously over her shoulder as she did so. 'Cook's worried, I can tell. She thinks Mr Martin might ask Mr Oliver to leave. But I don't believe it'll ever come to that, sir. Mr Martin might be on the outs with his cousin, but he won't chuck Mrs Sylvia out onto the streets,' she said judiciously, shaking her head. 'It'll never happen, sir, mark my words. The village wouldn't like it. They remember Mr Clive with too much affection for that to happen. They won't stand for his widow being treated shabbily, no matter how much he and Mr Oliver argue. And Mr Martin, he always does what's expected of him, sir.'

Trudy and Clement exchanged baffled looks. 'Mr Martin and his cousin Oliver have begun arguing have they?' Clement asked casually. 'Well, well, even the best of families *will* quarrel,' he agreed blandly. 'And over a lady you say? Well, again, these things do happen.'

The maid gave a slightly cunning smile, which suddenly belied her tender years. 'The American lady is rich they say, sir,' she said archly.

Clement blinked at this blatant bit of cynicism, but then had to smile. Trust the village grapevine not to mince matters.

'And both... ah, Mr Martin and Mr Oliver have shown an interest in this lady, I take it?' he fished carefully.

'Yes, sir. She lives in the city, sir. One of these American ladies who come over to study at the university they say,' she added a shade darkly, clearly having her suspicions about academic females.

'And all this has happened just recently?'

'Within the last six months or so, sir,' she confirmed easily. 'Anyways, I best get back to Cook. You can see yourself out, sir, can't you?'

'Oh yes,' Clement agreed. 'Much obliged, miss.'

The maid smiled, and stepped back inside.

Trudy waited until the door was shut behind them, and they had started to walk away, before glancing across at her friend. 'Rather interested in the de Laceys' domestic life, aren't you?'

Clement shrugged, unwilling to be drawn.

'Well, I can't see what their tangled love lives have to do with Eddie Proctor's death,' she said, then flushed a little, wishing that she hadn't sound quite so prim.

But the coroner didn't seem to notice. Instead he paused to open the garden gate to let her through, and then looked out across the meadow opposite, where several large horse chestnut trees were just beginning to form their distinctive white-and-pink 'candles'.

'You never know what might prove relevant and what won't,' he advised her. 'When you're groping about in the dark, any fact has to be worth uncovering.'

And with that, Trudy had to be content.

Chapter 11

Up on the top floor of Briar's Hall, Emily de Lacey stared out over her family's fiefdom through a small dormer window. From here, she could almost see all of it – the rolling, productive farmlands, the encompassing small wood, and some of the rooftops of the village itself. She knew, vaguely, that her family owned all the cottages in the village, as well as the pub. She'd once heard her father say to someone at a family party that the only thing the de Laceys didn't own was the church.

And for some reason, that had pleased her.

Now, though, nothing much pleased her at all.

She rubbed her eyes, which felt sore, and which any mirror would have told her were red from her constant crying. Her ribs also ached from all the sobbing that she'd done that morning, just after she'd woken up.

Mornings were the worst, Emily had decided. Because in that one fleeting moment when you first woke up, before you had time to remember things, Eddie wasn't dead. For a just a tiny amount of time, it was possible that she could get up, gobble her breakfast, and then race out of the house to meet Eddie by their secret place, and decide what to play.

But then she would remember. And cry.

And now, here she was, standing by the window, looking out on a sunny but breezy day, and wondering what she could possibly do with herself. Because she was bored, as well as everything else. Her family wouldn't let her leave the house just yet, although she knew of two ways that she could sneak out of if she really wanted to. But who was there to play with her if she did? Everyone she knew was back at school now. Normally, she wouldn't mind not having to go to school, but the trouble was, she couldn't seem to settle down to anything here on her own. Normally, on the rare occasions when she had to 'play quietly' by herself, she could play clock patience, or do a jigsaw puzzle, or read. She had a lot of books and had been halfway through *Treasure Island* when…

Easter Sunday.

Emily felt another sob rack her thin body and tried to think of something else.

She knew she should brush her hair, for instance, since Mrs Roper always said tidy hair indicated a tidy mind. But in a mutinous moment of defiance, Emily ran her hands through her long, brown locks and mussed them up even more.

But it was no use. Nothing would take her mind off things, and once again she let her mind drift back in time.

She'd been excited about the Easter egg hunt – everyone at school was. Even Eddie, who wasn't that much fussed about chocolate, was eager to get started, and they were among the first to congregate at the entrance to the kitchen gardens.

Of course, they'd all been warned not to trample through the vegetables and fruit, and had been told very firmly by Miss Reason, the indomitable leader of the Briar's-in-the-Wold branch of the WI, that none of the eggs were hidden in the vegetable plots. Instead, they were to stick to the grass paths, the walls, the potting sheds and outhouses.

And at ten o'clock they'd been allowed in – all of her friends giggling and laughing and splitting up, all bragging they'd find the most, whilst the adults looked on, and reprimanded anyone forgetting the warnings to keep out of old Crickie's vegetable patches or the flowerbeds.

But try as she might, she couldn't remember when Eddie had sneaked off and gone about his own business without her. Because he *must* have *deliberately* sneaked off, Emily had decided. They'd started the hunt together and had promised to share out their finds later, and usually Eddie kept his word. But when she'd been hunting around the water butt, sure that some of the stones around it must have hollows between them where an egg could be hidden, she'd looked up to say something to him, and he wasn't there.

She'd looked around but couldn't see him anywhere. She'd felt a little cross about it, but had gone on hunting for eggs on her own. After all, what did it matter to her if he'd gone off? He was probably trying to find more eggs so that he could give them to his brothers and sister, before 'sharing' whatever was left with her. Or so she'd reasoned at the time.

But now she wondered. Why had he gone into the old orchard at all? It wasn't as if it was the time of year to find any fruit there. (Lallie always let them scrump the fruit whenever they wanted, without even pretending to chase them!) So there was no reason why Eddie would have even gone there. He knew there wouldn't be any eggs there, because Miss Reason had said so. It just didn't make sense.

Emily shifted in front of the window, surprised to see two strangers come out of the arch to the kitchen garden, pause to talk for a moment, and then make their way over towards her Uncle Oliver's house.

She craned her thin neck a little better to watch their progress, but from this distance and height it was a little hard to make out much detail about the interlopers. She could see, from his thatch of white hair, that one of them was an old man. And the other was a girl, but she was wearing some odd-looking dark clothes.

And her hat didn't look like any hat that she'd seen Mrs Roper wear, either.

But then they disappeared from sight and, her momentary distraction gone, she sank back into thinking about Eddie.

She felt another tear run down her face, and brushed it away. What was the use of crying, she told herself angrily? It wouldn't bring her friend back.

She sniffed hard and wiped her nose with the back of her hand, then reached impatiently for her hankie. Ladies, Mrs Roper said, always used handkerchiefs. It had made Eddie laugh, for he'd never possessed such an object.

Emily wiped the back of her hand hard with the small square of linen and lace, then lost interest in it, and stuffed it unceremoniously back up her sleeve.

It was no good trying to run away from things, she reminded herself stalwartly. The truth, so the vicar said, always found you out. And it turned out that he was right about that. Which was sort of odd, Emily thought with a frown, when you stopped to actually consider Reverend Cryer. Old and dithery, Eddie had called him. He seemed, on the face of it, the last sort of grown-up you'd expect to actually know what he was going on about.

Oh well. Emily heaved a sigh, and dragged her thoughts back to 'the truth'. Which had to be 'faced'. Just like the vicar, Mrs Roper had always maintained that it was no use trying to hide from unpalatable facts. (Emily had had to look up the word in the dictionary, and finding it pleasing, used it whenever she could. It amused her father to hear her use it, which was always nice and gave her a pleasant feeling in her tummy.) Facts, Mrs Roper had gone on to lecture her at length, needed to be faced down and 'firmly dealt with'.

So, up in her room, 10-year-old Emily de Lacey faced down the facts.

She knew that Eddie wouldn't have tried to climb down that

well. Eddie didn't like heights, so he wouldn't have gone down the well on purpose.

And Eddie wasn't silly, so he didn't fall in by accident.

Which left only one thing. Somebody, Emily de Lacey thought tiredly, had put him in there.

And what if it was all her fault? What if the thing she'd told him all those weeks ago had got him into trouble? Or (an even more terrible thought this) what if someone had noticed what they'd been doing since then?

Would that same someone put her down the well too?

Alone, at the top of her house, surrounded by views of her family's fiefdom, little Emily de Lacey began to cry again.

Chapter 12

'The Bell' was busy enough for a small country village pub that lunchtime, which is why Clement suggested, after leaving the dower house, that they have lunch there.

He wasn't expecting more than sandwiches or an indifferent pie and a pint, and so was pleased to see that ham off the bone, fresh-baked bread, cheese and pickles were on offer. He ordered and paid for two hearty dishes, and returned to the window seat with them, where Trudy was waiting.

When they'd first stepped inside, her uniform had attracted immediate attention, but after a moment, the backs and faces that had been turned their way, turned back again, and conversation had slowly drifted back around the smoke-filled bar.

Most of the thirsty drinkers, Trudy could tell at once, were farm hands, but she made no attempt to engage them in conversation. Well, not just yet, anyway. She had an idea that Dr Ryder would want to talk to the locals about the Proctors and she didn't want to queer his pitch by making them nervous of her police uniform.

One whiff that this was to be a formal interview by the police and she could forget about them offering any real confidences.

So she smiled her thanks as Clement brought the food over

and accepted her glass of lemonade gladly. The coroner, she noted, had a modest half-pint of the local brew from Hook Norton.

She watched him take a sip, sigh, and then reach for the dish of butter and begin to spread a slice of bread generously. But her smile wavered a little as she noticed that the hand holding the butter knife was trembling slightly.

Should she just pluck up her courage when they were alone and simply ask him outright why he sometimes had the shakes? But the thought of being so outspoken made her go a little cold.

What if he took offence and reprimanded her for not minding her own business? She would hate to ruin their friendship! And it would be horrible if she never saw him again.

Surely it was better to just let sleeping dogs lie. Her dad always said you couldn't put the genie back in the bottle.

So she determinedly thrust the problem to the back of her mind and quashed it once more, then picked up her knife and fork and cut into her ham. 'Hmm, this is good,' she said, both truthfully and loudly enough for the landlord to hear and beam his approval.

Mine host was a small, red-faced man, going bald on top, but with a look of sincere bonhomie on his face that had probably stood him very well in his chosen profession over the years.

'Pigs be butchered fresh by the chap up at Manor Farm,' he called across amiably. 'And smoked in his own smokehouse. And the wife makes the cheese herself with Grandma's old churn out back, and milk from the Jerseys.'

'The cheese is spectacular,' Clement concurred, again quite truthfully. 'And the onions aren't bad either.'

An old man, who'd been playing dominoes in one corner with an even older crony, gave a sudden cackle. 'Don't you go trying Elsie's piccalilli mind, mister, or it'll blow the top of your 'ead orf!'

There was a general ripple of mirth at this, and the landlord grunted good-naturedly. 'That's what you want from a good piccalilli, Cyrus, you old coot.'

Clement, seeing that there was no time like the present, leaned back in his chair and grinned. 'I'll remember that. I'm Dr Clement Ryder, by the way,' he added, his bass, educated voice addressing the room in general, and sounding impressive, even to Trudy's ears. 'I was the coroner who held the inquest on little Eddie Proctor. We've just been up at the Hall, offering our condolences.'

There was a small, sad silence as the room digested his bona fides, then the landlord took up the mantle. 'Ah. That was a very sad business that. Very sad.' He nodded his head several times as he began to clean and polish some glasses with a spotless cloth.

Clement nodded. 'Yes. I see some very sad things in my profession, I'm sorry to say. The Proctors are having a hard time of it right now.'

There was another general shifting in the room. 'Vince, he's out over by Folly Meadow now. Reckons he's better off working, and who's to say he's not right?' one man, a large, muscular chap with the kind brown eyes of a spaniel and hands like spades, spoke up over his glass of cloudy cider.

'I take it you all knew his Eddie?' Clement asked, whilst Trudy, wisely, kept silent and got on with her lunch, trying to make herself as invisible as possible.

'Oh yerse,' the big man continued heavily. His work boots were caked with mud, and his big, chapped hands restlessly turned his glass around and around on the tabletop. 'A real bright spark he were. Happy chap, always out and about and up to larks.'

'Great pals with Emily de Lacey, or so I've been told,' Clement mused casually.

'Another bright spark that 'un,' someone else piped up from the back of the bar. Because of the smoke and the smallness of the windows, which let in little light, Trudy couldn't actually make out who it was who spoke, but his pronouncement seemed to meet with approval, because everyone nodded or smiled.

'Clever as a monkey, she is,' the old man with the dominoes agreed. 'I often seen her and Eddie conspiring together. Had a notebook, she had, and giggling like little gals do as she wrote stuff down. When they seen me coming they hid it right quick.' The old man laughed. 'Told 'em that diaries were good things to keep, for them that could read and write, and she told me it weren't no diary but their secret codebook.'

Clement smiled. 'Secret codebook eh? Sounds mysterious.'

'Oh, they be playing spies, or some such,' the anonymous voice again spoke up from the back. 'Eddie told me they suspected the milkman was a German spy, and they was making a note of his rounds, and checking to see no hidden messages had been written on his milk bottles!'

The room exploded in mirth at this. 'So that's why old Sissie Mayflower thought he was trying to snaffle her milk,' the big man said with a grunt of laughter. 'She stopped me one day in the road, and said I was to guard my milk. I thought the old maid had finally gone daft!'

Clement let the fond laughter subside, then said gently, 'Sounds like he was the adventurous sort. I dare say that old well proved a real temptation for him to explore. It's a pity the de Laceys didn't make sure it was better covered.'

There was a brief, hard silence, then the landlord, once again, took up the challenge.

'Well, that's true enough, no way around it,' he agreed gruffly. 'But I dare say they never thought nothin' on it. Who'd have thought a kiddie would fall in?'

There was a general murmur of agreement at this, which didn't surprise Trudy at all. After all, every one of these men worked on de Lacey land, and lived in de Lacey property. Even the landlord must have been given the licence and the living at the pub by the grace and favour of the powerful family. So none of them were going to criticise the likes of Martin de Lacey openly.

70

But she also sensed that their sympathy for the family was genuine.

'And they're filling in the well now, I understand,' Clement said, no doubt sensing the same thing, and not wanting to lose their goodwill. 'Which I recommended they do at the inquest. So at least nobody else has to worry about their own children playing in the orchard and not being safe.'

'Yerse, praise be,' the big man said. 'I told my own nippers I'd have their hides if I found 'em in there, mind.'

Clement nodded, then abruptly changed the subject. 'I tried to speak to little Emily, but the housekeeper wouldn't let me past the door.'

At this, there was another gust of laughter. 'Ah, she wouldn't. Old lady Vivienne's dragon we call her,' the old man said, and moved a double-six onto the line of dominoes in front of him with a small grunt of satisfaction. 'All starch and vinegar she is!'

Clement cast his net a bit wider. 'We also tried to call on Mr Oliver de Lacey, but he was out.'

'Ah, you'll be lucky to find him in, mister,' the old man warned. 'He's one of them nuclear bomb people.'

At this, Trudy nearly choked on her lemonade.

'Sorry?' Clement asked, just as startled.

'He means,' the landlord said, casting the old man a glare, 'he's one of those nuclear electric wallahs. Off to London whenever he's not teaching at the university, see. Advising the Gov'ment on them power stations them's set on building and all.'

'Oh I see. So he's a physicist,' Clement said. 'A clever man then.'

'Oh yerse, no doubt,' the landlord said slyly. 'Well, when it comes to having it up here.' He tapped his temple meaningfully. 'Mind you, he has other interests 'sides all that atomic stuff. And just as hot a topic, I'll be bound.'

And again there was a general ripple of mirth.

'Oh? Bit of a ladies' man is he,' Clement guessed, catching on pretty quickly. Given that he'd just been told Oliver and Martin de Lacey were showing an interest in the same woman, it seemed to him to be a good bet.

And from the guffaws that followed, he realised that he was right.

'Never get married and settled down, he won't,' the old man predicted. 'Having too much fun being the bachelor boy. Despair of his poor mother, no doubt. She might want grand-kiddies to dandle on her knee, but she'll have to wait a while yet, I reckon!'

'Good-looking chap is he?' Clement asked, polishing off the last of the bread with gusto.

'He thinks so,' the big man said, again to general merriment.

Wondering if news about the cousins' mutual interest in the rich American lady was known in the village, Clement took a sip of his excellent beer, and mused, 'Mr Martin de Lacey now – he seems a very different sort altogether.'

'Oh yerse,' the landlord said at once. 'Salt o' the earth, is Mr Martin.'

'Ah,' the big man said. 'He understands how things should be done all right. Got a real feel for sheep, he has.' He said this with such finality and reverence that it was clear that, as far as he was concerned, nothing more needed to be said.

'Installed indoor privvies in all the cottages too, he did,' the anonymous voice nevertheless piped up in affirmation from his hidden spot in the corner. 'My wife was in seventh 'eaven for months.'

'And he don't put up the rent, 'cepting every now and then,' the old man with the dominoes agreed.

Trudy, who'd been watching the pair of old fellows on and off for some time, had yet to see his even more ancient companion actually move, and she was rapidly coming to the conclusion that he must be asleep. She couldn't see much of his face under the peak of his cap, so his eyes might well be closed.

'He must be having a hard time of it now though,' Clement said sympathetically. 'What with what happened to Eddie playing on his mind. I know for a fact he's doing all he can to help Vincent Proctor, but that sort of thing must lay heavy on a man. Pity his wife's not still alive to comfort him.'

At this, there was a subtle but unmistakable withdrawal. One moment, the room had been inclined to be friendly and affable. And the next… it was as if Trudy and Clement became the instant outsiders again.

'Another half, sir?' the landlord inquired of Clement.

But Clement, no mean psychologist, understood at once that it would be pointless staying now. 'No thank you.' He got up, Trudy silently following suit. 'But please give my compliments to your wife. That was some of the best bread I've ever eaten.'

The landlord beamed. 'I'll tell her, sir.'

Trudy nodded her own thanks, but could feel the eyes boring into her back as she and Clement walked the short distance to the door.

Once outside, she drew a long, steady breath.

'Well, that was interesting,' she said, a shade ruefully.

'Wasn't it just?' Clement agreed with a grin. 'I wonder just what the late Mrs de Lacey did to get in their bad books?'

Trudy sighed. 'Let me guess. You want me to find out all I can about her, right.'

Clement smiled. 'You know me so well, young Trudy,' he teased.

But do I? Trudy wondered, as she climbed into the passenger seat in the Rover beside him.

As he turned the ignition, she plucked up her courage and said as casually as she could manage, 'So how have you been keeping lately?'

But it sounded unbelievably clumsy and out of the blue, even to her own ears, and she wasn't surprised when he looked across at her with one white eyebrow raised questioningly.

'I just wondered how you've been, that's all. There was that nasty bug going around a few weeks back. It seemed everyone I met had had it or was coming down with it,' she heard herself gabbling.

'Really? I must have been one of the lucky ones then,' Clement said briskly.

Trudy nodded, but having finally broached the subject, couldn't quite let it go yet. 'So you're feeling in the pink then?' she prompted. Surely, if there had been anything that he'd been trying to confide in her about his health, she'd just given him the perfect opening for it.

Again Clement shot her a swift, assessing glance. But his eyes had grown wide. 'Yes, I'm perfectly well,' he said flatly. 'And you?'

'Me? Oh I'm fine,' Trudy said, swallowing hard. 'But if I wasn't, I'd tell you.' She turned and smiled at him, hoping she wasn't grinning like a ghastly clown or something. 'As I dare say you'd tell me too. If you were ever under the weather.'

Clement smiled vaguely and put the car into gear. Trudy, feeling an idiot, stared miserably out of the windscreen.

*

They had been gone a few minutes, before two men in the back of the pub rose from their seats and also quietly left. In their mid-forties, they were both dark-haired and clean-shaven, with regulation short-back-and-sides, and wore good quality (but not ostentatiously so) suits. They'd arrived not long before noon, and had been ensconced in the darkest part of the bar for some time. Long enough, at any rate, for the regulars to have noted their presence, and then more or less forget about them, since neither had spoken much – not even to each other.

It was observed by those seated nearest to them that neither of them had finished their pints of beer, which made them even more of a distinct oddity.

The pub's inhabitants watched them go thoughtfully. But once rid of their surprising presence, the talk quickly turned to the coroner and the woes of the Proctor family. Some said that Doreen had begun taking to the drink too much, though her best friend, Flo Robbins, insisted that it wasn't so.

Outside the pub, the two men climbed silently into their car, and drove away.

Chapter 13

Clement dropped Trudy off at his office, where a pile of paperwork patiently and persistently awaited him. She retrieved her bicycle from the courtyard where she'd left it, and pedalled back the short distance to the station, mulling over all that they'd learned so far. Which didn't seem much, she mused ruefully. She certainly didn't feel confident that they were getting anywhere nearer to establishing whether or not Eddie Proctor's death had been an accident or a well-concealed and executed murder.

She briefly reported her actions to her uninterested DI, who brusquely gave her permission to spend some time in the local library on the research the coroner had asked her to carry out, and within twenty minutes, she was once more pedalling through the city streets.

With a grin, she had to acknowledge that she didn't mind doing paperwork of her own, when it involved researching something interesting like this, and she contentedly hummed the Everly Brothers' latest hit 'Walk Right Back' under her breath as she went.

The sun was out, making the city's Cotswold stone buildings shine palely, wherever they weren't blackened by the city's habitual pall of coal fire smoke and traffic fumes. A laden Foden lorry, carrying slack from a quarry not far away, made a blatant traffic violation near Carfax, but Trudy turned a blind eye to it.

During her first month on the job she wouldn't have done so, and would have flagged him down, forcing the driver to pull over and writing him a citation without a second's thought. Now, though, she felt as if she had more important things to do, but did wonder guiltily if she was committing the cardinal sin of 'relaxing her standards'. This, so her tutors had drummed into her during her training period, was something she would always need to be vigilant about.

But the lorry was now out of sight, so there was no use dithering about it, and with a shrug Trudy told herself that, of course, the case she was working now – the unexplained death of a small boy – had to take priority. Even so, she had to console her conscience by promising herself that the next violation of the law she saw would have her swooping down on the miscreant like a veritable avenging angel. Well, as close an approximation to that as a probationary WPC of the City Police could manage, anyway!

Once at the nearest library, it didn't take her long to find, with the help of a friendly assistant librarian, the archive of the city's newspapers.

She started, naturally, with the obituaries. The death of someone as prominent in local society as the wife of Martin de Lacey was almost sure to have been well documented, and a lavish if discreet obituary was an obvious starting-off point. It would provide her with date of death and some bare facts, although it was by no means certain that she'd learn much more, she had to acknowledge realistically. Old families, as she was fast learning, had a habit of keeping their business low key.

But she needn't have worried, since she immediately struck gold with a newspaper article that had been published just a day after Martin de Lacey became a widower. The story had simply been too newsworthy to keep out of the papers.

With her heartbeat steadily accelerating with every word she read, Trudy made copious notes of the very interesting particulars surrounding the death of Jennifer de Lacey, nee Wainwright, a little over three years ago.

Jennifer had been the only daughter of a wealthy banker from Sussex, who had come up to Oxford to study Fine Art at Somerville College. At one of the city's many soirées, she met her future husband, Martin de Lacey, and the couple fell in love and were married just after Jennifer finished her degree. She was 21, and from the photographs Trudy later managed to track down of their big, society wedding, had been a very beautiful woman indeed. With waves of long dark hair framing a heart-shaped face, it wasn't hard to see why Martin de Lacey had chosen her for his bride.

The marriage seemed to have been a happy and successful one, with Jennifer giving birth to two children – Emily, and then three years later, George. Trudy had little trouble tracing their activities through the archives, as they were featured prominently at charity galas, theatre first-night performances, and all the big annual balls. The glamorous couple were also photographed regularly at the Henley Regatta, and of course, Ascot and other such events.

But then, three years ago, tragedy had struck this golden couple.

One morning, Jennifer had taken her favourite horse, a handsome hunter named Seamus, out for his usual ride, which included a gallop over the hills on the de Lacey estate. She had been an acknowledged horsewoman from an early age, and was a regular at the local hunt, and the de Laceys, naturally, kept a large stable.

But that morning, Seamus, sweating and in a state of some agitation, had returned to the stables without his rider.

An immediate search was made, and Jennifer's body was found in one of the meadows, lying not too far from a large hawthorn hedge. Her neck had been broken, along with her collarbone and one of her legs, leading to speculation that her horse may have trampled her, or rolled on her, in their fall.

When she read this, Trudy had to pause to think of the odd coincidence that both the unlucky Mrs de Lacey, and the boy, Eddie Proctor, should both meet their ends in much the same manner – that of a broken neck.

It was all but a foregone conclusion at the inquest that the jury would decide that Mrs de Lacey had fallen after jumping the hedge, and that they would bring in a verdict of misadventure. She was duly buried in Briar's-in-the-Wold churchyard, and was mourned by her surviving husband, children and her parents.

Trudy made a note in her notebook to ask Dr Ryder if he could look up the inquest details and see what the witnesses had had to say about it all. She knew that he couldn't have been the coroner at the original inquest, or he'd have mentioned it before now, but she also knew that Clement wouldn't let that stop him from accessing the records. And if his fellow coroners didn't like it, they would no doubt be told to lump it!

Feeling satisfied with her progress so far, Trudy packed up for the day and went home.

Chapter 14

When he got back to his office, Clement Ryder checked that the door was firmly shut behind him, and that his secretary was safely and noisily tapping away at her Remington typewriter. He then went to his desk, sat down with a relieved grunt and, reaching into his desk drawer, withdrew a small brown glass bottle of pills.

He'd bought the pills during his Christmas holiday in Switzerland a few months ago, where he knew an old friend who would prescribe them for him with no questions asked.

He took two of the pills now with water and then leaned back in his comfortable chair. He felt a little tired, but ignored it. He was no spring chicken, and couldn't expect to swan around as if he were. Even so, he knew that the ennui that sometimes swept over him couldn't always be accredited just to his age. That was wishful thinking.

After a lifetime in medicine, he knew what it meant to have Parkinson's disease. Who better?

But he was confident that he was still in the very early stages, and that he'd done all that could be done to maximise his chances of continuing to lead a good and productive life for some years to come yet.

Of course, he'd had to resign as a surgeon. You couldn't

continue to operate when your hands might start trembling any moment. But he told himself he was reasonably happy with his new career as a city coroner. It was interesting and fulfilling most of the time, and allowed him to keep making his mark in the world.

His mouth felt dry – another symptom of the blasted disease that was slowly but inexorably making inroads into his health – and he poured himself a second glass of water.

And then he went over that moment in the car, when Trudy had asked him if he was feeling well. He wanted to believe that it meant nothing. That it was just his heightened sensitivity on the subject that made him think she had begun suspecting that there was something wrong with him.

But he knew he would be living in a fool's paradise. Trudy was a bright, clever, and observant young woman. Clearly, she was, at the very least, aware of something not being quite right. And she couldn't have made it any more clear that she was giving him the opportunity to talk about it, if she'd come right out and asked him.

But there was simply no way that he could confide in a young, serving police constable, that he was unfit for his duties. Burdening her with his secrets, and then asking her to keep them would be patently unfair on her. Even though he was fairly confident that she wouldn't report her knowledge to her superiors if he asked her not to, it still wasn't a risk that he was prepared to take.

Besides, he was a man who'd always kept his own counsel.

And what if she started pitying him? He shuddered. No. He would say nothing. Whatever little tell-tale signs she'd noticed, at this stage, could only have led to vague suspicions on her part. With luck, it would be a year or more before anything more overt made her sure that something was wrong with him.

And they would cross that bridge when they came to it. Not before.

Determined not to sit and brood, he turned his thoughts to

the Proctor case. It was early days yet, but he was beginning to think that perhaps the boy's father might just be on to something.

It was not so much that they'd learned anything *physical*. Nothing, for instance, that Trudy's hard-headed DI would accept as actual evidence. But the psychology was interesting. The players in the drama were slowly taking shape, and Clement's instincts were beginning to kick in. He was not a man given to outbursts of imagination or the kind to be influenced by atmosphere, naturally, but Clement was nevertheless willing to concede that there was definitely something 'off' at Briar's-in-the-Wold.

Not that he'd say as much to young Trudy! She'd accuse him of having 'intuition' which was nonsense. But he *was* an experienced man of the world, and you didn't get to be his age, and reach the heights of both his chosen careers, without learning how to read people.

And so far, he'd met several players in the Eddie Proctor case who were definitely afraid of something, and intent on covering up whatever it was that worried them. Whether or not that was actually something as bad as murder, though... Oh well, time would tell.

And so, telling himself that although he was feeling heavy-eyed, he really didn't need to take a nap (bloody Parkinson's be damned), Clement determinedly reached for the first of the folders in his In Tray, and opened it.

Chapter 15

The moment Trudy stepped through the front door, the smell of steak and kidney pudding wafted through from the kitchen, making her mouth water.

Her mother called out her usual hello, and Trudy answered back as she ran lightly up the stairs to change and have a wash, before coming back down.

As she stepped into the hall she heard her father's voice, then, with some surprise, another male voice answer him. As she swept into the small kitchen, Brian grinned up at her from the table and mumbled hello.

'Hello, Brian,' she said with a friendly smile, but inside she felt her spirits dip a little. It was not that Brian was an unattractive visitor to come home to. He had a mop of pleasing sandy-coloured hair, and a wide, handsome face, a little marred by freckles perhaps, but this was more than compensated for by his smile. He had a nice square chin, and clean white teeth, and was, as Trudy knew only too well, considered to be something of a catch by all the girls in Botley.

But after the lunch at the hotel, she'd sensed that things between them – and their lacklustre courtship – needed to be sorted out once and for all, and she was not particularly looking forward to it.

'Isn't this nice?' Barbara Loveday said cheerfully, hefting the suet pudding from her biggest saucepan of boiling water, and setting the glass dish onto the draining board. 'Brian just popped around to see if you were back from work yet, and since there's more than enough' – she indicated her muslin-topped steaming pudding – 'to go around, I asked him to stay for dinner.'

Trudy nodded, pulling back her chair. Naturally, her mother would invite him to dinner. Barbara Loveday spent a good deal of her time reminding her daughter of just how lucky she was that Brian Bayliss was so fond of her.

'Yes, Brian always could smell a good dinner from a mile off!' she teased him.

She'd known Brian for all her life, and felt as natural with him as she did with her own brother. He was just a year older than she was, and since his family lived just down the street, they'd gone through primary and secondary school together. There, although he had never exactly shone in the classroom, Brian had excelled at rugby, and now played for the local amateur team, who regularly managed to lift the available silverware on offer.

It had always been Barbara Loveday's and Mrs Bayliss's fondest wish that the two of them would make a match of their own, but for all their scattered dates and friendly outings together, Trudy had never really felt that this was going to happen. And now she was wondering if she was not the only one who'd been thinking that. For unless she'd misread the signs, her so-called 'boyfriend' wasn't all that keen on taking their relationship any further either.

'Brian's just told us he's got a new job,' her father said, folding his newspaper away and propping it up against a plant pot on the kitchen windowsill.

'Yes, with better pay than his old job, plus the chance of rising to foreman in five years' time,' Barbara put in eagerly as she mashed the potatoes and then moved to the sink to strain the swede and carrots that were to accompany their meal.

'Oh? Where's this then?' Trudy asked Brian obligingly.

'Working for the council.' It was, perhaps not surprisingly, her mother who swiftly supplied the answer, her voice indicating her pride at this coup on his part. Brian, so far, had yet to speak, and Trudy cast him a swift thoughtful glance, wondering if he resented having someone answer for him.

But he was smiling amiably at her, and Trudy supposed that he must have got used to it, since it was usually his own mother who did the talking in the Bayliss household!

'Doing what, Brian?' Trudy asked, stressing his name slightly, and looking at him firmly.

'Road-sweeping,' Brian said succinctly.

'Good job for a big strapping lad like you,' her father said approvingly.

Trudy nodded, glad because Brian seemed glad.

'Here we go then,' Barbara said, setting down two heaped, steaming plates of food in front of the two men, before bringing two much smaller portions to the table for herself and her daughter.

'We're that looking forward to getting a telly next week, did your mother tell you?' Barbara said to their visitor, passing him a bottle of Daddies Sauce. 'Your mum said she was going to see if she could get your dad to agree to renting one as well. That'd be nice, wouldn't it?'

Trudy speared a piece of steak as her mother battled to get her visitor chatting. Brian was a nice boy, but he needed to find some other girl to court, someone who wasn't interested in pursuing a career, perhaps. And there would be no shortage of offers, Trudy mused, glad to have her conscience appeased, as she thought of the string of girls who'd be happy to take him on.

Of course, it would upset Mrs Bayliss. Not to mention her own mother, but it had to be done. Her top priority right now was her job, and would be for some years to come.

Her parents simply wouldn't take her ambitions seriously. Not even her recent moment of fame had made a dent in the Lovedays' mainly unspoken – but deep-seated – conviction that Trudy's job was 'just a phase' she was going through.

With a sigh she smiled at Brian, who seemed to be gamely trying to think of something nice to say about television, and she nervously awaited her opportunity. She'd never had to throw over a boy before and even though she was convinced that Brian would be all right about it all, she still felt awkward.

Later, when the dishes had been washed, wiped and put away, the moment finally came as she walked Brian to the door.

'So, do you want to come to the cinema Saturday night with me?' he asked without any notable enthusiasm.

Carefully, she eased him outside and shut the door firmly behind her.

'Brian, there's something we really need to get clear,' she began gently but firmly, taking a deep breath. 'Do you think it's time we called it a day?' she asked clumsily. 'I mean, you and me… it's not really working out. Is it?'

She watched his shoulders slump in relief, and she let out a long, slow breath.

Chapter 16

The next morning, Trudy went to work in a solemn mood.

The talk with Brian couldn't have gone better. He'd instantly agreed that he'd been feeling for some time as if they were just going through the motions, and that he, too, had been trying to work up the nerve to break things off. It had ended with him kissing her on the cheek gratefully, and pressing a hand around her arm. He had left, if not with an actual spring in his step, then without any noticeable regret, which might have hurt her pride had she not been so relieved that neither of them had been left with any hurt feelings.

But that had been only the first hurdle.

Fearing a family row, she'd left it until this morning to break the news to her parents that she and Brian were no longer officially an item.

Frank Loveday, she'd noted without much surprise, hadn't looked that disappointed, but her mother had been a different story. Dire warnings about girls who were left old maids through being too fussy, were followed up by admonitions about young girls who didn't have any common sense, to a final, hurt and cold silence when she realised her daughter wasn't going to back down.

Now, as she entered the station, Trudy felt almost glad to see

DI Jennings, even though all he did was scowl at her and check the clock to see if she was late. (Which just went to show how bad the atmosphere had been at home!)

She spent the morning catching up on writing her arrest reports for the past week, but finding herself free at lunchtime, she called the coroner's office. Dr Ryder's secretary told her that he was indeed free from one o'clock onwards, and so she quickly ate her sandwiches (which she'd had to make herself, since her mother was so disgusted with her) and then pedalled over to Floyds Row.

Once ensconced in Clement's office, she filled him in on all that she had learned about Jennifer de Lacey's death. He immediately got up and asked his secretary to find the records and have them sent up to his office when she had a spare moment.

'So, where do we go from here?' Trudy asked. 'Do we talk to Eddie's brothers and sisters now?'

But her friend was already shaking his head. 'I'd still rather leave that as a last resort,' Clement said. 'Let's stick to the adults in the case first. Have you found out who this rich American woman is, who's causing so much upheaval in the lives of the de Lacey men?'

'Not yet,' Trudy admitted. 'But it shouldn't be that hard, should it?'

Clement grunted, thought about it for a few moments, then reached for his telephone. He picked up the black Bakelite receiver and then swore under his breath as he realised that he couldn't recall – from memory – the number that he wanted.

He thrust aside the painful realisation that he'd never had trouble with his otherwise excellent memory before, and reached instead for his diary, where he had a list of telephone numbers in the back pages. Finding the name of the particular friend he was after, he put his finger in the dial, and twirled the clear plastic around until he had dialled 128.

For her part, Trudy waited patiently. She had no idea who he was calling, but she'd learned very quickly that Dr Ryder knew many people, from all walks of life, and all of them, so it seemed, were happy to oblige him.

She listened to his side of the conversation, and from picking up the odd clue here and there, concluded that he was talking to the chairman – or whatever he was – of the local golf club.

As expected, Martin de Lacey was also a member. And, also as expected, with a little delicate probing, the wily old coroner was soon able to find out who he'd been seen dining with about town lately.

He hung up with a smile and a promise to his friend on the other end of the line that a box of the best Panamas would be winging their way to him come next Christmas. Trudy, after a moment's amused thought, decided Dr Ryder must mean the cigars, rather than the hat!

'Her name's Marjorie Chandler. She was up at St Hilda's, he thinks,' Clement said, forcing Trudy away from her rather whimsical musings, and back to the business at hand. 'Anyway, the grapevine has it that the lady likes to think of herself as something of an academic and is in no hurry to return to America, and the bosom of her family millions. She has a flat near the park, overlooking Keble, Lord help her!'

Trudy gave a splutter of laughter. She knew that the gaudy white-and-red checkerboard edifice that was Keble College was either loved or loathed, depending on who you talked to, and she concluded that Dr Ryder, clearly, was not a fan!

*

It didn't take long for them to drive from Floyds Row, past the Martyrs' Memorial, through St Giles', and then turn off right towards the park.

The coroner found a parking place easily right outside the house and beneath a spreading lime tree, which was just beginning to bring forth its lime-coloured leaves into a rather grey and overcast spring morning.

They stepped into the vestibule and consulted the small list of occupants, which had been pinned to the wall beneath a large and rather attractive arts-and-crafts wooden-framed mirror. Miss Chandler's flat, it turned out, occupied the entire top floor of the large, Victorian building, and probably would indeed command great views of the park and surrounding architecture.

'Well, if we didn't already know the lady was rich, we'd be left in little doubt about it now,' Clement said, huffing slightly as they climbed to the top floor. There, he reached automatically into his coat pocket for a roll of mints, and slipped one into his mouth, chewing quickly. Halitosis, alas, was yet another symptom of Parkinson's, and one he was particularly keen to combat.

Trudy gave a disinterested shrug, then reached for the doorbell and gave it a firm ring.

Chapter 17

A tall, thin woman with obviously dyed blonde hair answered the
door. She was not particularly beautiful, but she *was* dressed in a
beautiful Balmain suit that showed off her boyish figure to its best
advantage, and was impeccably made-up. Trudy instantly noticed
the flash of precious gemstones that caught the sunlight as she
lifted one hand to brush a stray strand of hair off her cheek. She
was wearing at least three rings plus a large, multifaceted bracelet.

'Hello. Miss Chandler?' Trudy asked pleasantly, since the
woman's eyes had gone instantly to her, widening in clear aston-
ishment at her uniform.

'Yes? Police?' she asked uncertainly, as if not convinced that such
a thing as a woman police officer were quite feasible. It made Trudy
wonder if they didn't yet have women in the police in the United
States of America. 'Oh don't tell me I've got parking fines *again*?'
the woman wailed, her broad American accident sounding odd to
Trudy's ears. She couldn't remember actually having met an
American before. She quickly smiled and held up a reassuring hand.

'Oh no, madam. We're not here about traffic violations. I'm
WPC Loveday, and this is Dr Clement Ryder.'

'Dr?' the American woman echoed, instantly transferring her
attention to Clement, and smiling widely. Clearly here she felt

91

on much surer ground. 'One hesitates to ask, in this city, but are you a doctor of medicine or…?' She left the question open-ended, at the same time stepping back and with a gracious wave of her bejewelled hand, inviting them in.

'Indeed, my doctorate is in medicine. But I've also studied law,' Clement admitted, belatedly remembering that he had, indeed, some very creditable initials that he could legitimately add after his name, since he'd crammed several law courses when he'd changed his career. 'I'm one of the county's coroners, Miss Chandler. Before that I was a surgeon at the Radcliffe Infirmary.'

'Really? How fascinating,' the thin blonde woman said, and clearly meant it.

And with this, Clement had no trouble at all in marking her out as (what a rather waspish-tongued friend of his always called them) an academic acolyte. They came in all shapes and sizes, he'd averred, but all of them had an overwhelming love for Oxford, academia, and themselves, in no particular order.

Wanting to get her onside immediately, he looked around the large living room, and beamed. 'How marvellous. I can see by your collection, you're a connoisseur of art. Have you come to Oxford to study it, by any chance?'

As expected, the wealthy American immediately looked pleased. 'Oh, I already have my BA – from Somerville. But I'm thinking about doing a more in-depth study as a post-graduate, specialising in the Surrealists,' she said enthusiastically. 'Please, won't you sit down?'

Trudy and Clement both did so, in a rather sumptuous leather settee overlooking big sash windows that gave a panoramic view of one of Oxford's more leafy streets. And glancing around, Trudy could see for herself that the walls were indeed choc-a-block with works of art. Most of which looked extraordinarily ugly to her eyes, she saw, with some surprise. At least, they certainly weren't what she thought of as pretty pictures.

There weren't many landscapes or paintings of flowers for

instance, she noted, trying not to stare at one really odd print of a clock that seemed to be melting…

'We're here to talk about the tragedy at Briar's Hall,' Clement said, dragging Trudy's rather bemused mind from the bewildering world of art and back to something with which she felt far more familiar. 'I headed the inquest into little Eddie Proctor's case.'

'Oh yes! Oh my word, that was awful,' Marjorie Chandler said. 'Poor Martin and Oliver were both so cut up about it.'

Trudy thought, somewhat cynically, that the death of an insignificant village boy probably wouldn't have made that much of an impact on the likes of the de Lacey family – and even less on someone like Marjorie, with her huge flat in the city, and her fancy clothes.

And once more, her thoughts went painfully back to the Proctor home – the boy's mother too tired to even see them and his father who seemed so helpless and beaten but determined to do right by his boy.

'I'm sure they felt guilty about it,' Trudy couldn't help but say, then flushed with her own guilt as the coroner shot her a quick, warning look of remonstrance. 'But they are going out of their way to be helpful in our inquiry,' she added quickly, hoping to redeem herself. Because Dr Ryder was right. It was no use antagonising the witness. They were here to get information, and her gran had always said that you caught more flies with sugar than vinegar.

'Oh, yes, well of course,' Marjorie said, clearly a little taken aback. 'But I don't see what *I* can do to help?' She turned once again to Clement, clearly feeling more sure of herself with an erudite, academic man, than with a spiky, unknown quantity such as Trudy.

'I take it you were at the Hall on Easter Sunday, when it happened?' Clement stepped in smoothly, and Trudy wisely subsided and let him do all the running, careful to keep her eyes off the bewildering artwork surrounding them.

'Oh yes. Martin had invited me to lunch. Oliver's mother wasn't there, but the rest of the family were,' Marjorie agreed instantly, again looking pleased with herself. Obviously she felt it was something of a feather in her cap to be on dining terms with minor British nobility. 'Briar's Hall is such a lovely and charming example of Georgian architecture, don't you think? And the de Laceys, of course, came over with the Conqueror.' As an American, she must find it almost unbelievable that families here could trace their ancestry back more than a thousand years.

Clement was happy to talk about the merits of several local architects, remarking that he quite liked the work of Dalrymple-Champneys, before guiding her back to the day that little Eddie Proctor had died.

'As I understand it, the adults didn't actually attend the Easter egg hunt itself?' he mused.

'Oh no. That was strictly for the local children, and Martin's own two, of course. Some members of the WI and the teachers at the local school oversaw it, I think,' Marjorie said. 'Cigarette?'

She opened a lovely Art Deco mother-of-pearl and jet cigarette box, and Clement accepted one, then used his own lighter to light first her own cigarette then his own. Trudy, who knew he preferred his pipe, bit back a smile. He certainly was intent on buttering up the wealthy American, and she wondered, with a sudden start, if he actually found her attractive.

She herself declined with a brief smile and a shake of her head. She'd only tried cigarettes a few times, and they just made her cough.

'Do you get on with Emily?' Clement surprised both women by asking next. But after only a momentary pause, the American woman recovered smoothly.

'Oh yes, she's a darling child. Very bright you know. I'm determined to persuade Martin that she should be encouraged to attend the university here. He, I'm sorry to say, still has a rather parochial Englishman country gentleman's view that proper education should be strictly for the boys only.'

'Oh, I'm sure if anyone can make him see the error of his ways, it's someone such as yourself, Miss Chandler.' Clement smiled urbanely. 'Yes, several people have told us that little Emily is a clever child. And probably mature for her age. I don't suppose you ever met Eddie Proctor?'

'The child who died? No, I'm afraid not, but I *do* happen to know that he was a particular favourite of hers. On the other few occasions I've been at the Hall, she did chatter on so about their exploits. It was awful, learning later that day that a child had died, and even worse to realise it was Emily's friend. I was so upset, I had to leave at once. I'm rather sensitive about that sort of thing, I'm afraid. Being so in tune with art and beauty, I find the realities of life rather unbearable sometimes.'

Trudy blinked at this blatant self-absorption but, having already learned her lesson, said nothing.

'I'm sure it was very upsetting for you,' Clement said smoothly, and only Trudy, who was getting to know him so well, could hear the hidden contempt behind his tone. 'So you never saw anything of the Easter egg hunt that day?'

'No, I'm afraid not.'

'I don't suppose Martin, or perhaps Mr Oliver de Lacey, mentioned anything about the boy? I understand you know them both quite well?' he asked, being careful to keep his voice mild and totally free of innuendo.

'Oh yes, I know them both,' the American said blithely. 'I met Martin first, and later I was introduced to his cousin. Oliver is such an interesting man, you know. Not only does he lecture in physics, he's also on a very important committee that advises your government on its nuclear energy strategy.'

'Yes, so I'd heard,' Clement said, hiding his amusement. Clearly, to a lover of all things cerebral, Mr Oliver de Lacey had it on points over his cousin, who, as far as Clement was aware, could claim no particular academic laurels for himself.

'Of course, Martin is so much the village squire and steeped in tradition, that he's equally fascinating, in his own way,' Marjorie mused, her voice taking on a slightly dreamy quality.

Ah, Clement mused wryly. Clearly the lady was torn between seeing herself as the wife of an Oxford don, and the lady of the manor.

'We're trying to discover what took the boy to the orchard – and the well – in the first place. I don't suppose Emily ever said anything to you about a secret meeting there?' Clement asked casually. 'We've been trying to talk to Emily, but she seems to be rather well guarded by Mrs Roper – the housekeeper.'

'Oh, *her*!' Marjorie sniffed, clearly not impressed by the likes of the de Laceys' guardian dragon. And probably, Trudy guessed with some amusement, that feeling was very much reciprocated. She couldn't see the likes of the swanky Marjorie Chandler impressing Mrs Roper much!

'Don't you worry, Dr Ryder, I'll be sure to talk to Martin for you, and make sure you get to speak to his daughter,' the American said, thankfully taking his hint. 'And to answer your original question, no, I can't say that she did mention anything to me about the orchard or the well. But having said that, she can be a rather secretive child you know. I noticed that. She likes to keep secret notebooks and all that sort of thing. But then, it's her age… Mind you, now that I think about it, I do believe her father told me that the dead boy was her ever-willing sidekick in her escapades. So if anyone does know why the poor boy went to the orchard that day, it probably *will* be her.'

'I see. Well, if you *could* just clear the way for us to see Emily,' Clement said, seizing the opportunity of making their visit worthwhile, 'I really would be grateful.'

'No problem. In fact, I can call Martin for you right now,' she said, taking a quick look at her wrist, which – Trudy was not surprised to note – was adorned by a diamond and platinum lady's wristwatch. 'He'll be in for lunch. He's always up early and lunches early too.'

She was supremely confident, not only that he would be happy to take her call, but that he would want to oblige her in any way he could, and Clement didn't doubt it either.

'Well thank you. We won't keep you any further,' he said, getting to his feet. 'I'm sure you must have a busy day ahead.'

'Oh yes. I want to see the latest Klimt exhibition at the Ashmolean.'

'Ah, you'll be impressed. I saw it a few days ago,' Clement lied with aplomb as Trudy scrambled to put her notebook away.

'You be sure to head over straight to the Hall now,' Marjorie encouraged them. 'By then, I'll have talked Martin around to letting you talk to little Emily.'

'Thank you,' Clement said, taking her hand and actually raising it to his lips and kissing it. Trudy found herself gaping at him, but after a quick look, saw that the American woman was almost glowing at this unexpected, continental chivalry.

It wasn't until they were headed back down the oak staircase to the public lobby, and he'd heard the door shut firmly behind them, that he glanced across at Trudy and smiled wryly. 'Rather hard work, isn't she, our Miss Chandler?'

'I'll say,' Trudy grumped. 'Did you see those clothes and make-up and all that jewellery? At this time of the day? And those *pictures*!' She shuddered.

'Ah, not a fan of modern art then, young Trudy?'

'Not if that's an example,' she said, looking upwards. 'What on earth were those melting clocks all about?' she demanded.

'Dalí,' the coroner said succinctly.

'Sorry?'

'Salvadore Dalí, a leading exponent of surrealism,' Clement said. 'That image, along with a gent in a bowler hat with an apple for a face, is a very famous…' And all the way on the drive over to Briar's-in-the-Wold, the coroner instructed her in the precepts of surrealism in art.

Trudy found herself wondering, almost constantly, whether or not her friend was pulling her leg.

Chapter 18

When they pulled up once more outside the Hall, she was glad to have a break from the coroner's dizzying lecture. It was not as if she didn't have other things to think about.

By the end of summer her probationary period would be over and then she'd be a fully fledged WPC. That deadline loomed larger and larger as the days went by, filling her with a sense of accomplishment, mostly because, when she'd first joined the force, everyone had expected her to have to acknowledge defeat and bow out before even six months had passed. But she had proved them all wrong, and now that her first goal – that of surviving her probationary period – was almost within her grasp, she felt nearly buoyant.

Of course, that ebullience was now offset, somewhat, on account of her being in the doghouse back home. She was not looking forward to tonight at all. She had a feeling that dinnertime was going to be something of an ordeal – either of silent recrimination, or yet another lecture on the perils of being 'left on the shelf'.

'Well, time to see if Miss Chandler's confidence in her influence over the lord of the manor is justified or not,' Clement said with a smile.

But it was clear, from the frigid look of bitter acceptance on the face of Mrs Roper when she answered their summons to the doorbell, that the American lady's word held sway at Briar's Hall. Or at least, for as long as Martin de Lacey had hopes of marrying into all her wealth.

'Miss Emily is in the library, and is expecting you,' Mrs Roper said coldly. 'Her father is with her,' she added, looking better pleased to be able to impart this piece of news.

She showed them through the hall and down a short corridor, veering off into one of a line of doors on her left, reluctance oozing from her every pore.

The de Lacey library was typical of many country house examples, displaying as it did shelves and shelves of (almost certainly) unread books, long, rather dusty-looking floor-length faded red velvet curtains, and the almost obligatory green-leather settees, armchairs, and chaises longues. Large sash windows let in bright rays of sunshine, which picked up the dust motes dancing in the air. Over in one corner, a large globe stood, with a vast swathe of pink around its circumference showing the extent of the British Empire. In another corner, a Georgian writing desk stood in solitary splendour, displaying a pen and inkwell set, carved out of ivory.

But it was to the two people in the room that Clement and Trudy immediately turned their attention.

Martin de Lacey rose first. He was dressed in a slightly shabby tweed jacket, sturdy trousers and country boots. All he needed was a filthy English Setter at his side, and he could have posed for a portrait of a Typical Country Gentlemen by any one of the noted Victorian artists, who would have had no truck with such things as melting clocks and men with apples for faces.

But it was the little girl sitting in one of the chairs facing them that Trudy and Clement had come to see.

The chair was a little too large for her, and she was sat right back in it, allowing her legs to swing to and fro freely. This motion stopped instantly, the moment she became aware of the adult eyes that were suddenly upon her. She was a rather sombre-faced child, with dark hair and grey eyes. She looked a little like her father, but Clement suspected that, in a few years' time, she'd probably surprise them all by turning into a great beauty.

'Mr de Lacey,' Clement said, coming forward and shaking the squire's hand, and then turning to beam down at the girl. 'And you must be Emily.'

'Yes, sir,' Emily said, watching him warily.

She'd been up in the nursery when Mrs Roper had come to fetch her, telling her that important visitors were coming and that she was to be quiet, and speak only when spoken to.

Now she looked at the coroner solemnly, but couldn't help but keep sneaking peeks at the other visitor. She'd never seen a woman in a uniform before. She recognised them at once, of course, as the visitors she'd seen from the window of the nursery.

'I'm Dr Ryder, and this is Woman Police Constable Trudy Loveday,' Clement said, matching her solemn tone, but allowing a smile to tug at his lips.

He wasn't surprised that the child was on her best behaviour, but he needed to break down that restraint as quickly as possible. With that in mind, he turned and glanced at Mrs Roper, who was definitely hovering.

Martin, catching the look, dismissed her with a slightly exasperated 'Thank you, Mrs Roper, that will be all.'

When the dragon had reluctantly departed, Clement noted the little girl relax slightly.

'Please, sit down,' Martin said, taking the chair beside his daughter, and regarding them closely. 'Are you making any progress?' he demanded.

'Some, sir, but it's early days yet,' Trudy responded first, mostly because she knew he'd made the remark to the coroner, and she resented being treated as if she was invisible. Also, *she* was the one wearing the uniform and *she* was the one – well technically at least – who had the authority here.

100

'I see,' Martin said. It was impossible to tell whether he was disappointed or relieved by the news.

'We hope you don't mind if we just have a little chat with your daughter?' Clement said. He'd selected another armchair, this one more or less facing the little girl, and as he spoke, he glanced around. 'There are a lot of books here. I've bet you've read all of them, haven't you, Emily?'

Emily gave a little snort of laughter. 'Not all of them,' she had to admit honestly. 'There are thousands and thousands!'

'Ah, that's true. But I've bet you've read the best of them,' Clement said. '*Lorna Doone*?'

'Oh yes. And *Black Beauty*. And *Swallows and Amazons*.'

'Ah. Do you have a boat for the lake here? I bet you do,' Clement said. 'I wish I had a lake in my back garden. I'd probably play at Swallows and Amazons all day long.'

At the thought of this white-haired man playing a game, Emily gave a little giggle. 'Yes, we have a rowboat, but I'm not allowed in it alone,' she said promptly, very conscious of her father's silent presence beside her. 'One of the gardeners always has to go with us. Usually Lallie – he likes rowing. And he knows where all the moorhen nests are, and sometimes he'll find us some duck eggs to take back to Cook. She likes to mix them in her cakes.'

Clement's eyes twinkled. 'Sounds scrumptious to me. Did Eddie like being in the boat?'

At the mention of her friend, all the joie de vivre abruptly left the little girl, and she bit her lip, looking down into her lap. 'He quite liked it,' she said at last.

'Could he swim?' Clement asked gently.

'Oh yes. So could I. But he didn't like swimming much. We preferred to play in the woods and stuff.' They had made a secret den there, but Emily wasn't about to mention that. It wasn't the sort of thing you told grown-ups.

'Ah, I bet you played Robin Hood in there.'

'Yes, I was Maid Marion,' Emily admitted proudly. 'We made

some bows from some willows, 'cause they're nice and bendy. And Eddie whittled some arrows with his penknife. We borrowed an old water bucket and painted a target on it, but we weren't very good at hitting it. It's jolly hard to get an arrow to fly right,' she said, sounding aggrieved.

Clement nodded wisely. 'It takes lots of practice,' he agreed. 'What else did you like to do?'

'Oh, all sorts,' Emily said, shrugging one shoulder. But she was too wise to be caught out that way, and let her eyes drift to the window in silence.

'Emily, do you know why Eddie went into the orchard that day when you were looking for Easter eggs?' Clement asked gently.

But Emily shook her head, looking genuinely baffled. 'No. They told us the eggs were only hidden in the kitchen gardens.'

'Did you know about the well?'

Emily shrugged. 'Oh yes. I do live here, you know,' she added, a shade scornfully.

'Emily!' her father reprimanded, and again she bit her lip and stared down at her lap.

'Sorry,' she muttered.

'That's all right, it was my fault.' Clement smiled. 'It was a bit of a silly question wasn't it? So had you ever explored it yourself?'

'Not really. It was a bit boring, you know – just a round wall with a wooden lid on top of it. We played "King of the Castle" on it when we were really little, but we're too old for all that kind of stuff now,' she added matter-of-factly.

Clement nodded solemnly. 'Oh yes, I can see you're far too old for that,' he agreed. 'Did anybody ever ask you to go into the orchard with them?'

He noticed her father stiffen a little at that, but the little girl only looked puzzled again. 'No. What do you mean? Who'd do that?' she demanded.

'Oh, I don't know. Anyone. A stranger, or somebody from the village? One of the gardeners here, or maybe the mummy or daddy of one of your friends from school?' Clement kept his voice level and off-hand.

'No,' Emily said, firmly. 'Why would they do that?' she repeated.

Clement shrugged. 'We're just trying to think why Eddie went to the well that day that's all,' he said simply. 'Did he say anything to you about it that morning, when you began searching for the eggs?'

'No,' Emily said firmly. Which was true, she thought mutinously. He hadn't.

'All right,' Clement said, sensing she was beginning to get restive. 'Had Eddie ever said anything to you about meeting a stranger in the area recently?'

'No, nobody ever comes here,' Emily said as casually as she could. It was jolly hard lying and not sounding sort of funny. She shot him a quick look out of the corner of her eye to see if she'd got away with it, and thought that maybe she had.

'Emily, you're obviously a very clever girl,' Clement said with a smile, 'and I dare say you've been thinking about what happened a lot. Do you know how Eddie came to fall down the well?' he finally asked outright.

He shot Martin de Lacey a quick look as he stirred in his chair. Clearly he was not sure whether he liked such a direct question being asked of his daughter, but before he could object, Emily was already answering.

'No, but you're right, I *have* thought and thought about it,' Emily said fiercely, her brow puckering and her tone conveying genuine frustration. 'But I just don't know what he was doing there.' It wasn't even one of their 'secret message spots' where they sometimes left messages for one another to find, like real spies did.

'And did you always tell each other everything?' Clement asked curiously. 'Or did you keep secrets from one another?'

Emily scowled. She knew Eddie liked to play tricks on her sometimes. And if he'd discovered a really juicy secret, she knew he'd keep it to himself for a while before he could spring it on her.

It always made him buzz with excitement when he knew something that she didn't. Not that such a thing happened often. No matter what Eddie thought, she nearly always knew about stuff that he was keeping from her, and just pretended that she didn't.

She shrugged graphically, realising that her adult audience was awaiting her answer. 'I dunno,' she eventually muttered truculently. She wished they'd go away. She was beginning to feel frightened again.

'I think that's really enough now,' Martin de Lacey said, sensing that his daughter was beginning to feel uncomfortable, and not wanting her to become stubborn. 'I think it's clear that she knows nothing about all this.' His tone of voice and the look he shot them made it clear that he was putting his foot down.

And Clement knew when to back off. 'Yes. Well, thank you, Emily, you've been very helpful. And we're really sorry about your friend,' he said gently.

'Yes, we're really sorry. You must miss him,' Emily heard the pretty police lady agree.

Emily blinked ferociously at this, but she wouldn't permit herself to cry in front of strangers.

But she was glad when they got up and left.

Only then, when her father came back in the room and stood in front of her chair with that look on his face, she suddenly wished they hadn't gone at all.

Nervously, she raised her face to look at him.

'Now then, my girl,' Martin de Lacey said quietly. 'I want to know just what it is that you're holding back. You might fool them, but you don't fool me. And don't' – he held up a hand warningly – 'give me any of your nonsense. I know you and that Proctor boy had your curious little noses poked in everywhere. I've seen you, playing spies and writing things down in that notebook of yours. Now you're going to sit there and tell me everything you've been up to.'

Emily gulped. 'Yes, Papa,' she lied.

Chapter 19

Master George de Lacey lurked behind one of his favourite columns on the front porch and tried not to fidget. He liked lying in wait there, hoping to make people jump by leaping out at them, roaring like a lion, or doing a Tarzan yodel.

Mind you, he'd had to give Nanny the slip first. But when he'd heard strange voices coming from the library he'd managed to accomplish that deed, and now he watched with glee as an old man with white hair and a woman in funny clothes stepped out of the porch, and Mrs Roper shut the door smartly behind them.

He carefully waited for his moment, hoping it would be the lady who passed by closest to him, since they were the ones who screamed in fright the best. He was in luck, and just before the strangers drew level with him, he leaped out, giving his most ferocious Tarzan wail. (Billy the boot boy had demonstrated this to him some time ago, as he himself had heard it being performed at the local cinema.)

Trudy didn't need to feign her jump of surprise, but let out little more than a squawk as she instinctively leaped back. Then she laughed as the little boy stood in front of them, arms akimbo, a ferocious scowl on his face.

'I'm Tarzan, and you no cross my jungle unless you cross my

palms with silver,' George said, somewhat confusingly. It had again been the boot boy (who'd not long since visited the local village fete) who'd told him all about the mysterious women who gazed into big glass balls and demanded silver in order to tell you your fortune.

'I'm not sure Tarzan would have any use for silver, m'boy.' It was Clement who spoke, reaching into his trouser pocket and producing a sixpence. 'But I'm sure this will come in handy for Master George de Lacey.'

George (not a member of the aristocracy for nothing) very quickly snaffled the bribe and shoved it deep down inside his shoe. Trudy watched, grinning openly. The lad was dressed in impeccably unsullied navy-blue shorts and a short-sleeved white shirt, but she doubted he'd remain clean for long, now that he was outside.

'Thank you, sir,' George said, mindful of his manners.

'Well, now I've crossed your palm with silver,' Clement said, looking at him with a sombre gaze. 'It's time you told my fortune.'

'Ah,' George said, slightly stumped at this. At 7 years old, he wasn't quite sure what a fortune was. The only fortune he knew about was the fortune that meant money – or treasure. But it didn't seem to make sense that you asked for money, in order to give money back.

'So,' Clement said, seeing his difficulty. 'Since you are now obliged to tell me my future' – here Master George's eyes opened fearfully – 'let's begin.'

'Er... I'm still learning how to use the glass ball, sir,' George said, then had a bit of a brainwave. 'In fact, it's in the wash,' he said quickly.

Trudy silently began to laugh, but was careful to keep her hand over her mouth so that the lad wouldn't see.

'Oh. In the wash, is it?' Clement mused. 'That's a bit of bad luck, isn't it?'

'Yes, sir. It gets frightfully dirty you know. And then you can't find the fortunes, see?' he tacked on, suddenly realising that his inspired fib actually made sense, when you took time to think about it.

'I can imagine. Oh well, never mind. We'll use my hand instead,' Clement said, in one stroke pleasing him inordinately, whilst at the same time, dismaying him utterly.

'Hand?' George said uncertainly, as the man with white hair leaned forward and held out his hand.

George promptly shook it, although it was rather hard, since he'd held his hand flat out, and facing upwards. Which was a funny sort of way to shake a chap's hand in George's opinion.

Clement thanked him gravely, but then held out his hand again, and tapped the bottom of his hand. 'That's my palm,' he explained helpfully. 'You're supposed to look at it and tell me my fortune.'

'Ah,' George said glumly. And how was he supposed to get out of this one? He could hardly suggest it was dirty. Mrs Roper and Nanny would both have his guts for garters if he were to be rude to a guest.

He sighed. There was no hope for it. He was going to have to give the sixpence back…

'But not to worry, I don't want to know anything really difficult,' the old man said next, and at this, George's heart lifted.

'You don't?' he asked hopefully, looking up at him winsomely with big grey eyes.

'No. Let's see,' the white-haired man considered for a moment, and then snapped his fingers. 'If I were to ask you who your sister's best friend is, what would you say?'

'Oh, that's easy,' George said with a proud grin. 'Eddie Proctor.' Then his smile faltered. 'But Eddie's with God now, so she won't be able to play with him anymore.'

'That's sad,' Clement agreed gravely. 'Did *you* play with him much?'

'Nah,' George said, dragging his toes across the path in front

107

of him and watching his foot's progress. 'They said I was too young.'

'You'll grow up,' Clement assured him briskly. 'Did you like Eddie?'

'Oh, well, he was all right I suppose. He played Tarzan with me sometimes. Not often. He was always playing with Emily.'

'I've heard about that,' Clement said. 'Playing spies, and stuff. Do you know who they were following about and spying on lately?'

'Oh, probably Uncle Oliver. But they were playing at something different now, I think.'

'Oh, why do you say that,' Clement said casually.

'I think they found hidden treasure!' George shot out, chest bursting with pride. Then he looked around nervously. 'But I'm not supposed to know about it. Do you suppose it was pirate treasure they found?'

'I don't think that's likely. We're rather a long way from the sea aren't we?' Clement pointed out logically. George heaved a massive sigh. 'But it might have been monks' buried treasure. Or an Anglo-Saxon gold hoard.'

George's eyes opened wide again. 'Really? Nanny told me about some old kings who buried their crowns and stuff. Do you suppose a king stayed at Briar's Hall in the olden days and buried his crown in the orchard?'

'He might. But why do you think he buried it in the orchard?' Clement asked, trying to keep the sharpness and the urgency out of his voice.

'Oh, I don't know. Perhaps the treasure was in the well, and that's why Eddie fell in, looking for it?'

'Did Eddie say there was treasure hidden in the well?' Clement asked casually.

'Oh no. I just thought… They must have found the treasure somewhere, so why not there?' George asked sensibly. It sounded right to him.

'What makes you think they found treasure? Did they tell you?' Clement asked next.

'No,' the boy said scornfully. 'They don't tell me things. They keep all their secrets between themselves.'

'That must have been annoying,' Clement commiserated. 'So how exactly do you know that they found treasure? Did you see them? Were you playing a game of spies of your own?'

'Nah,' George admitted, again dragging his toe across the path and watching it thoughtfully. 'I wasn't very good at it. They always caught me and told me to go home. But I did hear them talking once,' he said, his head shooting up and his face beaming again.

'What did they say?' Clement asked, as Trudy held her breath.

'They said they could buy a bicycle for Eddie. And Emily could buy a pair of roller skates for herself. Nanny wouldn't let her have any; she said they were too dangerous for a lady. But Eddie said, now they wouldn't have to rely on their daddies for things, or Lallie helping them build stuff like trolleys and swings and things. They could just get whatever they wanted from the shops themselves. So they must have found treasure, mustn't they?' George finished triumphantly.

'Did they say where they found this treasure?' Clement asked, not quite sure what to make of this tale.

'Nah. They were just laughing and naming all the things they could buy for themselves if they wanted to. But...' George frowned. 'I don't think Emily really meant it, cause I heard her say that they couldn't really, because the money wasn't theirs. So that would be stealing, wouldn't it?' he asked earnestly.

Clement soberly agreed that spending money that wasn't yours was indeed stealing, pretending not to see the crestfallen look on the lad's face at this unwelcome piece of news. 'So what did Eddie say when Emily said that?'

'He said it should be "finders keepers losers weepers". Which is all right, isn't it,' George said, nodding firmly. Clearly he had no doubts about this iron-clad rule, and Clement didn't want to get on the lad's wrong side by explaining the rather dubious merits of this axiom when it came to the finer points of the law.

'Did you hear where they found it? Whatever this treasure was?' he asked, but at this, Master George shook his head vigorously.

'No, 'fraid not, or I might have loo…' He suddenly flushed as he realised that he was about to admit to something that Nanny might have spanked him for, had she known about it. 'They saw me then, and changed the subject,' he said instead.

'Hard lines,' Clement said, and meant it. He'd have liked to know more about this intriguing incident. So far, it was the only sniff of a real motive they had. *If* Eddie's death had indeed been murder.

'You were at the Easter egg hunt, weren't you?' Clement said, but just then he heard the door open behind him, and with a sinking heart, could guess just what was coming next.

'*Master George!*' Mrs Roper roared, and the little lad wasn't the only one to jump. 'What have I told you about talking to strangers? Come in at once! Nanny has been looking for you. You haven't finished your geography lesson.'

George shot them an agonised glance, muttered 'sorry' and promptly scampered back inside.

Clement and Trudy watched him go, weathered the venomous look the housekeeper shot at them, and then watched as the door was slammed shut with a resounding bang!

Trudy let our her breath in a whoosh. 'Poor little tyke. I hope he doesn't get in any trouble,' she added kind-heartedly.

'I doubt it. I imagine he's quite good at looking out for himself, is Master George,' Clement said with a grin, remembering the lad's way with winsome looks. 'So, what do you make of his tale of his sister and Eddie finding treasure?' he asked.

By unspoken mutual consent, they began to stroll around the gardens, keeping to the paths and admiring the handiwork of Mr Cricklade and his small gang of gardeners as they went. Forsythia bushes were in full bloom, their yellow stems complimenting the massed beds of tulips and daffodils, and in the rose beds, the prickly, pruned bushes were beginning to show red leaves.

'I'm not sure,' Trudy said. 'Eddie and Emily may just have been playing a game of "what if". You know – "what if I were rich". You'd then go on to list all the things you'd do or buy. It's the sort of game nippers might make up.'

'Hmm. Maybe,' Clement said, not sounding convinced.

'You don't think they really found buried treasure, do you?' Trudy asked with a smile.

'Depends on what you mean by treasure,' Clement said. 'We know both children were curious and among other things, liked to play at spies. And we know Emily, for one, is a very intelligent child. Who knows what they might have found whilst playing one of their games?'

Trudy looked around. They were crossing a lawn, and in the distance, she could see the sheen of silver through the trees – and guessed it was sunlight on the lake. The whole estate was an ideal playground for children, with plenty of spaces for hiding and maybe eavesdropping on people or observing their actions.

They were rounding the area now where the formal gardens made way for more landscaped grounds. In the distance, Trudy could see a grey domed roof and suspected some folly or summer-house. Without consciously thinking about it, she turned her steps in that direction.

'Do you think it's possible someone was giving the children money?' she asked quietly, not liking the way her thoughts were going. 'You know… Perhaps they stumbled on a courting couple who'– aware that she was probably blushing now, Trudy kept her face turned resolutely away from her friend – 'may have had reasons of their own for slipping them a bob or two to keep quiet about what they'd seen. Especially if one, or even both of them, had been married. To other people, I mean.'

Beside her, Clement bit back a smile. 'Yes. Perhaps.'

'And don't forget, to children, very little could feel like a fortune. If I'd found tuppence when I was their age, I'd think I was rich.'

'But you'd probably know it wasn't enough to buy a bicycle and a pair of skates,' Clement pointed out.

Trudy frowned. 'But if someone was paying them *serious* money... Clement, you can't really think the children could have been *blackmailing* someone, do you?'

Clement sighed. 'It's not a nice thought, is it?'

'No! And I don't really think it's a feasible one either. I know I've never met Eddie Proctor, but from all we've learned about him, he seems a nice, straightforward sort of little boy.'

'Not a wrong 'un, as they say?' Clement mused.

'No. And what's more, I think his parents would have raised him to know right from wrong,' Trudy insisted stubbornly.

Clement nodded. He too, didn't much like the idea that Vincent's son might have been caught up in something ugly. And yet... somebody had wanted the lad dead.

'I take it we're agreed then that the boy *was* murdered?' he asked softly. 'And that we should proceed under that assumption?'

They had stepped off the gravelled walkway now, and were following a mulched path through the trees. Ahead, a pale white solid shape told them that they were reaching the summerhouse in the trees.

'Yes. I think so,' Trudy agreed. 'I'm not sure why – but it just doesn't *feel* as if died in an accident.'

'In which case, there has to be a motive,' Clement pointed out with unanswerable logic. 'We know he wasn't interfered with, so we're not looking for some sexual deviant. And there was no evidence of domestic abuse. So what does that leave us with?'

Trudy felt her eyes smart, and quickly shook her head. 'I just don't want to think...' But it was no good. Her throat began to clog and she knew she couldn't say her ugly thoughts out loud.

'That the lad might have been doing something wrong and got mixed up in something that helped contribute to his own death?' Clement obliged, by doing it for her. 'No. It's sick-making, isn't it.'

'Yes. And I still don't believe it's true,' she insisted stubbornly.

'I hope you're right,' Clement said heavily. 'Because if not... you must see what that means?'

Trudy blinked, looked at him, thought about it for a moment, and then suddenly went pale. 'Oh no! Emily!' she whispered, aghast. 'You can be sure that whatever Eddie knew, she did too!' Which meant yet another child could be in danger.

Just then, the trees – mainly beech, elms, and a few scattered hazels – receded, leaving an open area, in which had been built a large, hexagonal structure. A vista had been cleared in front of it to give it a view of the lake. Wild woodbine grew up the trellis attached to the walls, and a white-painted veranda surrounded it on all sides.

'Oh, how lovely!' Trudy said, her dark thoughts momentarily chased away by the romance of the scene.

Clement too, looked at it, but with far more thoughtful eyes. 'It looks in very good shape for a mere pagoda,' he mused, beginning to circle around it. The grey slate roof was immaculate, as was the woodwork. The windows were sparkling clean and... yes. He could see where a small stovepipe chimney had been set in one wall.

By the time they'd walked to the front, he could see that the building's only door was quite sturdy, and firmly shut. And that, off to one side and half-hidden in the laurel was an old-fashioned privvy.

Just then, the door opened and a large shuffling figure stepped out onto the wooden planking that led to the two shallow front steps.

'Hello. It's Lallie isn't it?' Trudy said, dredging her memory for his name from their previous talk with the head gardener. The last time she'd seen him, this man had been training pear trees against a south-facing wall.

What was it Mr Cricklade had said? He was a bit simple?

'Hello, miss,' he said, sounding and looking surprised to see them.

It was Clement who caught on first. 'You live here, Mr... er...?'

'Clark, sir. But everyone calls me Lallie,' he said. 'Yes, this my 'ome.'

He was a big man, Trudy noted, who rather gave one the impression of being soft and fat, which was, in fact, rather misleading. Perhaps it was his voluminous, obviously hand-me-down clothes that gave that impression, or the way he shuffled about with slightly stooped shoulders, as if he was constantly caught in the attitude of apologising for something.

'Hello, Lallie,' she said quietly. 'We're sorry for the intrusion. We didn't know you lived here,' she said, nodding at his unusual home.

'Oh, ar, 'ave done ever since comin' home from the war,' Lallie said, his face lifting in a smile as he looked around. 'Didn't always used to. Dad was a cowman on the farm before he died, and then Mum stayed on in the cottage. But when I come home, vicar told me she'd been took, see, the winter afore. New-monia, he said. And the squire had rented out the cottage to som'un else.'

'Oh no! How awful,' Trudy said. What a thing to come home to! This poor soul had probably lived in the village, man and boy, and had joined up, no doubt with all the others of his generation, to fight in the trenches. And when he returned...

'Ar – miss me old mum, I do,' Lallie agreed peaceably. 'So anyways, vicar, he says let me have a word with the squire, like, and next thing I knows, Mr de Lacey asks me if I wanna live here.' He turned and nodded at his modest home. 'He said I could use anything I needed to do it up, like. Tools and wood and whatnot. Let me have a good look round the sheds and the like. I found me a nice little old wood-burner stove, and fixed her up right good.'

'You've done a fine job,' Clement agreed, and meant it. He

could see the old wooden structure was perfectly weatherproof and well cared for, with a fresh coat of paint, and new putty around the windowpanes to help keep out the draughts.

'Old Cook, she found an old gas stove in the storerooms I could have, and a brass bed was found in the attic up at the Hall, which fits right nice against the far wall. People were right nice to me, they were.' He beamed a smile. 'Folks *are* nice, if you give 'em a chance, my old mum always said, and she was right. Do you wanna come in for a cup of tea? I have a pump that Mr Cricklade said draws water from the underground spring that feeds the lake.'

'Oh thank you, but we don't want to put you to any trouble,' Trudy said. And not because she had any qualms about drinking the water. Somehow she just felt it would be wrong to step into this man's humble home. 'We were just up at the Hall. Talking to Mr de Lacey about that poor boy who died.'

'Ah. Bad business that,' Lallie said, shaking his head. His mop of unruly brown hair probably hadn't been cut properly since his army days. 'I showed him a nest once, that a pair of throstles had built in an old teapot up in a damson hedge.'

Trudy hadn't heard of thrushes being called by their old English country name of throstles since she was a girl in pigtails and short skirts. 'I'll bet he liked that. Did he collect birds' eggs?' she asked amiably.

'Dunno.' Lallie shrugged his shoulders. Then he smiled. 'Nippers were always here and there, playing cowboys and injuns and what have you. I made 'em a trolley once, from some old pram wheels and a bit o' wood and string. Made Miss Emily squeal, it did, when they went down the hill.'

'We've just been talking to her and her father,' Trudy said softly.

'Ah. Dare say squire's not happy with that there well,' Lallie said heavily. 'Never said nuffing to me about making sure it was covered up though, honest,' he added quickly.

'We're all clever with hindsight,' Clement said sadly. 'I have no doubt, if he could go back in time, Mr de Lacey would have made sure it was safe.'

Lallie again shrugged his shoulders. 'I 'appen as he would, an' all,' he agreed heavily. 'Squire be all right, in his own way. But private like. Very private,' he repeated, shaking his head. 'Don't do to cross the squire, it don't,' he added.

And then, with an abruptness that took them both a little by surprise, he suddenly came down the two steps and set off into the woods. 'Got to get on, or Mr Cricklade will tell me I've been shilly-shallyin' and whatnot,' he called back by way of explanation, over his shoulder. 'Mind you keep to the paths then!' was his final admonition, before he disappeared from view.

Chapter 20

'We'd best keep to the paths then.' Clement grinned at Trudy as they turned and began to make their way back towards the car.

Trudy grinned back for a moment, but then her face fell again, as her mind continued to worry over a very nasty thought that just wouldn't go away.

'Dr Ryder, do you think Eddie might have been lured to the well with a promise of money?' she asked quietly. 'Regardless of what all this talk of treasure was about, it might explain what he was doing at the well in the first place.'

'Hmmm. It's possible. All kids like the thought of money.'

Trudy sighed. That was true enough. When you were just a kid, the desire for money wasn't really anything truly venal because you simply didn't really have any concept of greed as a good or bad thing. To your young self, money was just another one of those things that belonged to the mysterious world of grown-ups that you didn't really understand. If *you* had it, for instance, you would spend all day at the fair, or the cinema, or go to the sweet shop and buy bags and bags of goodies. (Unlike grown-ups, who seemed reluctant to spend it at all!) And if you didn't have any pocket money – which you mostly didn't – you then promptly forgot all about it and found something else to do that didn't require money at all.

But a promise of money would always be alluring and could pretty much guarantee a kid's compliance. 'Well, there are plenty of people with money in this case.' Trudy sighed heavily. 'Any one of the de Lacey family for a start – either the squire or his cousin. And Marjorie is loaded with it! Did you see all that jewellery she wore?'

Clement laughed. 'How could I miss it? But as you've already pointed out, we needn't be talking serious wealth here anyway. A boy of Eddie's age could have been lured with a promise of a shilling.'

Trudy sighed over this sad truism.

'Anyway, let's not get too sidetracked with this talk of treasure,' the coroner advised. 'Remember the source. Nippers of George's age can get things wrong or misunderstand things. But we *do* need to get back to the parents and see if Eddie had been unusually flush lately.'

'It might be a better idea to talk to his brothers and sisters,' Trudy warned. 'If Eddie did have some money, he might have kept it hidden it from his parents.'

'All right. You go and talk to them,' Clement said, 'but go carefully. Kids can sometimes surprise you by how resilient they are, but even so, they'll still be mourning their loss. But aren't you supposed to interview minors only with their parents present? Mind you, it's unlikely they'll rat Eddie out in front of their mum and dad if he *did* have some spending money stashed away.'

Trudy smiled. 'I was thinking that I might just sort of bump into them on their way home from school for their lunch and have a chat.'

Clement mock-sorrowfully shook his head. 'Probationary WPC Loveday,' he said, in sad, slightly scandalised tones. 'Are you becoming corrupted in your cynical old age?'

Trudy smiled. 'No, sir. I'm just using what the sergeant calls my initiative,' she shot back promptly.

'Oh. That's all right then.' He grinned.

'So what are *you* going to do?' she asked curiously.

'I'm going to talk to the cook up at the Hall,' Clement said. 'I want to learn more about the dragon who guards the de Lacey den.'

Trudy shrugged. She didn't quite see why the coroner was so interested in Mrs Roper. True, she seemed a bit fierce in her family loyalty, but some old retainers were just like that. And she certainly couldn't see why she would want to murder a village child – even if he did have the temerity to become friends with Emily de Lacey!

Chapter 21

Mrs Hilda Verney was slightly surprised by the visitor to her kitchen. For a start, she was not used to distinguished-looking gentlemen simply wandering through her kitchen door via the rear entrance. Nor was she keen on having her daily routine interrupted without good reason. But her initial suspicion was very quickly overcome when he introduced himself.

She hadn't gone to the inquest herself, but she *had* read the newspaper reports of little Eddie Proctor's death. How could she not? It would be the gossip of the village for decades to come. And one of the reporters, who'd obviously done his homework, had given a brief résumé of the coroner in his report, which included the fact that he'd been a renowned surgeon of many years' standing, before his change of occupation.

And like a lot of rural, working-class people, Mrs Verney held doctors – and surgeons in particular – in very high regard. Add that to the cut and quality of his suit, his air of power and authority, and his rich, very educated voice, and Mrs Verney was soon reassured as to his bona fides.

Besides which, the head of the house had informed all the staff that they might run into this man in the Hall or the village, and if he were to ask them any questions about Eddie Proctor's accident, they were to cooperate with him fully.

Naturally, this had led to wild speculation belowstairs as to what it might all mean, but the boot boy had said with confidence that it was all down to Vincent Proctor. The lad had been lurking outside the study when the farmworker had asked the squire to make sure that a proper investigation into Eddie's death would be done, and he had quickly spread it around belowstairs.

And whilst some in the village thought that it should all be decently laid to rest and least-said-soonest-mended, others had a lot of sympathy for the dead boy's parents. It was, after all, only natural that they'd want to know the truth about what had really happened that Easter Sunday.

And the cook was firmly in the latter camp.

Nevertheless, she took her time to prepare a pot of tea and set out two plates with a slice of her own-recipe lardy cake. It gave her time to think and arrange her thoughts in order.

Not that she knew anything that might actually help him. Like the rest of the staff, she hadn't had anything to do with the Easter egg hunt. But if the squire wanted his staff to answer the man's questions, then she'd go along with his orders.

And so, she took a seat at the table opposite him, and smiled politely.

'Do you know the Proctors well?' Clement asked first, leaning back easily in the kitchen chair and ignoring the slight squeak of protest it gave.

'Only as well as I know most folk in the village,' Hilda said comfortably. She was a comfortable-looking woman altogether, with a figure like one of her own cottage loaves, and a mess of grey hair done up in a surprisingly elegant chignon. She'd removed her pinafore as he'd been introducing himself, revealing a loose, soft, blue-grey dress, which matched her wide, rather watery-looking eyes.

The moment she'd sat down in her own chair, an enormous

tabby cat had leaped onto it, and had settled down with practised speed and continued to purr contentedly as she absent-mindedly stroked it.

'I see Doreen in the village shop and at church most Sundays,' the cook admitted. 'Her husband not so much – men tend to find excuses not to attend so often, don't they? And I don't go to the village pub, so…' She gave a shrug, but spoke without censure, and Clement got the impression that she was well content with her life here at the Hall. She seemed the sort who liked to keep herself to herself, but probably didn't miss much.

They quickly established that she'd been the cook here for over twenty years, and she informed him with another gentle smile that her title of 'Mrs' was strictly an honorary one, as she was quite happy being single.

He got the feeling that she was one of those rare people who was not inclined to ask life for more than they already had. No doubt, she had rooms up in the servants' quarters that she considered to be perfectly adequate, enjoyed whatever hobbies she had outside of work, and was probably a very good cook. Most importantly, she was an unbiased observer with no axe to grind, which, he felt sure, would make her a mine of useful – and untainted – information.

'Mr de Lacey feels guilty about the well not being covered properly,' Clement said. 'At least it's covered over now.'

The cook shook her head sadly. 'It takes something like this to remind you how hard life can be,' she agreed quietly.

Clement nodded. 'The poor little girl, Emily, misses her friend keenly.'

'Yes, she would,' Hilda agreed, chucking the purring cat under his chin. 'They were best pals, those too. They often came down here to help me mix cakes and do some cooking. They liked making orange butterfly cakes the best. All that butter cream icing meant they could lick the bowl.'

'And then have first pick of them as they came out of the oven?' he mused with a tolerant smile.

'Well, naturally, as is only fair!' Hilda agreed with a smile of her own. 'There was no harm in that boy,' she added quietly but firmly.

Clement nodded. 'That's good to know,' he said gravely. 'I've talked to Emily, of course, but she says she has no idea what her friend was doing in the orchard at all that morning. I think I believe her,' he said, letting his tone become slightly cautious.

Hilda Verney was silent for a moment or two, then sighed. 'Emily's a good girl. She wouldn't lie out of spitefulness or mischief. She's very clever, though, like a cartload of monkeys.'

Clement thought about this for a moment or two, then smiled. 'She was the leader of the pair?'

'Oh yes. Always full of ideas.'

'And Eddie was always happy to follow?' Clement mused.

'More often than not.'

Clement sipped from his mug of tea, and glanced out of the window. The kitchen was not quite below ground, but the windows were high, and sunlight filtered down from high up, meaning that they were without a view of the gardens.

'Mrs Roper seems a rather unfriendly soul, I thought.' He changed tack slightly, and wasn't surprised to see the cook's smile turn slightly wry.

'Yes, I can see how she might appear that way, especially to what she would term "outsiders". She is very loyal to the family who took her in after her husband died.' The cook sliced up more of the lardy cake, and pushed it across towards him. 'It's sometimes hard for people who have wealth and privilege to understand how frightening life can be for those who have neither,' she explained carefully. 'Mrs Roper felt the loss of her husband keenly. She'd left home, moved to a new place, and suddenly she was all alone.'

'I can see that must have been terrifying,' Clement said truthfully.

'Yes. But then old Mrs de Lacey took her in. Gave her a job as her maid – a roof over her head, a regular wage, and perhaps most importantly of all, a new purpose in life,' the cook said slowly. 'At that time, Mrs Vivienne was just beginning to get old you see – I mean truly old. Unable to get around much, and becoming forgetful. She was not the force she had once been, and she needed someone not only to see to her comforts and her needs, but also to be her eyes and ears in the house. And Cordelia needed someone to look after and make her feel secure. It was a match some might say was made in heaven.'

Clement cut a slice of his greasy cake with a fork and chewed it slowly for a moment or two. 'But you didn't think it was very healthy?' he finally said.

Hilda Verney shrugged her plump shoulders. 'Who am I to judge?' she asked simply. 'It suited them both, that was certain. As she got older, and her physical and mental faculties began to fail her even more, I'm sure Mrs Vivienne was happy in her choice of companion and confidante. But when she died…'

'Cordelia Roper was left rather bereft?' he hazarded. 'So where did she turn her energies then? I doubt Mr Martin would have welcomed her mothering.'

'Not he!' Hilda said with a snort of laughter.

'The children then?'

Hilda again shrugged. 'You'd have thought so, wouldn't you? But I'm not so sure. George was little more than a baby and had his own nanny. And Emily… Emily doesn't really like her, you know. Mrs Roper was too much her grandmother's creature, and Emily has a rather secretive nature.'

'Ah. So now Mrs Roper is a dragon without a hoard of gold to guard over? How sad.'

'Oh, I wouldn't be so quick as to presume *that*,' Hilda warned him, in her usual quiet but impressive way. 'She still sees herself as the guardian of the old lady's legacy.'

'Which is?'

'Family first and last,' the cook said promptly. 'Mrs de Lacey was fiercely proud of the family's place here, and its history. And its future.'

'Ah. So no wonder Mrs Roper isn't happy about all the fuss that's been kicked up by Eddie's death. She must have hated the press attention in particular, and the criticism of the family in not securing that well properly.'

'Yes,' Hilda said simply.

Clement, delighted to have found such a perspicacious witness, cast his mind around for anything else that he might need to know, and remembered the curious attitude of the village people in the pub when he'd mentioned Martin de Lacey's deceased wife.

'How did the old Mrs de Lacey get on with Jennifer, her daughter-in-law? How did Mrs Roper, come to that?'

Hilda reached for the teapot. 'Refill?' She got up to boil fresh water. It was clearly a device used to give her time to think, and Clement obligingly waited her out, then held out his half-empty mug for a top-up when she was finished doing her thinking.

He was well aware that, if this woman hadn't wanted to speak, he'd have been unable to make her. She would have responded to threats, bribes, flattery or guile with the same bland smile, routing him utterly.

'I'm afraid Mrs Roper always took her cues from the old woman and treated them like gospel,' Hilda said, and Clement began to pay even more careful attention. 'And Mrs Vivienne hated her daughter-in-law like poison.'

Although she spoke the words in her same, usual quiet tone, and with no undue emphasis, it only served to make her actual words all the more shocking.

Clement blinked, then shifted a little in his chair. From a woman so clearly not given to exaggeration, the words hit him with quite some force. Here, clearly, was evidence of raw emotion indeed within the usually enigmatic and aloof de Lacey family.

'Do you know why?' he asked at last. He was careful not to

insult Hilda Verney by trying to 'wangle' information out of her. Either she could tell him, or she wouldn't, and they both knew it.

But he thought he had the measure of the woman now. And whilst she might be careful who she spoke to and what she said, she was also the kind of woman who had a keen sense of her civic duty, as well as a moral compass of her own.

And the death of a little boy, by any standard, was wrong. Even if she could see no correlation between old family feuds and a village boy's recent death, she was not about to gainsay a man like Clement Ryder.

'I believe the old Mrs de Lacey had some doubts regarding her daughter-in-law's… fidelity to her marriage vows.'

Clement let out a long, slow, breath. 'Ah,' he said, then added carefully, 'And was she biased, in your opinion? Some mothers can be over-fond of their children, especially their sons, and in those kinds of cases, no girl can quite be good enough.'

Hilda Verney smiled a shade grimly. 'I don't think anyone who knew her would ever accuse Mrs Vivienne of being the "doting" mother type,' she said, and then rose from the table. 'And now, I really must be getting on with preparing the family dinner, Dr Ryder. It's been so nice chatting to you.'

She had gone as far as she was willing to go and would go no further. And as frustrating as he found it, he respected her limits.

'Well, it's been very nice talking to you too, Mrs Verney,' he said graciously as he rose from the table.

And he meant every word of it.

Chapter 22

Whilst Dr Ryder was letting himself out of the kitchen, and contemplating with some satisfaction his meeting with a rather remarkable woman and an even more interesting interview, Trudy was walking down the village lane. She was surrounded by Eddie Proctor's collection of brothers and sister, but was learning very little for all her careful questions.

Oh, she could tell that the eldest boy felt somehow guilty for not saving his brother from his fate, and was consequently inclined to be rather angry and aggressive with everyone and everything. And she had discerned that the youngest of them hadn't really understood the concept of death, and still expected to see Eddie sometime soon – perhaps sitting down for his share of the family dinner.

The ones closest to his age knew him and his habits best, but apart from the fact that he was always 'up at the Hall with Emily' or playing conkers or cards when it was raining, she could learn little more.

But one thing she had established to her own satisfaction – if Eddie had come into some money recently, he hadn't shared it with any of his siblings.

Trudy walked them as far as the turn-off to their house and

watched as they all rushed up the path, eager for their meal. She was very relieved to see that it was the children's mother who opened the door to them, but was careful not to let Mrs Proctor see her.

But at least Doreen Proctor was now up and about and had started caring for her large family. That had to count for something, didn't it? Even if she did look pale and washed out.

Feeling pensive, Trudy turned and made her way back towards the Hall.

*

Two men up on the edge of the woods, taking care to make sure they were concealed by the outer edge of trees, watched her movements through binoculars.

They were the same two individuals who had been sitting, unnoticed and mostly forgotten, at the back of the pub on the day that Trudy and Clement had gone there to chat to the regulars.

One of them meticulously noted her movements down in his notebook, whilst his companion turned his attention back to the Hall. *He* was just in time to notice Dr Clement Ryder emerge after his interesting chat with the cook.

Like his companion, he duly noted down details of the coroner's activities in his notebook.

After he'd done so, they watched in silence as the policewoman and the old man met up and began to talk.

'Do you think these two are going to cause problems?' one of them asked thoughtfully.

'I doubt it,' his companion said shortly. 'They're hardly Sherlock Holmes and Dr Watson, are they?'

*

Down below, Trudy told Clement about her mainly negative findings after talking to Eddie's brothers and sister, and Clement filled Trudy in on what the cook had been able to tell him.

'Sounds like you had a more productive time of it,' she said wryly. 'So that's why the villagers all went quiet when we mentioned Martin de Lacey's wife. If she caused a bit of a scandal, they would close ranks about it around strangers.'

'Poor chap,' Clement said mildly. 'Martin de Lacey, I mean,' he added, when Trudy shot him a slightly puzzled look. 'The cuckolded husband is always a figure of fun. If his wife had been the sort to have affairs, it must have made him very angry.'

Trudy nodded. 'So what do we do now?'

'Well, whilst we're here, we might as well go and see if Mr Oliver de Lacey or his mother are in,' Clement mused.

'*She* might be, but he'll probably be at the college, this time of day. Or up in London,' she added gloomily.

But for once, her pessimism was unwarranted, for after they'd made their way to the charming dower house, it was Oliver de Lacey himself who opened the door to their summons.

129

Chapter 23

At 35, he was younger than his cousin, and his head of plentiful, well-cut dark hair showed that, unlike Martin de Lacey, he was yet to be bothered by the prospect of incipient baldness. Also unlike his cousin, he preferred not to sport a moustache, and – in Trudy's opinion – was rather the better-looking for it. Nevertheless, there was no mistaking him for anything other than a de Lacey, with the same wide grey eyes and square chin that could be seen in many of the family portraits that were hung on the walls back at the Hall.

'Hullo?' His glance went first to Trudy, his eyes widening slightly as they took in her neat dark uniform and the cap perched pertly on her head of upswept hair. 'Police eh? Has mother been forgetting to pay for her dog licences again?'

Trudy smiled politely, introduced herself and the coroner, and somewhat coldly stated their business. Why was it that so many people mistook her for a meter maid?

'That poor young chap who drowned in our well? Bad business that. Better come in then,' he said at once, stepping aside to let them pass. 'Mother's not in. Playing bridge at some old pal's place, I expect. I'm not in for much longer myself – got a tutorial at four.' As he spoke, he eyed a grandfather clock that was ticking ponderously in the hall they were passing through. 'Into the sunroom I think. Second door on the left.'

The sunroom was aptly named, and resembled a sort of small mini-library-cum-lounge, with one wall dedicated to bookshelves. The rest of the room was taken up with a large low coffee table and several easy chairs. A generous amount of spring sunshine slanted in through a set of modern French windows, doing its usual party trick of flirting with the dust motes dancing in the air before falling across an ancient dog that was snoring in front of an unlit fireplace.

'Bit of a bad show on our part, that well not being properly covered and all that,' Oliver de Lacey admitted at once, taking a chair and indicating they should do the same. 'Not like my cousin not to be on top of stuff like that. Mind you, it's really the estate manager's job to… Yes, well, it's easy to apportion blame after the fact, isn't it?' he said smoothly.

He was dressed in a rather fine three-piece suit of dark navy with a fine red pinstripe, black Oxfords, and an Eton tie, and looked as unlike a country squire as it was possible to be. Clement found it easy to picture this man, dressed in the colourful and ornate academic gown that he was surely entitled to, striding towards the Sheldonian Theatre to attend some academic function or other, looking for all the world like the Oxford don he was. Little wonder the well-heeled Marjorie Chandler was having difficulty taking her pick of the cousins.

'I've spoken to your cousin Martin,' Clement began amiably, 'and on behalf of the boy's father, he's asked me to investigate the incident just a little further.'

'Oh? But surely there's nothing untoward in the inquest's findings?' Oliver said, one dark eyebrow rising in query. He neatly crossed one leg over the other at the knee, careful to smooth out the slight crease in his trouser leg that this motion instigated, and began to sway his loose foot lazily in the air. 'The poor tyke fell in by accident, didn't he?'

131

'Oh, we're not disputing that,' Clement lied smoothly. 'But obviously his parents would like to find out, if possible, exactly how that came about. Just for their own peace of mind.'

'Yes, yes, I can see that,' Oliver conceded immediately. 'It must be beastly for them not knowing the whys and wherefores. But I'm afraid I can't help you there,' he said, looking at Trudy, then back to Clement. 'Who can ever know what's in someone else's mind, especially at a time like that? Perhaps he saw a bird fly out and was looking for its nest? Robins and blackbirds *do* nest in some queer places you know.'

Clement shrugged. 'Anything's possible.'

'You *were* here on Easter Sunday, sir?' Trudy asked, deciding it was time to make this interview a rather more official affair. Besides, she didn't like the way that Oliver de Lacey was so obviously assuming that Dr Ryder was in charge here.

As if in confirmation of her suspicions, he turned a slightly surprised glance her way – as if he'd almost forgotten her presence – but he responded to her question quickly enough. 'I was, officer, yes. But I didn't take part in the Easter egg hunt of course. I remember doing so when I was a little whippersnapper myself. And I knew Martin's two would be out and about. But I didn't bother to go and watch. Besides, I was entertaining a lady. And later I had a paper to write.'

Trudy felt her lips twist in a wry smile. This man didn't need to point out just how important he was, or how precious his time had to be. His sense of self-worth and self-importance oozed out of every inch of him.

'Yes, sir, I'm sure you were busy,' she said quietly. 'But you were aware that Emily was friends with the boy who died?'

'I think Mother mentioned it later, yes.'

'Did your mother attend the Easter egg hunt?'

'Oh no. She was taking a holiday with friends somewhere on the south coast. Besides, that sort of thing wouldn't interest her,' Oliver said blithely, leaning back slightly in his chair and regarding his free foot for a moment as he continued to rotate it in heedless circles. Needless to say, the leather was spotless and perfectly polished. 'Even though Mother likes to think of herself as the interim lady of the manor, given that the position is vacant until Martin decides to remarry, she can't be bothered to actually carry out the duties of the same.'

Clement shifted slightly in his chair, and so in tune by now was Trudy with his methods, she realised at once that he wanted to take over, and took the hint by beginning to ostentatiously write down Oliver's testimony in her notebook.

'I understand your mother has lived here most of her married life?' Clement resumed, glancing around the pleasant room with a smile. 'It's a lovely old house. But not quite Briar's Hall?'

Oliver allowed a cool smile to flicker over his face. 'No, not quite. Mind you, we're lucky to have it at all, as I have to keep reminding my dear mama. Martin's under no real obligation to let us keep on living here rent-free you know. He does so out of a sense of family obligation and all that.'

'Still, it can't be altogether pleasant,' Clement mused, 'feeling as if your right to be here is solely by the grace and favour of your cousin?'

Oliver's smile was a few degrees cooler now. 'Well, Martin doesn't really have much option – not unless he wants to earn the disapproval of the village by chucking us out. And he does so like to be seen as the benevolent leader! Anyway, it may not matter for much longer. I've been thinking it was high time I got married and settled down, and the lady I have in mind would probably be much happier living in Oxford itself. Mama probably would be too, come to that.'

'Would the lady you refer to be a certain Miss Chandler, by any chance?' Clement asked casually.

For a moment, Oliver de Lacey went utterly still – including his swaying foot. Then he cocked his head slightly to one side, like a starling spotting movement under a lawn, and regarded the older man carefully.

'I can't see how we've gone from a wretched boy coming to a tragic end on our estate, to my future bride,' he said, making it clear that he suspected the older man of showing bad manners.

'Oh, I hadn't realised that things had progressed as far as *that*, between you,' Clement said breezily, unrepentantly ignoring the implied reprimand. 'Let me be the first to give you my congratulations. I shall be sure to do the same to Miss Chandler, when next I see her.'

Oliver sighed heavily. 'Hold your horses a moment.' He held up a languid hand, managing to sound both bored and wearily amused at the same time. 'I haven't actually got around to popping the question yet.'

At this, Trudy couldn't quite help herself, and interjected smartly, 'You seem to be taking it for granted the young lady will say "yes", sir, if I may say so.'

Oliver rolled his eyes slightly and once again sighed – rather more dramatically this time. '*Mea culpa*, officer. Let's just say, the young lady has intimated that she wouldn't be averse to a proposal, which has given me every reason to be confident of her response.'

'And is your cousin aware of this?' Clement asked mildly.

'Martin? Good grief, I have no idea,' Oliver said casually, then setting both feet firmly to the ground, he glanced at his watch and stood up. 'Now I really must be getting back to college before the little beast I have to mentor shows up to try and defend his latest essay. He won't be able to of course,' he added glumly. 'It's dire. I don't think he has the faintest idea how Einstein… Well, never mind all that.'

'Well, thank you for sparing us Einstein, sir,' Clement muttered, rising from his own chair and holding out his hand. 'And thank you for your time.'

'As I did warn you at the outset, Doctor, I knew I couldn't possibly be of much use to you, I'm afraid.'

Clement wisely said nothing, and the three of them walked in silence to the front door. In the hallway, Oliver picked up a set of car keys from an ornate marble and ormolu console table and stepped outside with them.

There he left them to walk around to the side of the house, where a small wooden garage had been constructed, probably sometime around the period when the first automobiles were beginning to make their appearances. He whistled something catchy from the latest show at London's West End as he went, and promptly disappeared from view.

Chapter 24

Clement and Trudy had made it up the drive and were nearly at the double gates before they heard the sound of his car coming up behind them on the gravel, and both stepped instinctively onto the grass verge to let him pass.

He gave a derisive toot as he swept past them, and Trudy was not surprised to see the long, low sweep of a Morgan in racing-car green shoot by.

'I don't like that man,' Trudy said as the car disappeared from sight.

Clement said nothing for a moment, watching as the car disappeared down the lane. 'Any reason in particular?' he asked eventually.

Trudy frowned. 'I'm not sure. Maybe it was just that he was so full of himself – in every sort of way. You know – he was so much *cleverer* than us. So much *richer*, so much more *important*. So much *better-looking*!'

'You speak for yourself, youngster,' Clement said, straightening his tie ostentatiously, shooting his cuffs and then sweeping a hand through his quiff of thick white hair.

Trudy burst out laughing. She wasn't sure why, but it always took her a little aback whenever Dr Ryder displayed his sense of humour.

'He doesn't like his cousin much, does he?' she said thoughtfully. 'I know he didn't say much about him, but you could just feel him sort of... I don't know... sneering underneath it all, whenever he talked of him.'

'Yes, I agree. And I'm pretty sure Martin de Lacey reciprocates the feeling in spades. No, there's not much love lost between those two.'

'Do you think that's why he' – Trudy nodded her head towards the now empty road – 'is so keen to marry Miss Chandler? Well, that and for her money, of course. To put one over on his cousin?'

Clement nodded, but in truth he was pretty sure that Oliver de Lacey's motives for wanting to marry and settle down with his rich American lady probably went far deeper than that.

He knew Trudy hadn't picked up on it – not surprising for a young girl who'd led such a relatively sheltered life – but he was quite sure that the opposite sex held little appeal at all for the likes of Oliver de Lacey. Clement found it quite easy to spot men who had no sexual interest in women – often it had something to do with the way they watched the opposite sex with a detached, uninterested eye that was, to him, unmistakable. So he was more than willing to bet a guinea or two that the don's reputation as a ladies' man had been very carefully cultivated – and was utterly meaningless.

However, he didn't really want to take the time right now to give his protégé the somewhat tricky and awkward explanation that would be needed to make clear to her why such a man would eventually need to consider marriage as a suitable cover. Presumably though, since homosexuality was a crime, she must have been taught about such practices in her training.

'Well, apart from confirming that the cousins aren't very friendly with each other, I don't see that we're any further forward, are we, sir?' Trudy said, a shade forlornly. 'We seem to be finding out interesting things all right, but nothing that explains why Eddie Proctor either fell or was pushed down that well.'

But Clement wasn't so sure. 'Oh, I wouldn't say that. The lad had to die for *some* reason,' he pointed out with grim logic. 'Which means that *someone* must have wanted or needed him to be dead. And a young lad, living in a small village – the only people he could have made an enemy of must be around here somewhere.' He looked around at the Hall, the dower house, and in the distance, towards the village of Briar's-in-the-Wold itself.

'So everything we learn about the people in his orbit could be significant, because it might lead us towards finding out why Eddie had to die.' Trudy nodded, willing to be convinced. 'All right. So, with that thought in mind… shouldn't we take a detour to the stables before calling it a day?'

Clement looked at her in surprise. 'The stables?' he asked, confused. 'Why the stables?'

'Well, we know that Jennifer de Lacey was a horsewoman, and that she died as a result of a fall from her horse,' Trudy said, wondering if she was being foolish. 'So if we're looking for dark deeds that might have a bearing on the residents, don't you think we need to chat with one of the grooms or…'

'Yes, yes of course,' Clement said hastily, angry with himself for not following her train of thought sooner. Uneasily, he wondered if he would have been so obtuse just a year ago.

Trudy smiled in relief. For a moment there, she thought her idea had been a stupid one. Usually it was Dr Ryder who came up with leads and ideas, so she felt rather proud of herself as they made their way to the Briar's Hall stable block.

Clement Ryder was unusually silent beside her.

Little was yet known about Parkinson's disease, but he knew from the studies he'd been doing ever since being diagnosed that its main symptoms were tremors, slowed movement (or bradykinesia), and rigid muscles. More mundane (but annoying) symptoms could include bad breath, hence his recently acquired habit of popping breath mints regularly throughout the day.

But although he experienced tremors and uneven footsteps

occasionally, he had not, as yet, noticed any of the other problems that could accompany the illness. Such as depression, swallowing problems, sleep disorders or thinking difficulties.

And the thought of the latter, especially, was truly terrifying. For he'd always been able to rely on his intelligence and brains. But when those inevitably and inexorably began to fail him…

His heartbeat quickened sickeningly as they made their way to the stables, but he forced himself to confront his fear head-on. Because Trudy's suggestion that they needed to talk to the grooms, for a horrifyingly blank moment, had made no sense to him at all.

Of course, it had only been momentarily, and then he'd quickly followed her reasoning. But was that simply a momentary lapse, due to his age? Or was it the first sign of the onset of cognitive problems? His mind instinctively shied away from the word dementia. But he knew that later, when he was alone in his house and darkness fell, it would come back to haunt him.

Then he noticed Trudy look across at him with a slightly puzzled glance, and told himself angrily to get a grip.

Granted, although research on the 'shaking palsy' was still in its infant stages, it was widely agreed that dementia usually occurred in the latter stages of Parkinson's. And he was still in the very early stages. So he mustn't let himself become paranoid over every little thing. He was nearly 60, after all, and it was totally natural that his reactions and thoughts should be slowing down just a fraction.

Yes, that's all it amounted to, he reassured himself. For just a fraction of a second, his young protégé had been ahead of him. Which, considering the great pains he was taking in order to teach her logical and lateral thinking, was surely an encouraging sign?

'That must be the stable block, don't you think?' Trudy's voice interrupted his melancholy mood, and he looked up to where she was pointing. Through a large arched entrance in the wall where, in days gone by, the de Lacey coach and horses would have exited, they could see a cobbled yard and a long half-brick, half-wooden structure behind it, with tell-tale half-and-half stable doors.

'Looks like it,' Clement grunted, still having trouble shaking off his maudlin thoughts.

They stepped through into a clean and well-maintained yard, and as they did so, a graceful equine head appeared inquisitively over the top half of a door. He had a black glossy coat and a white lop-sided star on his forehead, and Trudy couldn't help but go over immediately to stroke his irresistibly soft and pink velvet nose.

'He reminds me of Black Beauty,' Trudy said. 'That book made me cry buckets when I was 12! I wish I had a carrot for him,' she added wistfully.

'Here, try one of these,' Clement said, sacrificing one of his mints to the cause. Trudy took it, laid it flat on her hand and offered it to her new four-legged friend, who, with a deft manipulation of his soft lips, accepted it gracefully.

'Can I 'elp you?' A somewhat sharp voice had them turning around, to eye the stable 'boy' confronting them – who looked to be in his late sixties, maybe even early seventies – if he was a day.

'I'm Dr Clement Ryder, and this is WPC Loveday,' Clement said, and he saw the other man relax slightly. He was wearing impeccable but old grey trousers, and a grey V-necked, sleeveless jumper over a white shirt. His cuffs were rolled up to his elbows, and he was as wrinkled as a walnut – and about the same colour too. An outdoorsman all his life, his head was now host to uneven tufts of white hair, and two white caterpillars of eyebrows guarded deep-set dark-blue eyes that watched them cautiously.

He was holding, a little alarmingly, a long-pronged pitchfork, which he let drop to the ground on hearing the coroner's cultivated voice.

'Ah, squire said as you might be about sometime,' he owned amiably. 'I'm William Kirklees, Head Boy here. It's about poor little Eddie? Squire said you'd be talking to us about him. Nice lad.'

'Did he often come to the stables?' Trudy asked.

'Only sometimes, and always with Miss Emily. Usually when they had pinched some sugar lumps or carrots or apples from the gardens.' He smiled, revealing a missing front tooth. 'All kiddies like feeding the 'osses. Not that the 'osses minded that. Greedy beasts, is 'osses,' he said fondly.

And so saying, he walked towards them and gave the black horse a fond pat on his neck. The horse responded by head-butting him affably in the shoulder.

'I don't suppose you were here on the Sunday of the Easter egg hunt?' Trudy asked.

'I was, then, but only to see to the 'osses. Didn't do a full day's work, it being Easter and all. Came in early then off to church. So I didn't see the young 'uns scampering around. Went home after church, see,' the Head Boy explained.

'Yes I understand,' Trudy said, never really having expected anything else. Artlessly, she turned to the horse and stroked it again. 'He's a beauty. Does he belong to the squire? Or is this his poor wife's horse? I understand she died in a riding accident?'

'Ah, no, this ain't Miss Jennifer's horse. The squire, he sold 'im on. Couldn't bear to have 'im around, I reckon. Nice 'oss, mind, was old Seamus. Very nice 'oss.'

'I've been told Mrs de Lacey was an excellent horsewoman. It must have come as a real shock when she was thrown, as she was,' Trudy continued artlessly.

'Oh ar,' the Head Boy said nodding. 'Miss Jennifer had one of the best seats in the Home Counties, I reckon. Can't think what could have happened. Seamus adored the missus, he did. And she knew how to handle him like a dream. Sorry to see 'im go, I was, but there you are.' He heaved a massive sigh.

He seemed a simple soul, and willing enough to talk, so Trudy nodded and decided to push her luck a bit. 'You must have thought about it a lot. Did you come to any conclusions about what must have happened that day?'

The old man rubbed his chin thoughtfully, and Trudy could have sworn she could almost hear the rasping sound made by his white stubble as his stubby thumbs swept over them. 'Only thing that makes sense is something spooked 'im,' the old man said at last. 'And the missus was so taken by surprise, he unseated her afore she could get control of him.'

'And is that what all the grooms here thought?' Trudy said craftily. 'I dare say they were all upset?'

'Oh ar. Yerse, I reckon that's what most of us thought. Except maybe John.'

'John?' Trudy prompted.

'Blandon. He was Seamus' groom. Well, he worked with all the 'osses, like, but Miss Jennifer, she preferred John looking after Seamus special like.'

'Oh? Do you mind if we talk to John?' Trudy asked, sensing something a little wary in the old man's manner now.

'You'd have a job, I reckon,' William Kirklees said, and gave a rather fruity chuckle. 'Not lest you can shout real loud! He moved up north somewhere, not long after the missus went. Married someone who owned a pub, or so one of the other lads told me. Mind you, that don't surprise me. He was always the sort to land on his feet, was John.'

Trudy glanced at Clement, whose eyes were now twinkling.

'A man with ambitions, was he?' Trudy said, careful to keep her voice light and jocular. 'I know his sort all right. Rather good-looking I imagine?'

'Oh, ar. Well, so the womenfolk told me. Couldn't see it meself, like. He had a head and pair of eyes and a nose and a mouth, the same as the rest of us.' The old man shrugged, as if the vagaries of women were so unfathomable that he'd long since given up trying to understand them.

'He must have been very upset. Do you think he left because the squire got rid of Seamus?' she asked, looking at him innocently.

The Head Boy shrugged. 'The missus's death hit him hard, that's all I know. And he just ups and puts in his resignation.'

'I don't suppose you know where up north he went do you?' she asked, but wasn't unduly surprised when the old man shook his head. 'Haven't a clue, my duck, sorry.'

Well, she would find him, Trudy thought. The one thing about being shunted off and having to work in records so often was that it had taught her to handle paperwork!

'Well, thank you, Mr Kirklees,' she said, and glanced at Clement, to see if he had anything to add.

The coroner nodded slightly. 'Yes, thank you, Mr Kirklees. You've worked here long?'

'All me life, man and boy. Well apart from the war, like. The first 'un, I mean.'

'So you would have known the squire's mother, Vivienne de Lacey? I'd lay bets she was a fine horsewoman too.'

'Oh ar. A real lady, she was,' William Kirklees said proudly. 'Once or twice she nearly got me with that riding crop of hers!' he said fondly. 'Didn't do to get on her wrong side. She had a bit of a temper on 'er, she had.'

Trudy gawped at him. 'She tried to hit you with her riding whip?' she asked, scandalised.

The old man looked at her and grinned. 'Oh, ar. Like I said, a real lady she was,' he said approvingly.

Clement coughed to hide the sudden bark of laughter that he could no longer repress, and turned away.

'Well, we won't keep you, Mr Kirklees. It's getting on, and I dare say you'll be wanting your tea,' Trudy acknowledged.

Even as she spoke, the church clock began to strike four.

'Ah, dare say,' the old man said evenly.

Trudy followed Clement back through the arch and towards the front of the house, where the coroner had left his Rover.

'Are these people all mad?' she huffed, once she was sure they were out of range. 'If someone tried to hit me with a crop, I'd… I'd… I'd *brain* them!'

'I'll bear that in mind,' Clement said solemnly. And a moment later, her sudden peal of laughter made his lips twitch. And for a moment, the gloom that had overtaken him before was suddenly lifted.

Trudy, in contrast, began to feel slightly gloomy on the short ride back to town. Once she'd reported in to DI Jennings, she'd have to go home, and she didn't for one moment think that she had heard the last about her break-up with Brian!

Chapter 25

Trudy was held back at the station for a while, since DI Jennings was in a particularly sarcastic and bloody-minded mood and demanded a practically word-for-word account of the Eddie Proctor case so far. This meant that she only just caught the last bus home, and was consequently late for her tea.

Not an auspicious beginning!

She changed into her civvies in super-quick time, washed her face and hands, and arrived at the tea table as silently as possible. Her dad was still sitting at the table reading the evening paper, although it was clear that both he and her mother had already eaten their meal at the usual time.

On seeing Trudy enter, her mother moved wordlessly from the sink where she'd been washing up and over to the oven. There, she donned a pair of oven gloves, opened the main oven door and removed a tin plate from one of the shelves. On it was a slightly congealed-looking mound of Lancashire hotpot and some slightly shrivelled peas. She then picked up an old newspaper from the countertop that she kept especially for just such purposes, slapped it down on the Formica table and then set the hot tin plate down on top of it.

'Mind you don't burn yourself,' she said tersely.

Trudy nodded glumly. She hated being in the doghouse with her parents – it always made her feel uneasy and uncomfortable. She picked up her knife and fork and tentatively pried a piece of lamb from the plate, blew on it, and carefully popped it into her mouth.

'Hmmm, lovely,' she said with forced cheerfulness.

On the wall, the sunburst wooden clock (a Christmas present from Auntie June a few years ago) ticked away neutrally, like a disinterested observer.

Her father rustled his paper, drawing her eye, and when he caught her gaze, offered her a slight smile.

Trudy grinned back at him, saw her mother begin to turn back to the table, and quickly wiped it off her face. Barbara Loveday sat down portentously, and leaned back slightly in her chair, arms crossed.

Which was not a good sign.

'Right, our Trudy,' she began – another sure indication that she was going to get a good talking-to! 'Your dad and I want to have a little chat with you.'

Trudy selected a piece of sliced potato, blew on it, chewed it, swallowed, and tried to look nonchalant. 'What about, Mum?' she asked mildly.

'About Brian of course,' Barbara said. 'I've had his mum around, asking if it was true that you'd thrown him over. I didn't know where to put my face. Madge has been my friend since we moved in here!'

'I'm sure she'll carry on being your friend, Mum,' Trudy began to try and placate her but, like most other of her 'little chats' with her mother, she was barely able to get a word in edgewise.

'Of course she will, our Trudy, that's not the point.' Barbara Loveday huffed shortly, her pretty, slightly plump face beginning to flush with anger.

Recognising the signs, Trudy hastily returned her gaze to her meal, although her appetite was quickly waning. She forced herself to fork up some peas and took her time chewing them.

'She says her Brian was right upset. He says it came right out of the blue. Naturally, Madge asked him what he'd done to upset you like, and he swears he doesn't know.'

'He didn't do anything, Mum,' Trudy said, trying to be patient, but feeling her own anger begin to stir. 'He's a nice enough chap, but I just don't want to marry him. I don't think we're suited. It's as simple as that.'

For a moment, silence reigned. Then her mother stirred in her seat. 'You've been seeing him since you were 16. That's nearly four years. When a lad's been going steady for that long... Well, he has a right to expectations.'

Trudy mutinously studied her plate. 'We barely went out,' she said at last. 'A few visits to the cinema and to the local dance a few times. And I never ever said... I never encouraged him... We never exchanged rings or got anywhere close to something like that. It was always you and his mother who assumed...' It was always the same when she got angry or upset – she just couldn't seem to link a coherent sentence together.

'And Brian assumed it too, don't you forget,' her mother admonished flatly. 'Madge said he was right upset about it all.'

Trudy bit back the smart retort that sprang to her lips, and took a long, slow, breath instead. 'I think you'll find that Madge is exaggerating a little. Brian didn't seem that upset about it to me. A little surprised, I know, and yes, disappointed. But I hardly broke his heart, Mum! Honestly.'

For a moment her mother stared at her flatly, then her shoulders sagged in defeat and she cast her silent husband a quick look that clearly said she could do with some reinforcements.

'It's not just about Brian, though, is it?' her mother swept on, her voice flatter, and somehow a little more bitter now. It sent a slight chill running down Trudy's spine, since it was a tone of voice that she'd never heard her mother use before.

'It's this job of yours, Trudy,' Barbara began, and instantly Trudy felt herself prickle.

147

'Oh, not this again, Mum!' she all but wailed. 'I thought we had this out when I first applied for training!'

'No we didn't then,' her mother shot back, her voice beginning to rise. 'We never wanted you to join, and you said you were going to, and that was that. And if you remember, young lady,' her mother carried on, with growing heat, 'you agreed that we would discuss it again when your probationary period was nearly up. When we'd all had some time to take in just what you being a woman police officer really meant. And now that time is up!'

Trudy frowned, trying to remember if she had, indeed, made this concession, and seemed to recall, vaguely, that she probably had. But at the time she'd made the offer, she was hoping that they would soon forget about it altogether.

Clearly, they hadn't.

'All right then,' Trudy said, taking the bull firmly by the horns, 'let's do that. You know as well as I do that I'm practically nothing more than a glorified clerk. I spend most of my time in records, or doing the filing, or making the tea. I might as well be working in an office as a secretary! When I'm not doing that, I'm called upon to do strip-searches of female suspects and root about in their handbags. Occasionally I get to sit beside the beds of people in hospital, waiting to hear if they wake up and say anything useful or incriminating. And I get to go and knock on people's doors and give them bad news, and sit and hold their hands – which is awful, and makes me sad, but it's hardly dangerous. And when I'm not doing any of that, I walk a beat. And so far…'

She hurried on as she could see that her mother was about to explore that promising avenue further, 'I've earned nothing more than a few scraped knees and elbows chasing down purse-snatchers and what have you. And I got far worse injuries than that on the hockey fields at school.'

She paused to take a much-needed breath, but it gave her mother time to jump in.

'And *that's* why you've just been commended for bravery is

it?' Barbara said angrily. 'That little shindig at the Randolph Hotel wasn't about a scraped knee was it, my girl? You tackled a murderer, our Trudy!'

'I thought you were proud of me,' her daughter shot back, clearly hurt.

'We were. We are! But that's not the point!' her mother all but shouted now, but looked, and probably felt, close to tears of frustration. 'How do you think we felt, your dad and me, when we heard what you'd done? We were sick with worry!'

'Mum! I was never in any danger! Not really – the suspect never wanted to hurt me!' she tried to explain, but even as she spoke, she realised she might as well not have bothered.

'And what about next time, Trudy?' The male voice, interjecting between them, brought Trudy up short. She turned her exasperated gaze away from her mother's equally tight face, and turned to her father.

She felt inexplicably betrayed by his sudden advent into the argument, especially since he was siding with her mother. Something of it must have shown on her face too, for her father sighed, and lowered his paper. He leaned over the table and reached for her hand, grasping it in his slightly callused fingers.

'You've been lucky so far, love,' he said gently. 'But luck won't hold forever. It never does.'

Trudy opened her mouth, then realised she didn't know what to say.

'I don't think you've fully realised yet, that the job you're doing can be really dangerous, our Trudy,' her father continued. 'Whenever we read about policemen dying in the line of duty in the papers, it makes our blood run cold. You can understand that, love, can't you?'

'Yes, but, Dad…' Trudy caught herself, and wondered, in growing despair, how she could explain the reality of things to them. 'For a start, that's police*men*.' She emphasised the gender strongly. 'There are loads of duties that they do that I would never have to do. And most of those incidents happen in London anyway – or in the big cities. Not in Oxford! Really, what I do is mostly office work. I promise.'

'Is that what you're doing now?' her mother asked abruptly.

Trudy blinked. 'That's not fair. You know I'm helping Dr Ryder with one of his cases – that poor boy who was found dead in a well up in Briar's-in-the-Wold. We're trying to help his parents find out what really happened,' she finished, on a note of growing triumph. 'Don't you think that's something that needs to be done?' she asked challengingly, sure she was winning the argument now. 'Just think what that poor little boy's parents are going through. And Dr Ryder and I are trying to give them answers. Don't you think someone *should* be doing that?'

She saw her mother look across at her father with a look of near-despair, and instantly her sense of triumph turned to one of shame. Which made her feel angry. But surely they couldn't deny that she was doing a good thing? So why did she feel so shabby all of a sudden?

'Yes, someone should,' Barbara said heavily. 'But why does it have to be you?'

Her father leaned back in his chair, and as he did so, his fingers, which had been holding hers across the table, slid away, leaving her hand feeling suddenly cold.

'We just worry about you, that's all, love,' her father said sadly.

Trudy, feeling herself close to tears, pushed her plate away. 'I think I'll have an early night,' she said miserably, and fled.

Chapter 26

If Trudy Loveday was alone in her bedroom, close to tears and feeling alternately bewildered, angry, distressed and rebellious, Marjorie Chandler was having a much more interesting — although equally emotional — time.

She was in her flat, regarding a lovely diamond and ruby ring, that Martin de Lacey had just offered her.

Outside it was growing dark, and the city lights were beginning to glow. She had just cooked them one of the few dinners in her repertoire — a pasta dish she'd been taught by an Italian grand-mother — and now they were sitting on her settee, in front of a flickering fire, sipping a rather nice Merlot.

Martin had chosen his moment well.

He was dressed in a rather fine but old suit, and had simply slipped his hand into his pocket and withdrawn a small, square turquoise-leather box, and lifted the lid.

'This belonged to my great-great-grandmother, Elizabeth de Lacey,' he said casually. 'She got it, I believe, from the younger son of a Marquis, who shall remain nameless,' he said with a smile and in that rather self-deprecating way Englishmen had. 'Needless to say, the minx kept the ring, but didn't marry the suitor. Created a bit of a stir in her day, did Elizabeth. She was rather known for that sort of thing – being a bit flighty, and all that,' he added with a smile. 'Scandalised the court any number of times – but she did increase her personal fortune quite considerably.'

Marjorie felt her heart thrill as she looked down at the gem. 'Which court would that be? Victoria's?' she asked, eyes gleaming.

Martin shrugged. 'Hers, or maybe the one before that. I'm not sure.'

Marjorie laughed. 'How cavalier you Brits are about your ancestry,' she said, with real envy in her soft, American drawl. 'In Boston, people would kill to be able to trace an ancestor back to any royal court.'

Martin shrugged. 'Back in the late seventeenth or early eighteenth century, I think we de Laceys had a title of our own. Baron, maybe, or something like that. But I think that line abruptly halted during the Napoleonic wars. Can't carry on the title through daughters you see. So I can't promise you'll be "Lady" de Lacey. Well, not technically anyway,' he said. 'But you'll be lady of the manor to everyone in the village, nevertheless.'

Marjorie laughed, slightly nervously. 'Is that your idea of a proposal?' she asked archly.

''Fraid so, old girl,' Martin said with a smile. 'I think I'm a bit past getting down on the old one knee and all that.' He regarded the splendid ring for a moment, then looked up as the woman beside him rose, and walked slowly over towards the fireplace. There she rested one hand thoughtfully on the mantelpiece and stared down into the flames.

Martin regarded her nervously. Had he mistimed it?

Tonight she was wearing some sort of fancy lounging trouser-suit in shot blue silk. Her long blonde hair had been left artfully loose and she looked younger than her thirty-one years.

'Of course, if I've overstepped the mark…' he began, putting the ring down on the coffee table in front of him, and coughed uncomfortably. 'I know Oliver… well, Oliver is much better-

152

lookin' than me, and a bit of a brain-box to boot. But... well, Oliver isn't exactly the marryin' sort, if you know what I mean?'

'Oh, Martin, don't be silly. You don't have to worry about Oliver,' Marjorie lied brightly. 'We're just friends, that's all.' She compounded the lie without compunction. 'It's just... well, you did rather spring this on me.'

She returned to the settee and picked up the case with the ring in it, that Martin had left to sit, so temptingly, on the table.

Of course, the proposal wasn't a surprise at all. She'd been aware that Martin had been building up his courage for some time. It was just that she still hadn't made up her mind.

Oliver, too, had been making discreet overtures, sounding out the lie of the land, as it were. But unlike his cousin, who had a far more straightforward approach, the physics don was much more cautious. In a way, she admired this evidence that proved the younger cousin was a more sophisticated, man-of-the-world sort. On the other hand, there was something brave and admirable about the way Martin simply laid it all out on the line. Had he lived in an earlier age, she could just imagine him as a cavalry officer, riding into the French battlefields.

And the ring *was* gorgeous.

And she'd be 'unofficially' lady of the manor. Pity the title wasn't still extant though. It would be something to make her friends jealous back home.

But did she really want to become just one of the 'green wellie' brigade? She'd first heard this phrase from friends in London, who found it screamingly funny. And it did give her pause to think. She was hardly the country wife type, after all.

But was being the wife of an Oxford don the best she could do either? Marjorie had always been aware that being wealthy was her biggest advantage and her greatest asset in life. She was not, she'd had to admit, particularly beautiful, although cosmetics and great clothes could create the illusion of beauty – just ask Coco Chanel or Christian Dior!

'Let me think about it, Martin,' she said at last, and sitting down beside him, she let her hand wander to the side of this face, and caress his cheek gently.

'Fair enough, old girl, you do that,' Martin said casually.

But his heart was beating sickeningly. He knew, once Oliver found out what he'd done, he'd up his own game.

And then they would see.

Chapter 27

Clement Ryder, unaware of his protégé's distressing family argument, or the angst being suffered by Martin de Lacey's family rivalry, had plenty of troubles of his own.

He had poured himself a very small brandy, and was sitting in front of a blazing fire, watching the flames moodily. A widower for some time now, his two children had long since flown the nest. But it wasn't the quietness of the house – a pleasant Victorian terrace in one of the city's more desirable areas – that was making him feel uneasy, so much as his own, unquiet thoughts.

With a grunt, he finished his glass of spirits and set it down on the inlaid walnut table beside him, and slowly leaned his head back against the headrest.

All right then, he thought grimly, let's have it. He closed his eyes, and began to think.

If he *was* beginning to lose either his memory or his cognitive reasoning, he'd need to find some way to measure his deterioration. Or lack thereof. He was still apt to believe that his momentary lapse this afternoon wasn't anything really ominous or significant. But he had to face facts. His illness was only going to get worse. Very slowly worse, he thought, and hoped, and actually believed. But even so… He needed to keep track of it.

So he would have to set up a system. Journals. Yes, he could start keeping journals, making a note of every episode – every set of tremors, every slurred word, every dragging of his feet. That way, he would have statistics – real, proper data – that he could study.

Facts had always been his ally. You could never rely only on your emotions. He simply couldn't afford to become afraid of every little slip that he made. Why, if he let himself dwell on every little thing that *could* go wrong, he could make himself afraid to get up in the morning. What if he accidentally cut his throat shaving if he had a sudden hand tremor? Choked on his piece of breakfast toast if he should begin to have difficulty swallowing? Got wiped out in his car by some maniac overtaking on a bend when his own reaction time was slower than usual?

No. That way lay madness.

There were other tests that could be of use as well. Tests that he could do every week that would check the progress and state of his mental abilities... Yes, there were plenty of those.

He reached for a pen and paper, and began to make his lists, feeling calmer and more reassured, the more he made a plan of action.

*

As the coroner made his lists, over at Briar's Hall, little Emily de Lacey lay in her bed up in her nursery room, and contemplated grown-ups. They could do some truly bewildering and baffling things. Things that made no sense to her or to Eddie either.

She turned on her mattress and stared at the wall. Familiar shadows, mostly cast by the trees outside, danced against the faded wallpaper.

Was Eddie in heaven, looking down on her? She thought he

must be, because there had been nothing wicked about him. She wondered if you knew all there was to know when you died. If so, why didn't he come back and tell her what had happened to him that day? Maybe you weren't allowed? The vicar sometimes said that it wasn't man's lot to know everything – that omni... omni-something-or-other belonged only to God.

She turned and sighed, trying to get comfortable, but she just couldn't fall asleep.

She was afraid.

What if something happened to her, like it had to Eddie? Well, it might be nice to be in heaven... But she rather thought it would be scary to get there. She didn't want to die.

But perhaps it would be all right. They hadn't told anyone else about the things they'd seen. So nobody else knew that *she* knew.

Unless Eddie had told somebody.

But Eddie wouldn't. Would he?

Chapter 28

The next morning, Trudy deliberately got up very early and slipped out of the house before either of her parents were awake. She caught the first bus into work, surprising her colleagues working the night shift, by joining then a good two hours before she was due in.

She didn't waste her time, but set about trying to track down John Blandon, the groom from the Hall, who'd gone 'up north' somewhere. With a relatively common name and not much to go on, it wouldn't be easy, she knew.

By the time the Sarge and the DI had arrived, she'd made a good start, if only in eliminating most of the John Blandons who definitely *weren't* her man.

Jennings, still in his sarcastic mood of the day before, told her she'd best get off to the morgue and see what the old vulture wanted this time. By now, Trudy never even winced at this unkind nickname for her mentor, and with a muttered 'yes, sir' was happy enough to go.

By the time she'd collected a bicycle and had pedalled down St Aldate's towards Floyds Row she was beginning to feel in a better mood. Her parents were bound to get over their unreasonable grump sometime, and who knew what the day might bring?

That was what was so glorious about doing what she did. You never knew what might happen next. But how could she explain this to her parents? Especially since they valued routine so highly, as well as the predictability that came with a safe and steady job? When she got to the coroner's office however, it was to learn from his secretary that he was sitting in court that morning and wouldn't be available until after lunch. Annoyed with herself for not checking his diary before she came, she trailed back outside, and stood for a moment in the spring sun feeling slightly despondent.

Around her, the city went about its normal business, and a fitful sun played tag with grey-tinged clouds. Two men went past her, discussing work, both of them rent collectors, from the little she overheard.

She didn't want to go back to the station, although she knew she ought to. But Inspector Jennings wouldn't really be glad to see her and would only have to root around and find something boring for her to do, so really, she would be doing him a favour if she saved him the bother, right?

Pleased with this bit of sophistry, she cast around for something she might usefully do, and after a moment's thought, went to the nearest phone box and rooted around in her police satchel for some pennies. She got through to the operator and asked for the telephone number for the dower house at Briar's-in-the-Wold, and was eventually put through, after duly feeding the telephone box some coins.

A maid answered on the other end. She began by primly reciting the number in full, stating the name of the residence and then asked diligently, 'How may I help you?' She sounded young, and said it all in such a rehearsed and expressionless manner, that Trudy was sure that the poor girl must have had the proper telephone etiquette drummed into her – probably by the mistress of the house.

'I would like to speak to Mrs Sylvia de Lacey please,' she said clearly.

'Certainly, madam. Whom may I say is calling?'

'WPC Loveday. It concerns Eddie Proctor.'

There was a sharp gasp on the other end of the line, and Trudy couldn't help but smile. Of all the possible scenarios she must have been taught on how to deal with people over the telephone (from how to correctly address a Bishop, to politely dealing with a wrong number) she doubted that receiving a phone call from the police had been included among them.

'I'll see if madam is at home,' the girl finally managed to stutter. There was a click as the telephone receiver was put down at the other end, and Trudy searched her satchel for another penny, just in case Mrs de Lacey was in a room far away or took her time about deciding whether or not to take the call.

But curiosity, as her old sergeant at training college had told her, was indeed a powerful motivator, for not long after, another far more confident voice came across the line.

'Yes, this is Mrs Sylvia de Lacey.'

'Hello, Mrs de Lacey, this is WPC Loveday. I'm calling from Oxford. I was wondering if, by any chance, you were thinking of coming into town today?'

There was yet another startled pause at this somewhat peremptory question, then, 'Well, I wasn't, but I can do so if you think it's important?'

'Yes, madam, if you'd be so kind. As you may or may not know, we're investigating the circumstances surrounding young Eddie Proctor's… accident?' She allowed a slight and significant pause before the final word, and thought she sensed a sudden tension over the line. Of course, that might just be wishful thinking on her part, she acknowledged to herself ruefully.

'But I thought that was all over and done with?' Sylvia de Lacey said sharply. 'The inquest said it was an accident or misadventure or something, didn't it? Surely there's nothing more to be said about the matter?'

So Martin hadn't told her that he called in people to run a

more thorough investigation, Trudy mused. Interesting that, since he'd informed all those belowstairs to expect them, and to cooperate. Was it possible that he'd neglected to tell his aunt because he suspected she wouldn't approve? Or did she just rank so low on his radar that he'd simply forgotten about her?

Even more interesting, she suddenly realised a moment later, is that this woman's own son, Oliver, couldn't have mentioned their visit to him either. Otherwise surely she wouldn't sound so surprised now? What was it about this family, she wondered, that they never seemed to tell each other anything? Little Emily was guarded from talking to them by both her father and the ever-faithful Mrs Roper. Oliver and his mother clearly didn't communicate. And Clement had told her that even during his initial interview with Martin de Lacey, the squire hadn't exactly been very forthcoming.

'We still don't know any details about how Eddie came to be in the orchard or to fall into the well, Mrs de Lacey,' Trudy explained patiently. 'Naturally, the poor boy's parents need to be reassured that everything is being done to find out more. I'm sure, as a parent yourself, you can sympathise,' she added, allowing her voice to sound gently chiding.

'Oh yes, yes, of course I do,' the other woman said at once, sounding a little irritated and flustered. 'It's all so dreadful! But I'm not sure how I can help?' she added stubbornly.

'We're talking to everyone who knew Eddie, of course, and all the staff at the Hall, as well as members of your family. We've already talked to Mr Martin de Lacey and your son, and young Emily. And the servants – Mrs Roper, the gardening staff and so on. We're trying to build up a picture of the boy, and what went on that Easter Sunday. Would it be possible to meet here in town?' Trudy was sure that by listing all the others that she'd spoken to, it would leave the other woman feeling reluctant to be left out. If only to try to find out what everybody else was saying.

'At the *police station*? You want me to come to a *police station*?' Sylvia de Lacey said, sounding truly astonished.

Trudy gave a small inner sigh. Obviously, ladies of Sylvia de Lacey's ilk would never expect to set foot across the doorstep of such an outlandish place. 'Oh no, of course not, Mrs de Lacey,' she reassured her quickly. 'I was thinking that we could meet up in town somewhere, perhaps over a cup of tea?'

'Oh yes, of course, that would be fine. Do you know Elliston & Cavell's?' She named a department store, which boasted a popular tearoom. 'Or would you prefer Fuller's?'

Fuller's, Trudy knew, was a rather expensive and upmarket cake shop and tearoom that neither she nor her parents had ever dared venture into, knowing they simply wouldn't be able to afford a cake between them! 'Elliston & Cavell will be fine, Mrs de Lacey,' she selected hastily. 'What time this morning would be most convenient for you?'

'Oh, I have a little runabout of my own. I can be there in about forty minutes?'

'That would be fine. I'll meet you in the tearoom then,' Trudy said with some relief. And then she wondered how nice it must be to have 'a little runabout' whenever you wanted to go somewhere. Of course, once Dr Ryder had taught her how to drive, she would start saving up, and in a few years she might be able to have a little car of her own. A Morris Minor perhaps or…

'How shall I know you?' The somewhat cool voice on the other end of the line interrupted her pleasant daydream and brought her back to earth with a bump.

'I'll be in uniform, ma'am,' Trudy said, and then almost giggled as another sudden silence at the end of the line showed that she'd succeeded in startling the lady yet again.

'Oh, of course, how silly of me,' she recovered swiftly. 'Until then, WPC…'

'Loveday, ma'am,' Trudy said gently, trying not to feel offended that she had forgotten her name, and hung up.

With a little time on her hands she indulged herself in some window-shopping, feeling alternatively guilty over not really working, whilst at the same time glorying in that freedom you felt only when you found yourself on an unexpected (and not actually sanctioned) holiday.

She felt proud of herself for getting Mrs de Lacey to come to her – since she didn't fancy bicycling all the way out to the village, but then her smugness abruptly fled as an appalling thought suddenly hit her.

Did she have enough money to pay for her share of the bill at the tearoom?

Once more, she quickly delved among her accoutrements in her police satchel, and was relieved to find that she could at least afford a cup of tea – but probably not a cake.

Reassured, she made her way slowly along Cornmarket Street to the department store, pausing outside a hair salon, where a photograph of a model displaying the latest bouffant style made her stop and stare. If she ever dared go home with a hairstyle like that, her mother would have a fit!

Hastily dragging her thoughts away from the idea of yet more maternal anger and disappointment, she hurried to the store and spent the rest of her remaining time wandering past the various counters, contemplating the wares on offer. This caught the attention of the store detective, who watched her curiously for some time, perhaps wondering why the police were in his store.

The shop girls too, watched her unobtrusively and then gathered together to whisper about her once she'd passed on. But Trudy was getting used to that sort of reaction. She was convinced, though, that more and more women would join the police force in the coming years, and then maybe she wouldn't be considered such an oddity.

The tearoom was a mixture of genteel efficiency and old-fashioned decor, and she chose a table in a far and rather dim corner, suspecting that Mrs de Lacey would appreciate a measure of privacy. She took a seat, told the waitress who immediately approached that she was expecting a friend, and looked around her with pleasure. She'd been here only once or twice before with her mother, and with a friend or two on special occasions – like birthdays – but never for a professional business meeting.

A woman with lavender-tinged hair and draped in a large but rather old mink stole appeared in the doorway, making Trudy sit up and take notice. But after a quick look around, the matron quickly spotted her quarry and moved across to join a table where two other, similarly well-to-do women were sitting.

For the next ten minutes or so, she contentedly watched the doorway as various people came and went, indulging herself by making up little stories about who they were and what their lives were like. But when a slim, elegant woman entered and paused to look around, Trudy straightened in her chair instinctively. The newcomer had salt-and-pepper hair that looked really attractive and striking, swept up as it was into a simple but elegant chignon, which helped highlight her high cheekbones and strong jawline to their maximum advantage. She was wearing a severely tailored jacket in navy blue, which matched a pencil skirt of the same colour. Only a froth of lace at the front of her oyster-silk blouse displayed a touch of femininity.

Her eyes quickly found Trudy, and she made her way to the corner table, all the while looking around quickly at the other customers, in case there should be someone present that she knew. Evidently there wasn't, for her expression seemed relaxed enough when she arrived in front of Trudy.

'WPC Loveday?'

'Yes. Thank you for coming, Mrs de Lacey.'

The older woman took a chair, removed her gloves, and was instantly attended by the waitress. 'A pot of tea and a plate of scones, please,' she said at once, without consulting the menu – or Trudy.

'So, how can I help?' she asked, getting to the point straight-away, and spearing Trudy with a pair of hazel eyes that seemed to miss very little. She wasn't exactly hostile, but Trudy could sense a certain impatience in her tone that warned her she'd better not shilly-shally.

'Did you know Eddie Proctor?' she asked first. 'I understand he was a particular favourite of your great niece, Emily.'

'Yes, I knew him,' Sylvia said at once, rather surprising Trudy who, for some reason, had been expecting a blunt negative. 'Or rather, I often saw him and Emily about the place,' she qualified. 'You know, playing in the grounds and that sort of thing. He seemed a nice enough lad.'

'You spoke to him?' Trudy asked, again, for some reason, feeling surprised. She simply couldn't put this elegant woman and a probably grubby, 11-year-old village boy together.

'Well, we didn't exactly have conversations,' Sylvia said, her lips – coloured in the latest fashionable lipstick – twitching slightly in amusement. 'But he was polite, and if we ran across each other in the grounds, we'd exchange a few words. I like to walk in the grounds, you see. I've always enjoyed walking in the countryside.'

Ah, Trudy thought. That might explain it. 'Yes. We've been told that he and Emily liked to play Robin Hood or cowboys and Indians in the woods and what have you. Did you ever see him talking to strangers?'

'In the Hall grounds?' One of Sylvia's elegantly plucked and shaped eyebrows rose in surprise. 'I think not,' she said emphatically. 'If anyone had been lurking around, the head gardener would have tackled him and asked him his business. And that hulking chap of his, who looks impressive enough but probably wouldn't say boo to a goose, would help him send anyone on their way who had no business being there.'

Trudy recognised Lallie Clark from this description, and smiled slightly. 'But the grounds are rather large, and some of them wooded. A stranger would be able to avoid notice easily enough,' she pointed out.

'Is that what you think? Some trespasser – a tramp or someone

– actually killed the boy?' She kept her voice down, but Trudy could sense the alarm coming from her in waves.

Just then, annoyingly, the waitress arrived with the tea things and a plate of delicious-looking scones. A small dish of clotted cream, and one of apricot and another of strawberry jam added to the temptation, and Trudy, (who'd forsaken breakfast for a quick getaway) felt her stomach rumble.

She blushed, hoping it hadn't actually been audible.

'Thank you. I'll pour,' Sylvia told the waitress, who murmured something and discreetly withdrew.

Trudy both admired and resented the cool but effortless way Sylvia talked to the girl, and wondered what this woman would do if she was ever actually forced to make her own way in the world. Would she be able to find work? Was she fit for anything, other than being Mrs de Lacey, of Briar's Hall estate?

She abruptly reminded herself to keep her mind on business, and watched the older woman's face as she set about pouring two cups of tea.

'Is it such a surprising theory, Mrs de Lacey?' she asked, fishing cautiously. She'd sensed something in the woman's manner just before the interruption, and tried to recapture it. 'From everything we've learned about Eddie so far, he doesn't seem the sort to just accidentally tumble into a well. He was afraid of heights, for a start.'

The hand on the teapot seemed to tremble just a little, but her face, when she glanced up and across at Trudy, revealed nothing. 'And you think that's really significant? As a mother myself, I can tell you that children can do some surprising things, sometimes.'

'Thank you,' Trudy said, as the older woman pushed her cup towards her. She reached for the silver-plated sugar tongs and somewhat awkwardly managed to get two lumps into her tea.

As she stirred, she contemplated her next question with care. Instinct told her that this woman had something to offer, but she couldn't quite get a handle on what it might be. She wished

Clement hadn't been tied up in court. She was sure he would know how to charm the information out of her. Or perhaps frighten it out of her!

'Have you ever seen anything odd during your walks in the woods, Mrs de Lacey?' She decided on a broader approach, not expecting anything to come of it, but she was sure that the woman paled slightly. It was hard to be sure under the artificial lighting, and her immaculate make-up didn't help either. But she seemed more tense and alert, and Trudy felt again that tiny thrill that told her she had hit a nerve.

'Odd in what way?' she asked sharply, and now Trudy was sure that her witness was temporising.

'Did you see Eddie – or maybe Emily – talking to someone you didn't know?' Trudy asked.

'You've already asked me that, and I've already told you – I didn't,' Sylvia said calmly.

Had she? Trudy thought back. She rather thought Mrs de Lacey hadn't said so – not in so many words. Was she just being cautious and slippery out of habit? Did she resent having to come into town and lower herself to talk to an officer of the law? Or was there more to it than that?

'A boy has died, Mrs de Lacey,' Trudy tried next, but apart from a certain tightness and thinning of her lips, her admonition seemed to have little effect.

'Yes, it's tragic. I know Martin feels very badly about it. Of course, the well has been made safe now, and there's even talk of having it filled in, but… The family feels very bad about it, I assure you,' Sylvia said politely. 'Scone?'

'No thank you,' Trudy said primly. She couldn't afford to split the bill, she thought resentfully. Then again, she had to tell herself not to lose control of the interview. She was allowing this woman, and her smug acceptance of her privileged lifestyle, to get to her, and it had to stop.

'Your son seemed…' Trudy began, and then her eyes sharpened

as she noticed the older woman's shoulder stiffen imperceptibly, '… to think it possible that it might not have been an accident,' she lied blatantly, but with some confidence. Since it was clear that Oliver hadn't told his mother about his own interview, she felt fairly safe that she wouldn't be called to account for it if she ad-libbed somewhat.

A look of puzzlement and surprise briefly flashed across Sylvia's face, but she managed to shrug elegantly. 'Oliver has his own ideas, no doubt. He always has had.' Then she smiled, a rather false smile, Trudy thought. As if she was trying to be seen to be friendly. But it didn't sit well on her, and Trudy didn't like feeling patronised. 'He's a very clever man you know – with a genius IQ,' Sylvia swept on, with another artificial smile. 'But… well, like a lot of great men, he isn't always very… practical or reliable about everyday and mundane matters. He might understand what nuclear fusion is, but if his car breaks down…' Sylvia smiled and waved a hand in the air '…he has to call a mechanic. He's always thinking of such big things that the little things… well, he hasn't a clue, really. He can be very socially unaware sometimes too. Like a lot of academics, he can be a little inattentive to things going on around him. As a result…' she again waved her hand in the air '…he's not always the best person to ask when it comes to opinions on people or everyday things.'

Trudy blinked, trying to understand what the woman was attempting to convey. Clearly, she was intimating that her son's points of view weren't always reliable. But why? What was she afraid of exactly? What did she suspect that her son might have already *said* to them?

'I see,' Trudy said, but actually didn't. 'I understand he's contemplating marriage soon?' She changed tack, desperate enough to throw anything into the mix and see what happened.

'Marjorie? Yes, a lovely girl,' Sylvia said placidly and with such evident relief at the change of subject that Trudy had to admit defeat there.

168

'He spoke fondly of Emily,' she tried next.

'Yes. She's rather fond of her Uncle Oliver,' Sylvia agreed smoothly, and glanced at her watch. 'I really must call in at Coopers before I return to the Hall. Was there anything else you wanted?'

There was – a lot more – but Trudy realised that she simply wasn't going to get it. Not from this woman, and not now, at any rate.

With as good grace as she could muster, Trudy thanked her for her time and watched her go, feeling a sense of frustration and failure.

She sat there for some time brooding, before becoming aware of the waitress hovering at the table. 'I hope the scones are all right, madam?' she asked punctiliously.

Trudy jumped, then felt her heart lurch as she stared at the plate of untouched scones still sitting at the table. Oh good grief! *The bill!* She'd been so distracted by her failure to get Sylvia de Lacey to tell her anything, that she'd forgotten about the bill!

*

'I could have died on the spot,' Trudy said, two hours later, as she sat in Dr Ryder's office, once more sipping tea.

'So what did you do?' Clement asked, highly entertained.

'I blurted something about not being able to pay for it. I felt such a fool! Then I felt even more embarrassed when the waitress said that it had gone automatically onto Mrs de Lacey's account. Apparently, she has a running account there, and they send a bill up to the Hall every month. The rich certainly do live differently, don't they?' Trudy mused.

Clement, who had similar arrangements with a number of clubs, shops and restaurants in town, nodded neutrally. 'I hope you had the good sense to eat both scones,' was his only response.

Trudy laughed. 'I did! And scraped clean every last morsel of jam and cream from the pots whilst I was at it!'

'That's my girl. So, what do you think she was hiding exactly?'

He'd listened patiently to her somewhat rambling and unsatisfactory account of her interview with Oliver's mother, but hadn't really been able to pinpoint the source of her angst. Which was not surprising, since she hadn't been able to either.

'I don't know,' Trudy said now, still sounding aggrieved. 'But I swear there was *something*. She was very cool, and superior, and polite and all that, but once or twice, I just felt as if I'd hit a sore spot. I could just feel that something was off, but couldn't quite track it down and take advantage of it. Once or twice, I even wondered if she might not be afraid, and desperate to hide it. Do you know what I mean?'

'Yes. Well, let's trust your instincts then, and follow up on it.'

'You mean go and see her at home?' Trudy asked doubtfully. It felt far too soon to her to tackle the inimical Mrs de Lacey again – especially without any fresh ammunition in their arsenal.

'No,' Clement said, watching the look of relief flash across her face. 'I meant, let's beard her son in his den. Since you seemed to think she was most sensitive when talking about him?'

Trudy nodded in confirmation.

'All right then,' Clement carried on. 'We've seen him at home, let's see how he reacts when we invade his place of work. Men feel most secure and comfortable where they're in their castle. But at their place of work... Not so much. They're always aware that their boss might be looking over their shoulder. Which, in Dr de Lacey's case, would be the principal of his college!'

170

Chapter 29

St Bede's College comprised a rambling set of buildings, built mostly in the early nineteenth century, when there was still land to be had between the Woodstock Road and Walton Street. It boasted a rather fine library, a not-quite-so-fine chapel, and three residential blocks for the students that were given various (mostly nefarious) nicknames by the successive generations of students forced to live in them.

The dons, like their students, had their rooms scattered around these domiciles, and the lodge porter was happy enough to direct them to 'Webster' the true name of one of the square, mock-Georgian buildings.

Finding staircase VI, they climbed to the second floor and found a door bearing Dr Oliver de Lacey's name, plus a set of impressive initials after it. They knocked and waited, and after a while heard a voice curse and call out.

'Go away, you numbskulls!'

Trudy's lips twitched as she glanced at Clement, who smiled back. 'Not the first time I've been called that,' he said with mock modesty, making her giggle.

He knocked again, more firmly, and from within there came another curse, and then the door was violently thrown open. 'The

171

tutorial is not for—' He broke off, his handsome face looking momentarily comical as he gaped at them.

Then the thunderous look was swept away, and was replaced by a sheepish grin instead. 'Sorry, I didn't realise it was you. Er, I take it you forgot to ask me something when me met before? Come on in. I can send for a scout if you'd like some tea or coffee?'

'No thank you, sir,' Trudy said. She'd learned, after one of their earlier investigations concerning the death of a student, that scouts were what students and dons called the college servants, and so this time wasn't taken aback by the phrase.

'Well, sit down. Oh, let me remove that pile of books…'

The room was pretty much what Trudy had been expecting of an Oxford don – it was lushly decorated with expensive oriental carpets and flock wallpaper, with old-fashioned, expensive-looking chairs and a sofa littered around. Books seemed to spill over every surface, mostly congregating on a large walnut desk. Framed portraits of landscapes and luminaries (which *were* much more her idea of proper art!) caught the eye, and through large, sash windows, the fitful sunshine reflected off long, floor-length, dark-green velvet drapes. In a large white fireplace, a fire flickered dully, in need of a replenishment of logs or coal.

'What a lovely room,' Trudy said.

'Is it?' Oliver said, sounding genuinely surprised. For a moment he looked around, as if seeing it for the first time.

But then, having worked here for some time, Trudy mused, he probably took it all for granted and never thought about it. But her mum would be over the moon about those curtains. Again she angrily tore her thoughts away from her mother.

They took seats on the Queen Anne look-alike chairs that Oliver cleared for them, but he himself chose what was obviously his usual and far more comfortable armchair. Trudy had learned that in Oxford, you didn't have classrooms as such, like the ones she remembered from her schooldays, but rather students – either individually or in small groups – came to a tutor's room for a tutorial.

Remembering that Oliver de Lacey was a physicist, with some sort of speciality in nuclear energy, she wondered, with an undeniable sense of awe, what things must have been discussed in this very room. Certainly things that were well over her head.

'So, what was it you forgot to ask?' Oliver said, glancing, yet again, straight at Clement.

But this time, Trudy wasn't having any of it. Her recent arguments with her own family had made her feel resentful and in no mood to take any prisoners.

'We hadn't forgotten anything, Dr de Lacey,' she began sweetly. 'It's just that after speaking to your mother, several points were raised that we'd like to explore a little further.'

And this time there was no mistaking the reaction. In the light falling in through the ample window, it was clear to see the Oxford don definitely went pale. Not only that, his vague smile seemed to freeze in place for a moment, and when he finally shifted in his seat, his shoulders looked rigid.

'You've talked to my mother? Good grief, why? She can't possibly know anything.'

Trudy, sensing weakness, smiled even more gently. 'Oh, I've found that mothers tend to know far more than anyone ever thinks they do, sir. Doing the job I do, I can't tell you the number of times I've arrested someone, usually some young chap or girl, who are utterly convinced that their parents couldn't have the least idea what they'd been up to. But they invariably did. Parents, you see, are in a unique position to know their offspring inside and out.'

Opposite her, Oliver managed to give a small laugh. 'Really, er... constable... you terrify me! What a hideous thought.'

But although he'd said it lightly, and as an obvious joke, Trudy could tell by the small beads of sweat that popped out on his forehead, that the idea had truly worried him.

Beside her, Clement was happy to see that she had the man on the back foot and was content enough to just sit and watch the show, but occasionally he let his eyes wander curiously around the room. A silk banner, hung up carelessly over a doorway, told him that this man had been a rower in his days, but the pale-blue colour of Cambridge gave him a momentary jolt. Then he recalled that, although de Lacey lived and now worked in Oxford, he had chosen to join the enemy and study for his degrees at Cambridge.

'So, er, what was it that mother said that brought you hot-foot to my door,' Oliver asked, the epitome of an amused man about town. He had recovered his poise now, and he watched Trudy with an idle smile on his lips. But his eyes were alert and alarmed.

Trudy, now that she was forced to be specific, found herself stymied once more. Because thinking back on her conversation with this man's mother, she still hadn't pinpointed exactly what it was that Sylvia de Lacey had said that intrigued her so much.

Aware that he was waiting, and that she needed to retain control of the situation, Trudy cast about for something. 'She told me that she liked to walk around the estate a lot,' she began, and was astonished to see the colour once again fade out of his face – even more dramatically this time than before.

She sensed Clement, too, suddenly sharpen his attention, and felt a warm sense of triumph wash over her. She might have been lucky in her choice of fishing bait, but sometimes luck was what you needed most.

'Did she?' Oliver said, his voice sounding dry.

'Yes, she did. Nothing surprising in that, sir, a lot of us like to walk about in the countryside, and your cousin's estate is very pretty.'

'Yes,' he agreed shortly.

'And your mother told me… well, obviously I can't discuss an ongoing investigation,' Trudy said smoothly, again feeling proud of herself for adroitly finding just the perfect excuse not to display her real ignorance. 'But we did talk about strangers…' She'd been about to carry on and add something innocuous along the lines of the likelihood of Eddie Proctor running into them, but quickly changed her mind.

For at her words, Oliver gave a very slight but perceptible jerk in his chair. She hoped Clement had noticed it too, but suspected that he had. Nothing much escaped the coroner's slightly watery grey gaze.

'I can see you've noticed strangers in the village too, Dr de Lacey,' Trudy decided to make it a statement, not a question.

For a second, they could both squarely see the momentary panic in the man's face, and could almost hear his mind racing. What was he thinking? No doubt he was wondering what his mother had told them. But what was there that she *could* tell them that would cause him such alarm?

Not for the first time, Trudy wished she could have a super-power, like Superman or one of the other characters from the comic books her brother had loved to read, because given the choice, she'd opt to be a mind-reader every time!

'Strangers?' Oliver repeated, frowning slightly. 'Well, you always get the odd hiker or two.'

Trudy had to reluctantly concede the cleverness of that answer. Not knowing what his mother might have said, or what Trudy was leading up to, it was so broad and general – and undeniable – that it could cover almost anything. And people *did* still hike about a lot. Walking holidays had been all the rage for a few decades, and if the advent of the car now made them less popular than they once were, there were still plenty of ramblers to go around.

And still, annoyingly, she was no further forward in figuring out just what mother and son were hiding. Because, by now, she was sure they were hiding *something*.

'Do you think it likely a hiker came across Eddie Proctor in your family orchard and pushed him into the well, Dr de Lacey?' Trudy asked heavily.

'I think it highly *un*likely,' Oliver said flatly.

'Your mother seemed to know the boy quite well.' Trudy tried another tack, and again succeeded in surprising him. Although the look of near-panic had now gone from his eyes.

'Really? I wouldn't have thought they'd have been bosom buddies,' he drawled, with that hint of lazy amusement that was beginning to get on her nerves.

But mostly she was annoyed with herself because she knew that, somehow, she had been successfully steered away from the 'danger zone' – whatever that was.

Now she was the one who felt her shoulders tighten with tension, because she had no idea what to ask next.

Clement, sensing her dilemma, chose that moment to rise and walk to a sideboard, where a range of silver-framed photographs had been displayed. He picked one up, showing a younger, just-matriculated Oliver de Lacey in front of a splendid building.

'That's Trinity, Cambridge, right?' Clement said, and with some relief, Oliver left his chair to join the older man.

'Yes, that's my old alma mater,' he agreed. 'But I came back to Oxford to do my DPhil.'

'I'm surprised you chose Cambridge to do your undergraduate studies. Living locally, as well,' Clement mused, 'that must have raised a few eyebrows?'

'Ah, see, that was the problem. It felt somehow too… parochial,' Oliver said with a smile. Clearly he felt much more comfortable talking to a fellow egghead. And Trudy had no objections now to letting them get on with it. It wasn't as if she had any piercing, insightful questions of her own to ask him, was it?

'You know how it is when you're 18.' Oliver laughed. 'You get these ideas! I wanted to be far away from home, and it gave me a sense of rebellion to fly the light-blue colours!'

Clement laughed. 'Yes. But you live and learn, I've found. And now you're back in Oxford, where it's much more convenient for your work in London, if nothing else.'

'True! Rebellion is all very well, but a comfortable train, and an hour's commute into town has its benefits.' Oliver laughed again. 'Especially when you work in such a high-pressure field as nuclear physics.' He deliberately kept his back turned to the unnerving young woman police constable, and began to talk shop.

He'd always found that his work tended to overwhelm and overawe most people, and it gave him a comforting sense of superiority. 'I began working for a government committee following the 1953 announcement of a civil nuclear power programme. Shortly afterwards, the Atomic Energy Authority Act created UKAEA, which took responsibility for the nation's nuclear energy programme. Naturally, they need experts, and… well, I was recruited,' he finished modestly.

'It must be challenging – and nerve-racking work,' Clement said, deciding to stroke his ego.

'Oh it was. I was one of those who oversaw the first FBR – fast breeder reactor – in March of '54 up in Dounreay in Caithness.'

'I remember the young Queen opening some site or other…' Clement snapped his fingers. 'Where was that?'

'Calder Hall, probably. I was there too,' Oliver said blandly. 'The reactor was the first of eight small prototype Magnox units. The codename for Calder Hall was PIPPA – pressurised pile producing power and plutonium. But I mustn't bore you. Marjorie often warns me that I tend to run away on the subject, making people go cross-eyed.'

'Not at all, I'm fascinated,' Clement assured him. And, in a way, he was. Oliver de Lacey was clearly not only a clever man but an also an influential one in his own world. He probably had the ear of quite a number of ministers and boffins in Whitehall, for instance. And men like that often needed watching, in his experience.

'Well, we won't keep you any longer, Dr de Lacey,' he said, clearly to the younger man's relief. 'And once again, thank you for your time.'

Trudy rose silently, and with a brief nod and a murmur of thanks of her own, allowed herself to be ushered out of the room.

By mutual, unspoken consent, they were silent as they walked down the stone spiral staircase and stepped out onto the open, large green lawn that was the centre of the quad.

'Well?' Trudy finally demanded eagerly. 'I was right, wasn't I? He was definitely hiding something. You saw that, yes?' she asked nervously.

'Oh yes. He'd got the wind up about something,' Clement agreed. 'And I found it very interesting that he chose to go to Trinity, in Cambridge, as a youth.'

'Did you?' Trudy said vaguely. She knew that clever men set a lot of store by such things, but that didn't interest her. 'I think his mother saw something in the estate grounds. And probably he did too. Something to do with strangers.'

Clement didn't disagree with her, but his mind was thinking along different lines altogether. Because ever since he'd seen that photograph of a young Oliver de Lacey, posing happily at Trinity College, Cambridge, a thought had struck him, so outlandish, and yet so plausible, that it blotted out almost everything else.

Of course, it was highly unlikely… And even if it wasn't, there was no possible way he could pursue it. And even if he was right… Could any of it fit in with Eddie Proctor's death? Well, yes, it just might, Clement conceded. They'd heard that Emily and Eddie often played spies, and were inquisitive little mites. No, wait a minute, Clement thought, he was letting his imagination run away with him. Which was usually an accusation that he cast young Trudy's way!

Even if – and it was an enormous if – what he was thinking had any basis in reality, was it really *likely* that there would have been anything for an 11-year-old boy to discover in the woods surrounding Briar's Hall?

No, Clement thought reluctantly, there wasn't. It was absurd. He was just indulging himself in a sheer flight of fantasy. He just couldn't see how little Eddie Proctor could ever have proved enough of a threat that he would need to be removed. It was preposterous.

'*Dr Ryder!*' With a start, he heard Trudy say his name loudly, and realised it couldn't have been the first time she'd done so.

He looked at her sheepishly. 'Sorry, I was thinking.'

'I'll say,' Trudy said, clearly exasperated. 'You were miles away.' Then she stared at him closely. 'Have you thought of something about why Oliver might want to kill Eddie?' she asked accusingly.

Clement blinked. Had he? Yes. No. Probably no. 'I can't see… No, I don't think so. Come on, I have to get back to the office,' he said abruptly. Absurd idea or not, it wouldn't hurt to do just a little checking around. He must have friends of friends who could ask a question here or there… but he'd have to be discreet.

Very discreet indeed.

Trudy was silent as they walked back towards his office, and kept shooting him suspicious glances. Clearly, she suspected he was on to something, and resented the fact that he wasn't sharing his thoughts with her. But the more he thought about things, the gladder he became that she hadn't picked up on his hint about Trinity College and Cambridge.

Because if there was even a hint of truth about what he suspected… or even if there was no truth in it at all, they might find themselves in very hot water indeed.

Chapter 30

Feeling distinctly uneasy about things, Trudy and Clement parted company, with the coroner striding away towards St Giles. She made no attempt to match his long strides, but wondered, resentfully, what he was going to do now. Because she didn't think for one minute that it was his duties as a coroner that were making him so anxious to get back to his office.

Somewhere in that interview with Oliver de Lacey Trudy was sure that something had occurred to him, and it frustrated her mightily that she didn't know what it was. And it made her even more angry that he clearly wasn't going to fill her in. Did he really have so little respect for her abilities? Even though he treated her with far more respect than any of her work colleagues, it was becoming more and more obvious to her that their partnership was by no means an equal one.

And not for the first time, it gloomily occurred to her that she just might not have the brains to rise much higher in her chosen career. But then she thought of Sergeant O'Grady, and told herself that you didn't need to have a brain the size of Dr Clement Ryder or Oliver de Lacey in order to be a good police officer!

And if Clement had things to do, then so did she!

Abruptly cancelling her intention to go back to the station

and lick her wounds, she detoured to the library instead, and then several other civil buildings, determined to track down the whereabouts of one John Blandon, former groom at Briar's Hall.

People had to live – which meant they had to pay utility bills, pay their rates and taxes, apply for drivers' licences, and all sorts of other things that left a paper trail.

And eventually – by dint of spending three hours ploughing grimly and determinedly through various county censuses and cross-referencing with several other bodies, – she felt flushed with success.

She had finally found her man!

Tomorrow, she would inform Clement that she had done so, and let him keep his secrets to himself. She would show him that good, honest, detective work was worth just as much as fancy brainpower any day of the week!

*

As Trudy Loveday went wearily home on the bus after a hard and frustrating day's work, Emily de Lacey crept down the stairs of Briar's Hall and glanced around the newel post.

The hallway was silent, but even so, she went on tiptoe to the front door, reached up to the latch – and almost jumped out of her skin.

'And where do you think you're going, young Miss Emily?' Mrs Roper's voice cut through the air, making Emily whip around and swallow convulsively.

'Nowhere,' she said instinctively.

'Indeed? But clearly "nowhere" is "somewhere" outside, since you were about to open the door,' the housekeeper pointed out, her eyes fixed beadily on the little girl.

'I just wanted to play, Mrs Roper. I've been indoors all day,' Emily whined.

'And you know why!' the older woman hissed. 'What has your father told you?'

Emily sighed, but repeated dutifully, 'I can't go outside unless someone is with me.'

Mrs Roper made a vastly exaggerated show of looking around. 'And is anyone with you?' she demanded archly.

Emily heaved a sigh. 'No, Mrs Roper.'

'No. And it'll be dark soon. Have you no sense, Miss Emily?'

The girl sighed. 'It'll be ages yet before it gets dark,' she pointed out stubbornly.

Mrs Roper glanced automatically out the nearest window, but wasn't to be distracted. 'And just who were you going to play with?' she asked flatly, making Emily freeze on the spot.

Sometimes, not often, but sometimes, Emily underestimated the housekeeper.

'You said you were going out to play,' Mrs Roper went on relentlessly. 'That implies you had a playmate in mind. But most of the village children are at home having their tea.'

Emily nodded. 'I just meant, I wanted to go out and play by myself.'

Mrs Roper's eyes narrowed. 'Miss Emily, were you trying to sneak out to meet someone?'

Emily stiffened. 'Don't be silly, Mrs Roper. There's no one in the garden to meet, is there?'

For a moment, the two of them stood there, so vastly different in almost every way, staring at each other across an equally vast gulf.

'I think you should go back upstairs. It'll be your own teatime soon,' Mrs Roper finally said heavily. 'And if I catch you trying to sneak out again, I shall tell your father. Do you understand me, young madam?'

Emily nodded soberly. 'Yes Mrs Roper,' she said, and turned and ran back up the stairs, her heart pounding.

Chapter 31

The next morning, rather gratifyingly, Clement was wise enough to congratulate Trudy heartily on her diligence and perseverance in finding the de Laceys' former groom, and declared himself more than happy to drive her to Northamptonshire, where John Blandon was now the landlord of his own pub.

'When they said he'd moved up north, I have to confess I was thinking that they meant a little further north than just the next county,' he commented with a wry smile as they left tthe city behind.

Trudy shrugged. She herself had never left Oxfordshire, and she supposed a lot of people she knew hadn't either. To her, Northamptonshire *was* north. But she was becoming more and more aware that people like the coroner – and certainly the de Laceys – probably thought of the north as grouse shoots in Scotland, where, no doubt, they had a small hunting lodge. Or perhaps the Lake District, where they probably had a small motor launch they could take out on summer days around Windermere.

'What's the name of the village again?' Clement asked, glancing across at her and no doubt seeing a rather sour look on her face.

'Forge Keating. It's in the east of the county. Shall I find it on the road map for you?' she offered dully.

'Yes please. You all right, Trudy? You look a bit down in the dumps.'

Trudy sighed. Where to start? She'd ditched a boyfriend, had a row with her parents, didn't like the way her so-called 'partner' was happy to keep her in the dark about things, and was beginning to feel resentful of anyone who had money! Although she knew that the latter was only a reaction to feeling so disgruntled about things in general. In truth, she didn't really envy the rich. In her experience, they didn't tend to be any happier than most other people.

'I'm fine,' she said simply. But contented herself for most of the journey by simply watching the way her friend drove, noting the movement of clutch and gear stick, when and how often he braked, and how much he used his mirrors. Since her driving lessons would start soon (for she almost had almost saved up enough to buy her learner's permit) it made sense to learn as much of the theory as possible before getting behind the steering wheel herself.

The coroner, not liking her unusual silence, continued to watch her thoughtfully. Perhaps it was because he was so intent on her that he failed to notice a nondescript Hillman that followed him all the way from Oxford, being careful to always keep one or two cars between them.

*

Forge Keating was a decently sized village, which tended to sprawl somewhat around a large Norman church, a slightly more modern manor house, and a bend in a river. Larger houses were clustered along the riverbanks, having the best view across the meadows, whilst smaller, mostly farmworkers' cottages had to be content to straggle along small lanes in a maze of unnamed roads and cul-de-sacs.

It had only one pub though, called 'The Tench'. Its painted sign depicted the eponymous fish flying and arching through the air, fighting against the hook and line of an unseen fisherman.

'Probably attracts a lot of anglers,' Clement commented, as they parked outside. It was a pleasantly warm day, and the rear of the pub did indeed overlook the river. Garden tables and benches had been placed outside in the pub garden, no doubt hoping to attract the attention of the first of the season's holidaymakers. Although Trudy thought Mr Blandon was being a bit optimistic there. It was only spring, after all, and the breeze could still be a trifle arctic at times.

The pub – a large, white-painted, picturesquely thatched place – looked well maintained and had two tubs full of bright yellow and red tulips standing either side of the main door, like two colourful sentinels.

It was only just opening time when they arrived, and the place was still all but deserted. Only an old man and his dog sat at the bar, the old man supping a rather muddy-looking pint, the dog stretched out on the red-tiled floor below and trying to doze.

'What can I get you… er lady and gent?' The man behind the bar caught sight of Trudy's uniform and looked surprised.

He was indeed a handsome man, at a little over six feet tall, with black hair and bright-blue eyes, with the classic, square-jawed chin so beloved of Hollywood leading men. His accent held a soft, Dorset burr.

He did like to move around, Trudy thought.

'A pint of the best local bitter for me,' Clement said. 'Trudy?'

'A lemonade, please.'

The old man's shaggy dog lifted his head long enough to look at them, then drooped back onto the floor with a sigh.

185

'And one for yourself,' Clement said, handing over a generous amount of coinage.

'Thank you, sir. I'll have half a shandy,' the landlord said.

'You wouldn't be John Blandon would you?' Clement asked, accepting his drink and some change, and taking an experimental sip. It obviously wasn't too bad, because he took a slightly larger sip, and settled himself more comfortably at the bar.

Trudy, who'd found the tall barstool a bit of a trial to get onto with any real decorum, shifted to a more comfortable position as well but left her fizzy drink untouched.

The landlord looked at Clement closely. 'Can't say as I recognise you, sir.' He avoided answering the question cautiously.

'No reason why you should,' Clement reassured him. 'I'm a coroner from Oxford. I understand you once worked in a village nearby – Briar's-in-the-Wold?'

The old man sitting at the bar sighed and took his pint to a far corner. Clearly, he was a man who didn't like his drinking to be interrupted by idle chatter. His dog dutifully traipsed after him, then sprawled out again with a world-weary sigh. Trudy had a feeling both of them spent a lot of time at 'The Tench'.

'I did, then. Four or five years ago now, must be,' John Blandon agreed, still wary. 'Mind if I ask what this is all about?'

Clement explained about the death of a young boy, and when he'd finished, the landlord sighed and leaned his elbows on the bar. 'Sounds like a bad business, right enough.'

'Did you like the de Laceys?' Clement asked bluntly.

'Can't say I thought much about them one way or the other,' Blandon said carefully. 'But I wouldn't have thought they'd have been the kind to leave summat knowingly dangerous just hanging around the grounds, like. They couldn't have known the well cover had rotted away at one end. Leastwise, not the estate manager.'

'What about the squire?' Clement asked. 'The estate manager is mainly responsible for the farms. The immediate house and gardens are more in the squire's remit, I understand?' Clement wasn't sure that any such delineation existed, but if this man had indeed (as local gossip seemed to have it) played fast and loose with the squire's wife, he wanted to know how he viewed the cuckolded husband.

'Can't see the squire being careless neither,' Blandon said flatly. 'He had nippers of his own who might have fallen in, didn't he? That little girl of his – I forget her name – was always into everything.'

Trudy didn't for one moment think that his man had forgotten the name of Jennifer de Lacey's children. But she was content to sit and listen and watch.

'You were there when another family tragedy struck, I believe?' Clement said. 'Didn't the squire's wife die in a riding accident?'

'Yes she did. Mind if I ask why you're asking all these questions?' The tone wasn't quite belligerent, but it wasn't happy either.

'This is an official police investigation, sir,' Trudy said, not very truthfully, but feeling pleased that her presence was once again being fully justified. Clement might be older and cleverer and a man, but *she* was the police officer here. And as such, carried authority, whether people liked it or not. 'And we'd be obliged if you'd cooperate. After all, it's not as if you have anything to hide, is it?' she added craftily.

As her old sergeant at training college had told her, a reminder that you shouldn't get on the wrong side of the law was usually enough to get any law-abiding citizen talking. And if it wasn't – well, then it told you something about the person you were dealing with.

'Of course I haven't,' John Blandon said at once. But he cast a quick glance over his shoulder as he did so, and Trudy guessed that Mrs Blandon must be in the kitchen. The one with the money – and thus, the one who had to be kept sweet, she mused cynically. 'What do you want to know?' he asked, lowering his voice just a touch.

'You were friends with Mrs Jennifer de Lacey, I understand,' Clement said. 'The lady of the house?'

The landlord began to polish his beer taps thoughtfully, his face partly averted. 'So that old chestnut is still floating around is it?' he muttered bitterly.

'Which old chestnut is that?' Clement challenged.

The younger man flushed slightly and shot him an angry look. 'You tell me! Just because people say I'm a good-looking lad, and was a groom at the stables, and Mrs de Lacey was a fine-looking, older woman… Dirty minds, some people have,' he finished flatly.

'So you and she weren't… friendly?'

John Blandon drew in a long, slow breath. 'I don't see how that's anybody's business but our own,' he said stoutly. And for a moment, Trudy felt a certain amount of admiration for the man. He might be an adulterer, but at least he was willing to defend his lady.

'Some might say it was her husband's business,' Clement pointed out dryly.

John Blandon flushed again. 'Never had much to do with the squire,' he muttered. 'Oh, he rode at the Boxing Day hunt, and sometimes just to get to the further farms. But he was more of a sheep man. Knew a lot about the arable side of things too, but didn't have much time for the horses.'

'So it was only Mrs Jennifer de Lacey who took much interest in the stables?' Clement mused. 'I understand her mother-in-law was something of a horsewoman too, in her day. We've been told she had a fine seat.'

'Perhaps she had. But she was too old to do much riding when I was there,' the former groom said flatly. 'The old lady didn't even have a favourite horse of her own that she visited anymore, since she'd sold her hunter a few years back… Funny that…'

For a moment, the handsome former groom looked startled, as if thinking over old times had brought something back.

'What's funny?' Clement asked swiftly.

'The old lady... talking about it all... I remember that day, when Seamus came back without his rider. In a right state he was. I knew right away something bad – I mean *really* bad – had happened. You know, the way you just do?' His voice thickened slightly. 'Well, we went out looking for her – Mrs Jennifer – and we found her soon enough. In the water meadow, just lying there. Neck broke...'

He broke off suddenly and gave the beer taps a last, rather vicious swipe, then slung the white towel over one shoulder in a practised sweep. 'Well, no use dwelling on that, is there? She was too young to go that way. Too full of life and fun...'

He shrugged helplessly.

'But you said there was something "funny" about that day. When we were talking of the old lady – Vivienne de Lacey,' Trudy prompted him, and he looked at her blankly for a moment, as if reluctant to leave thoughts of his dead lover behind, and then slowly nodded.

'Yes, that's right. I just remembered. She was there that day – at the stables I mean. I remember thinking at the time that it was a bit odd,' he continued, 'because, like I said, she didn't really ride anymore, and her favourite horse had been sold on. So what was she *doing* there?'

'She was there when Seamus came back without his rider?' Clement asked, needing to get the timeline straight in his mind.

'No, not then,' John said, a touch impatiently. 'Before. Before Jen... Mrs de Lacey went out riding. I remember, I'd been mucking out the far stables when the head groom told me the missus was going out, and to get Seamus saddled and ready.'

He looked past them, out of the window and across the river, but was clearly seeing another time and another scene as his blue eyes became thoughtful. 'I was just walking back to Seamus's box, when the old cow came out.'

He paused, then shrugged. 'As you can no doubt tell, I didn't like her much.'

'Why not?' Trudy asked bluntly.

'She was just... poisonous. Yes, that's what she was. Dried up and old and ill and she just wanted everyone to be as miserable as she was. And she never liked Jen... Mrs de Lacey. Never accepted her into the family or tried to make her feel welcome. Never thought her good enough for her precious son – as if the squire were any great catch,' he snorted.

Trudy and Clement exchanged brief looks.

'So you saw her *before* her daughter-in-law went riding that morning?' Clement asked, still seeking clarification.

'That's right, I did,' John said with a scowl, as if he suspected them of doubting his word. 'And like I said, I was surprised. It's a bit of a walk from the house to the stables – and in them days she wasn't that inclined to walk far. But she made the effort that day, leaning on that ebony cane she always had. What's more, she was coming out of Seamus's box. Now then,' the former groom said, his voice hardening. 'You tell me what she was doing in there.'

For a second, the deserted pub seemed to shiver in a cold draught.

'You think she did something to the horse?' Clement said flatly.

But the man wasn't willing to go quite that far. Perhaps even here, in the far reaches of Northamptonshire, the name of de Lacey still carried with it enough residual power to remind him he would do better to be discreet. Instead, he contented himself by shrugging sullenly. 'Well, I know there was nothing wrong with the tack, cause I saw to all that myself,' he defended himself obstinately. 'And Jenny was just too good a rider to take a tumble in the ordinary way of things. Besides, Seamus was the least skittish horse you ever saw. What's more, that horse wasn't right, not for a few days afterwards. Off his feed, shaking, the sweats...'

'That might have been a reaction to losing his rider though, mightn't it?' Clement mused. Although no horseman himself, he had friends who were and insisted that horses could be delicate, sensitive creatures. 'Was he fond of her?' he asked, for again, the same friends swore blind that horses could be as loyal and affectionate as dogs.

'Oh yes, he loved her right enough,' John Blandon agreed sadly.

'But you really do think, don't you, deep down, that the old lady had something to do with her daughter-in-law's accident?' Clement persisted gently.

But again, the handsome landlord was too wily to be drawn into any outright admission. And try as they might, they could get nothing more out of him. If Jennifer de Lacey's former lover knew any more secrets, he was not willing to share them.

Chapter 32

Clement and Trudy left the pub after finishing their drinks, and once back in the car, sat in silence for a few seconds.

'Do you think he's right?' Trudy asked at last.

'He could be,' Clement said, rather unhelpfully. 'But after all these years, there's no way to prove it, is there? And even if we could, what would be the point? Both the poisonous old lady and the full-of-life young lady are now dead.'

Trudy heaved a heavy sigh. 'But what if Eddie Proctor somehow found out something about it? Or maybe Emily overhead something? Her father or grandmother talking when the old lady had still been alive? And then she passed it on to Eddie?'

'And Martin de Lacey threw him down the well so that he wouldn't repeat it?' Clement asked, sceptically. 'Our squire is no fool. He must realise its common gossip in the village anyway that his wife and our handsome friend in there' – he nodded to the pub – 'were a bit of an item. If he could weather that with his pride intact, he could weather any other gossip about his old mum!'

Trudy sighed. Perhaps he was right. 'Don't forget though,' she pointed out stubbornly, 'that one or two people have mentioned the squire has a bit of a temper, and it's not a good thing to get on his bad side. That would probably include a nosy little kid poking his nose into delicate family business. Perhaps the boy said something that touched him in the raw and he just lost control of himself and…' She shrugged graphically.

Clement nodded. 'It's a thought.' He reached for the key and felt his hand begin to tremble. He fumbled the ignition slightly, but managed to turn it, and then slipped the car into gear. He'd have to concentrate very carefully on his driving now. Damn this bloody Parkinson's!

But Trudy had noticed his difficulty, and felt a chill of alarm ripple through her. If Dr Ryder was really ill… Her heart contracted in fear and denial. The man *had* just drunk a pint of strong bitter, she reminded herself. So perhaps the lunchtime tipple had had an effect on him?

Then again… maybe it hadn't.

To distract herself, she turned on the radio, and the current top of the hit parade, Elvis Presley's 'Wooden Heart', filled the air. She had a feeling, though, that this might not be to the coroner's taste, and quickly turned it off again.

Once again, Trudy was unusually silent as they drove back towards Oxford, her mind chasing around and around in circles. Sometime soon she would simply have to take the bull by the horns and ask him outright if his health was all it should be. But even as she thought it, she could feel herself quailing from the idea. It was so irrevocable. Once she'd asked the question, she wouldn't be able to take it back. And what did they say about letting genies out of their bottles?

With both of them so distracted by their various thoughts, neither of them noticed the Hillman that still kept pace a safe distance behind them.

*

Inside the car were the two men who'd been watching them on the hillside at Briar's Hall.

'So what do you think all *that* was about?' the driver of the car asked casually.

His companion shrugged. 'I'll find out who owns the pub when we get back.' It had been left to him to reconnoitre the pub, which he had done by simply peering in carefully through the nearest window. He'd seen at once that the main bar was virtually empty, but that both the subjects were having an intense chat with the man behind the bar.

'You think they're actually getting anywhere?' the driver asked.

'You know, I wouldn't be surprised. I've been asking around, and our Dr Ryder is known to be the perspicacious sort.'

'Yeah, there have already been mild rumblings of discontent,' the driver said. 'If they start to become a real nuisance, I expect we'll get orders to pull the plug on them,' he agreed casually.

The man in the passenger seat reached into his pocket. 'Want a humbug?' He rattled a white paper bag at his companion enticingly, but the driver didn't want a sweet.

*

'So, what do we do next?' Trudy, oblivious to the car that was tailing them, looked across at the coroner.

'We need to go back to the Hall, I suppose,' Clement said. 'Just in case Emily really *did* hear something about the deep, dark family secret and passed it on to Eddie.'

Trudy's eyes widened. 'We can't ask a little girl if she thinks her granny killed her mother!' she objected with squeak.

Clement sighed. 'Of course not. But there's someone else in that house that we *can* talk to about it.'

'Not the squire,' Trudy said promptly. 'He'd just deny it. And

194

probably stop us from investigating further as well,' she muttered gloomily. 'Don't forget, we're only in this thing in the first place because he asked us to snoop around. But he could always change his mind.'

'No, I wasn't thinking of him either,' Clement said. 'But who else would know all of Mrs Vivienne de Lacey's secrets?'

Trudy could have kicked herself. 'The dragon!' Of course – Mrs Roper.

*

Mrs Roper answered the door promptly, her face tightening instantly at first sight of her visitors.

'Mr de Lacey is out up at Three Trees, seeing about some fencing that's come down. And Miss Emily is not well, and can't be disturbed,' she said frigidly.

'That's all right, Mrs Roper, it's you we've come to talk to,' Trudy said, forcing her voice to sound friendly. Which wasn't easy in the face of such unbending animosity.

'Me?' The housekeeper couldn't have looked or sounded more astounded. 'I have nothing more to say to you. I didn't know Eddie Proctor that well, I didn't see him at that wretched Easter egg hunt, and I believe he just fell down that well by accident. So…'

She began to shut the door in their faces.

'We'd like to talk to you about Mrs Vivienne, and Mrs Jennifer de Lacey,' Trudy tried again quickly. Which at least had the effect of stopping the closure of the door.

Mrs Roper's mouth had fallen slightly open. 'The mistress of the house?' she said, and both of them instinctively knew that she wasn't referring to Jennifer. 'What on earth can *she* have to do with anything?'

'We believe Eddie might have learned some secret about her, something that might not show her in a good light,' Clement said flatly. He was beginning to think that trying to get this woman to talk to them was pointless, since she was so hostile, but she might let slip something if he could shock her badly enough.

His words made her go white, then red. 'Mrs Vivienne was *a lady*,' Mrs Roper all but hissed at them. 'And there's nothing that can have been said about her that would show her in a bad light, unless it was all lies. Lies, do you hear me?'

'Did she really hate her daughter-in-law?' Clement said. 'We...' But before he could finish, the door slammed with a contemptuous and furious bang.

'Well, if the old lady did confide anything bad to her,' Trudy said grimly, 'not even bamboo shoots under her fingernails will make her tell us about it!'

'You've been reading too many Sexton Blake novels,' Clement reprimanded her with a smile. 'Bamboo shoots under her fingernails indeed.'

But although they both smiled at that, they trudged around the side of the house feeling distinctly thwarted.

And then they both stopped abruptly, as they heard a weird sound.

'Pssst...'

Trudy glanced at Clement, who wore an equally surprised expression.

'Psssst! Over here!'

Suspecting young Master George had once again slipped his leash, they turned, but saw, emerging from a laurel thicket underneath an open window, not George, but his sister Emily.

Her hair was a little mussed from her passage through the leaves, but her eyes were big and round and fixed on them urgently.

'I need to tell you something,' she whispered. 'About Eddie. Quick, let's get away from the house, before Daddy or Mrs Roper finds out I'm not upstairs.'

Trudy glanced around quickly, and saw the wall of the kitchen garden. 'Let's go in there,' she said. Its tall red-brick walls would hide them from any prying eyes.

Quickly, the three of them trotted up the path through the lawns and shot into the privacy of the kitchen garden. A quick look around showed them that Mr Cricklade was nowhere to be seen.

'All right, what is it?' Trudy asked breathlessly. Could the answer be about drop into their lap at last?

Chapter 33

'It's about Eddie's secret code spy book,' Emily said solemnly. 'The one he used to note down the car number plates.'

Trudy looked at Clement, then back to the little girl. Perhaps because her thoughts had been so taken up recently with the death of this girl's mother, it took her a moment to adjust to the new topic. 'What number plates were these, Emily?' she asked, careful to keep her voice calm and mild.

'Uncle Oliver's friends. The ones who were teaching him to wrestle.'

Trudy blinked at this, totally at a loss. She'd had no idea what the little girl was going to reveal, but this reminded her somewhat of Dr Clement's lecture about surrealism. *Wrestling teachers?*

Beside her, she could sense that Clement was shifting about from foot to foot a little uneasily.

'Perhaps you'd better start at the beginning,' Trudy said, hunkering down so that she was face to face with the girl, instead of looming over her. 'Was this one of the spy games you were playing?'

'Yes, but I thought of it first,' Emily said, smiling proudly. 'I was on my own when I first played the game, and I only did it because I saw Uncle Oliver down by the lake looking all suspicious, and I thought I'd follow him. That's when I made up the spy game and I became Lola, the beautiful French spy. I made Uncle Oliver a nasty German. Of course, he's not really. He's as British as you and me,' she confided.

'He certainly is,' Trudy said. 'So you were playing on your own and you saw your uncle. What made you think he was acting suspiciously?'

'He kept stopping and looking all around, as if to make sure there was nobody about who could see him. Like Lallie working in the garden, or one of the villagers, using the shortcut. They do sometimes,' Emily explained. 'The lake has a footpath that leads to the lane by the village green. Daddy says technically they're trespassing, but he doesn't mind.'

'All right,' Trudy said, ignoring the largesse of the lord of the manor. 'So you thought your uncle was making sure that nobody could see what he was doing?' she encouraged.

'Yes, which is when I thought of the spy game. So I crept up on him, ducking behind the bushes and all sorts. But he only went to the boathouse,' she said, her voice clearly echoing the disappointment she must have felt. 'I thought he was just going to take the rowboat out. I almost gave up then, but the more I waited, the more I realised that he was taking a jolly long time getting out on the water. That's when I noticed his friend. He went into the boathouse too.'

'Friend?' Trudy asked, careful to keep her voice calm. This was the first time they'd caught even a sniff of a new suspect and she must be careful to get a description. 'What did he look like?'

'Oh, I don't know, I was quite a long way away – I didn't want Uncle Oliver to catch me, see? So I couldn't really see his face.'

Trudy bit back a groan of frustration, but wasn't about to give up. 'Could you see the colour of his hair?'

'Oh yes, it was blond.'

'Could it have been white?' Trudy asked.

'Oh no, he wasn't old, because after a bit, when they still didn't come out in the boat, I sneaked up to the boathouse, like an Indian, and looked in the side window. It wasn't half hard, too,' the little girl told them earnestly, 'because all the windows were high up. You have to climb up on something to see in, but around one side there's this old water vat. So I climbed up on that and looked in. And I could see Uncle's friend wasn't old. I think he was a bit younger than him.'

Once more, Clement began shifting about a little uneasily and Trudy shot him a quick, questioning look. He was watching the little girl closely, and Trudy was sure she could see concern on his face, but so far he seemed content to let her do the talking.

'What did you see?' Trudy asked simply.

Beside her, Clement Ryder held his breath.

'Nothing much, it was too hard to see in,' the little girl confessed. 'The window was absolutely filthy!' Emily added, with such obvious disgust that both Trudy and Clement had to smile.

Clement let his breath out again, loud enough for Trudy to hear him. But she was too busy concentrating on her witness to wonder what had been worrying him.

'So I left, and when I saw Eddie again, I told him about this great new game I'd invented – spies – and how I was Lola, and he had to be James Bond,' the little girl gabbled. 'We started off spying on the gardeners, but that was boring, since they didn't do anything but hack about at weeds and stuff,' Emily continued with a sigh. 'So then we tried spying on some of the grown-ups in the village, but they sometimes caught us and told us off. We'd almost given up when, one day, we were staking out the boathouse again. That's what they call it, you know, when you keep watch on a place. And Uncle Oliver came back again. Of course—' here she broke off to beam proudly at them '—by this time, I'd already gone back there when I was sure it was empty and cleaned the side window, so if we needed to, I could see inside properly.'

'That was very clever of you, Emily,' Clement said, and meant it. But his voice was once more tight with tension.

'Thank you,' Emily said with a pleased smile. 'Anyway, as soon as we spotted Uncle Oliver go in, Eddie wanted to climb up to the window, but I said we had to wait, and see if his friend came again. If they were passing on secret messages, we needed to catch them doing it and make a note of it properly. The date, time, all that sort of thing,' she explained airily. 'Of course, we knew it was only pretend,' she added anxiously, just in case they should think her silly. 'We knew Uncle Oliver wouldn't *really* be passing on classified information.' She'd clearly heard that phrase from somewhere, and she repeated with a solemn nonchalance that again had the pair of them smiling.

'And did his friend come back?' Trudy asked, still not sure where all this was going, but getting drawn into the drama nevertheless.

'Oh yes. Well, no,' the little girl hastily amended, somewhat confusingly. 'Another of his friends came, but it wasn't the same man. This one didn't have blond hair like the first one did. But he came to the boathouse, and then we sneaked to the side and both of us climbed up to look in. We had to be jolly careful to be quiet.'

'And what did you see?' Trudy asked, amused.

'They were wrestling,' Emily said. 'Or at least, that's what Eddie said they must be doing. They were sort of lying on the floor and moving about.' She gave a brief shrug. 'We couldn't see all that much, because they were behind one of the rowboats.'

Beside her, Trudy was sure the coroner muttered something under his breath, but she wasn't to be distracted.

'I expect Uncle Oliver wanted to learn a new sport,' Emily swept on with her tale. 'He already knows how to row and play tennis and golf and stuff. Eddie says wrestling is something only boys can do anyway,' she said with disgust. 'It's so boring! Anyway' – she shrugged – 'after a bit we went away. I said I was getting bored of the spying game, but Eddie said he wanted to keep on with it for a while. So I said, if he *really* wanted to be James Bond, he should follow Uncle Oliver's friend when he left and see if he could tail him back to wherever it was he went when he wasn't meeting Uncle.'

'And where did he go?' Trudy asked.

'Only to a car parked on one of the farm tracks just off the village green. At least, that's what Eddie told me later. So he couldn't follow him any further.' Emily shrugged again. 'But he copied the number plate, by writing it in the dirt with a stick. So I loaned him one of my exercise books and a pen so that he could go back and note it down properly, and the make of the car as well. Eddie was good at knowing all about cars. There weren't many he didn't know the name of,' Emily said proudly. 'Eddie was really clever, in a lot of ways that I'm not. Anyway, after that, he'd sometimes report back that Uncle Oliver took more wrestling lessons, sometimes with the blond man, sometimes with other men. And he followed them, and made a note of all the number plates too. Of course, that didn't really get us anywhere, since we couldn't figure out how to find out who they were from that. In the films, the police or whoever can find that sort of thing out. But we couldn't.' The little girl took a much-needed breath. 'But after a while even Eddie got bored with it and stopped following them.'

'Well, thank you for telling us all this, Emily,' Trudy said.

'It's just that I overheard Daddy talking on the telephone to Aunt Sylvia. I got the feeling Aunt Sylvia was cross about something, because I heard Daddy telling her that the police had every right to consider strangers in the grounds. That's what made me think of Uncle Oliver's friends. But I suppose they're not really strangers, are they, if Uncle Oliver knew them?'

'No, I suppose not,' Trudy conceded.

'Anyway, I just wanted you to know,' the little girl said. 'I'm not allowed to play on my own anymore. Mrs Roper says it's not safe,' she added forlornly. 'And... sometimes I get scared,' she admitted.

Trudy reached out and put a hand on her shoulder. 'Is there anyone in particular that you're afraid of, Emily? You can tell us if there is, you won't get into trouble, I promise,' she said softly.

'No. Not really. It's just… grown-ups can be so funny sometimes, can't they? I mean, do really odd things. I don't understand them. I told Eddie…' Suddenly her garrulousness dried up, and she looked down at her feet uneasily.

'Yes?' Trudy said sharply. 'What did you tell Eddie?' she asked more gently, careful not to sound too pushy or insistent. 'You can tell us too, you know. I'm a police lady.'

The little girl heaved a sigh. 'Well… it's just that, once, when Eddie wasn't here, I saw Uncle Oliver leaving the boathouse, but only because I was down by the lake trying to catch damselflies in a jar. I don't hurt them, and I let them go very quickly,' she promised. 'Anyway, I noticed he and his wrestling teacher were holding hands,' Emily blurted. 'So I told Eddie. I mean… only little kids hold hands, don't they? So they don't get lost. It seemed strange. Eddie thought it was strange too, and he said, next time, instead of hiding in the bushes and waiting for the teacher to come out so that he could follow him, he'd climb up and look in the window again. I told him not to do it again after that first time, in case Uncle Oliver or his wrestling teacher saw us. We'd have got in trouble then. We'd already learned that grown-ups don't like being spied on.'

Again, Trudy noticed that Clement was looking very uneasy, and wasn't surprised when he finally asked a question of his own.

'Did Eddie say what he saw?' the coroner asked gently.

'No. He just said that I was right, and that grown-ups can do some very strange things. But after that, he said he was fed up of playing spies too and didn't want to go back to the boathouse, so then we invented a new game. Well, not new, really, because it meant building forts in the bushes, which we'd done before.'

Clement nodded. 'Emily, do you know what happened to Eddie's notebook?'

'Oh, I expect he hid it,' the little girl said simply. 'He thought it best. Every good spy knows you've got to have a secret hiding place that the baddies don't know about.'

'And do you know where Eddie's was?' Clement pursued.

'Of course,' Emily snorted. '*I* spied on *him* one day and followed him. He never spotted me either,' she boasted. Then her smile faltered as if she suddenly realised that she'd never be able to play spies, or anything else, with Eddie again.

Her lower lip began to tremble ominously.

'Can you tell us where it was,' Trudy put in hastily, hoping to stop the tears before they could begin. The distraction worked, because Emily nodded, swallowing hard.

'Yes. It's in the hole in the old oak tree by the tumbledown wall opposite the orangery. Do you want me to show you?' she added helpfully.

'That would be a good idea, thank you,' Trudy said, getting up and then rubbing her calf ruefully as she felt a touch of cramp shoot through her leg.

'It's this way.' Emily, looking serious, led them through the kitchen garden to one side of the outer wall, where a long, low, glassed-in lean-to did indeed grow a variety of small, pruned citrus trees. 'See, that's the oak tree over there,' Emily said pointing across a small meadow, and setting off almost at a run.

It was a lovely spring day, and the buttercups were out, with a few orange-tip butterflies fluttering about and taking advantage of the early source of nectar. The oak, just greening, was indeed a veritable old tree, and halfway up the trunk was one of those naturally framed, round boles that such trees sometimes acquired. Too low to the ground to house a woodpecker or an owl's nest, it might have been a former resting place for squirrels or perhaps field mice. For, after somewhat gingerly putting her hand inside it, Trudy felt some old fallen leaves that would have made a comfortable bed for some small mammal.

But no notebook.

'Are you sure this was his hiding place, Emily?' she asked.

The little girl nodded. 'I know that's where he kept all his things,' she insisted. 'Here, let me have a feel,' she said, a shade condescendingly. 'You need to get your arms and hands right in. You're not afraid of woodlice are you?' she scoffed.

Trudy wasn't – but earwigs were another matter.

But the little girl's face quickly fell as she, too, had to admit defeat. 'It's not there,' she said, sounding amazed and angry. '*Somebody took it!*'

'Maybe Eddie moved it,' Clement said consolingly. 'Could we see *your* notebook do you think? You said you loaned it to Eddie so that he could copy down the number plates of the cars. So it should still be in there, right?'

Emily's shoulder's slumped and then she shrugged morosely. 'Sorry, but Eddie tore out the piece of paper so he could put it in his own codebook. That's what he hid in here,' she said moodily. 'I suppose I'd better get back before Mrs Roper finds out I'm not still in the nursery,' she said heavily.

'Bad luck,' Trudy commiserated with her.

The little girl gave them a woebegone smile, and they watched her go all the way to the house, before Trudy turned to Clement and shrugged. 'All right, so what was all that about? All the time she was talking, you were looking like a right nervous ninny,' she accused him, a shade crossly.

Clement grinned, liking the phrase – but not at all so sure that he liked it being applied to *him* – and then very concisely told her just what it was that had been making him so nervous.

When he was finished, Trudy knew her face must be red as a beetroot.

Of course, she knew all about homosexuals – she'd been taught about them during her training. Homosexuality was a crime, after all, but she knew the likelihood that she'd ever have to arrest anyone for it was slight. Both DI Jennings and Sergeant O'Grady made sure that she was never called to make up the numbers whenever one of those sorts of clubs were raided. Nor was she allowed to do patrols at night at certain gentlemen's lavatories, which were also known hotspots for that sort of thing.

Of course, now it was clear what the 'wrestling lessons' had really been.

'But I thought Oliver de Lacey wanted to marry Marjorie Chandler,' Trudy said, with a frown. 'So he can't be, you know…'

Clement sighed, and once again set about educating her.

When he was finished, Trudy was silent for a while, and then sighed. 'We need to warn her, don't we? I mean, suppose she actually marries him, and then the poor woman finds out…'

'Yes, I'll have a discreet word,' Clement promised. And then wondered. Was it possible that Martin de Lacey had called them in, not so much because he cared about Eddie Proctor, but because he was hoping that they would discover his cousin's secret? Which would, in turn, seriously boost the likelihood that Marjorie Chandler would come to find out? His mind went back to that first interview with the squire, when he'd come to his office. Hadn't he felt then that Martin de Lacey had a hidden agenda of his own?

Clement gave a mental shrug. It hardly mattered now. 'I'm more interested in Eddie's missing notebook.'

Trudy frowned. 'Why?' Then her eyes widened. 'You don't think it has something to do with Eddie's death do you?'

'Well, we've been looking for a motive for murder,' Clement pointed out. 'Just suppose Oliver discovered Eddie peering in through the boathouse window during one of his… er… wrestling matches? As you more than most can appreciate, if the boy reported back to anyone what he'd seen, he would be facing actual jail time. He'd certainly lose his job at the university, not to mention his high-flying job in the city, that's for sure. And the scandal alone would ruin him.'

Trudy nodded. Yes, she could see all that. His poor mother would be devastated. The proud de Lacey name, dragged through the mud, the courts, the press. 'But… Would he really *kill* the boy to keep him quiet?' she asked, appalled. 'And wouldn't it be much easier and safer just to pay him off? 'The money!' she suddenly cried out, so loudly she almost made Clement jump. 'You remember, young George told us that he overheard Emily and Eddie talking about money. Perhaps Oliver de Lacey was paying him to keep quiet?'

'Hmmm, it might explain it,' Clement concurred. 'We certainly need to speak to Oliver again. Come on, let's go back to my office. You need to make notes of that conversation with Emily while it's still fresh in your mind, and I want to do a bit of discreet investigating of my own. If what we suspect is true, we'll need to have more concrete evidence against him than merely young Emily's say-so. And there are people, and places, that men such as Oliver like to go. I need to put out a few more feelers – it might just be possible to find somebody willing to testify about his proclivities. Even so, it's going to be tricky.'

Trudy nodded, eager to get going, and quickly the pair made their way back to the house.

The church clock struck three as they hurried past the house and headed for the front drive where they'd left the car.

*

And the person who, on Easter Sunday, had stood on the hill looking down at the Hall and decided that Eddie Proctor needed to die, watched them go with narrowed, angry eyes.

So Emily had been talking.

And the boy's hiding place had been found to be empty. Things were getting out of control. Yes. It was time for some rapid action.

The killer of Eddie Proctor began to plan quickly.

Chapter 34

The moment they stepped into the coroner's office, his secretary pounced.

'Oh, Dr Ryder, I'm so glad you're back. Inspector Jennings has been on the phone all afternoon. He wants you or, better yet, WPC Loveday to call him back, urgently. He's been most persistent.'

'Oh no. Does he sound angry?' Trudy asked, her heart plummeting. Although she couldn't think what it was she must have done to bring about his ire this time.

'Yes, a bit angry. But more excited, pleased but irritated, I'd have said.'

Well that didn't sound much better, Trudy thought gloomily.

'Come on through, you can phone from my desk,' Clement offered.

'Thank you,' Trudy said. At least whatever dressing-down she was going to get would be made easier for having to take it over the telephone. At least then she wouldn't have to withstand his withering and contemptuous eyes!

Sitting down and taking a deep breath, Trudy lifted the receiver and dialled the station's telephone number.

PC Walter Swinburne answered it. The oldest PC was something of a grandfather figure to her. The moment he heard her voice, his own lowered dramatically.

'What the hell have you been up to?' he all but hissed. 'Whatever it is, you've really gone and done it this time.'

'What do you mean?' Trudy whispered back. 'I haven't done anything!' she protested.

'You must have done *something*,' he insisted. 'The big boys from London arrived an hour or so ago, and have been closeted with the inspector in his office ever since. There have been some raised voices, I can tell you, and not all of them coming from the inspector! Every now and then he charges out here, demanding to know where you are, and if you've reported in yet. You'd better have a good excuse, my girl, I'm telling you,' he warned.

'I've been in Northamptonshire,' Trudy said. 'So I could hardly check in, could I?'

'I'd better transfer you over. Take a deep breath, 'cause you're in for it, I reckon,' the old constable warned her again.

Trudy gulped, quickly beckoned Clement over, and indicated he should lean close. She half-lifted the receiver away from her ear and held it out, so that they could both hear what was being said.

'WPC Loveday!' The booming voice of her irate inspector carried clearly across the wire. 'Where the Dickens are you?'

'I'm at the coroner's office, sir,' Trudy said smartly.

'Are you? Well in that case, I want you and the old vulture to get over here right away. Is that clear?'

Trudy gulped. She was so tense that she didn't even wince at the fact that the coroner must have heard the cruel nickname they had for him at the station. 'Yes, sir. But I'm not sure if Dr Ryder is free…' She tried to save her friend, at least, from whatever storm it was that was breaking, but Clement was already shaking his head.

'*The old vulture* is free to come over, Inspector,' Clement said, raising his voice to be sure that it would carry to the other end. 'Expect us in five minutes or so.'

Slightly disconcerted – but also mollified – the inspector muttered something that might have been a half-hearted apology and rang off.

Trudy hung up. 'Well, don't say I didn't try to spare you,' she said ruefully. 'The inspector in a tizzy is not a pretty sight.'

'Nonsense, wouldn't miss the fun for all the tea in China,' Clement assured her robustly. And meant it. He enjoyed a good blazing row now and then. And he'd never yet met an argument that he couldn't win.

'I'm sorry about… you know, the old vulture thing,' Trudy muttered, but Clement merely laughed. Did she really think he didn't know what they called him behind his back?

'Any idea what it's all about?' Trudy asked glumly, as they went back to where he'd parked his Rover.

Clement thought he might have a pretty good idea. But he shook his head. 'Let's just wait and see, shall we?' he advised brightly.

Chapter 35

DI Jennings was sitting behind his desk when they knocked on the door. Two men, who had also been seated, rose slowly as Trudy and Clement walked in.

'Ah, WPC Loveday, and Dr Clement Ryder,' Jennings said. 'This is Inspector Robinson and Inspector Brown.' He made the introductions with a deadpan voice, but Trudy could tell her superior officer was feeling an excess of emotion.

From his glittering eyes she suspected amusement, but there was also a certain tension about him that suggested he was not too far off becoming angry. An unusual and intriguing mix that didn't do much to soothe her already heightened nerves.

'I'm sorry I've been out of touch, sir,' Trudy said smartly. 'Dr Ryder and I have been interviewing a witness in Northamptonshire.'

Jennings shrugged slightly. 'Yes, well, there'll be no more of that. I'm pulling you off the case,' he informed them flatly. 'The Chief Constable concurs with me.'

Trudy stared at him uncertainly, then turned to look at the two strangers. They appeared to be somewhere in their late thirties or early forties, both were dark and clean-shaven, were neither ugly nor attractive, fat nor thin, or in the least memorable in any way. They were dressed in near identical suits, and both smiled meaninglessly at her. But something about them made her shiver slightly.

'The inspectors are from Special Branch,' Jennings said, again with that odd mixture of excitement and resentment. 'It appears that your investigation into the Proctor case has caused a few ripples in places where they don't like ripples,' he explained dryly.

Trudy blinked. She'd never expected to meet anyone from Special Branch! But at least it explained Inspector Jennings' odd behaviour. On the one hand, he'd be delighted to have an excuse to shoot down Dr Ryder's pet project, but on the other hand, he wouldn't have appreciated another division coming onto his patch and usurping his authority.

Clement slowly pulled up a chair and sat down. 'Ah, I take it this is to do with Oliver de Lacey's hush-hush work in atomic energy? Has he been complaining?' he asked casually.

'Not at all, Dr Ryder,' Inspector Brown – or was it Robinson? – responded smoothly. 'But I'm sure you can appreciate that the powers that be don't see the need for a man in such a sensitive and stress-related profession to be needlessly harassed.'

'I wasn't aware that he *had* been harassed,' Clement said mildly. He looked relaxed, almost indolent in the chair, his hat resting nonchalantly on his knees, but Trudy could tell that he, too, was feeling angry. And it heartened her somewhat. At least she had one ally in the room.

In truth, though, Clement was feeling angry with himself, rather than with the two strangers, or the anonymous government lackey who must have sent them. Evidently, the feelers he'd put out recently hadn't been anywhere nearly as discreet as he'd expected or hoped.

'Oh, I'm sure you've behaved impeccably, Dr Ryder,' Inspector Robinson put in smoothly. 'But it's time to call it a day now. The boy's death was an accident, plain and simple. I take it you haven't got any evidence that says otherwise?' he added blandly.

Clement's lips twisted slightly at the gauntlet that had just been thrown down. 'Not yet,' he was forced to admit, careful to keep his voice as bland as before. He certainly wasn't about to give them – or Jennings – the satisfaction of knowing they'd got under his skin. 'But the de Laceys are certainly a family with a lot of secrets.'

He met the level gaze of both men with one of his own.

Behind his desk, Jennings watched the showdown with a sort of nervous fascination that left him undecided just who he should be rooting for. For whilst there was no doubt that the curmudgeonly coroner could be a right pain in his backside at times, there was something so oily and superior about the Special Branch men that they got his back up. They wielded so much power, and they knew it. What's more, they were so used to people backing down whenever they spoke that he was almost hoping the coroner would give them a bit of a shock. Just for the fun of watching the resulting fireworks.

'That may well be, Dr Ryder,' Robinson – or was it Brown? – said mildly. 'But no purpose would be served by bringing them into the light.'

'Unless it had something to do with the death of a young boy.'

'Are you saying that it does?' the slightly taller of the two officers demanded shortly.

Trudy, who so far hadn't dared say anything, wished with all her heart that the coroner could claim otherwise, but she knew how few really solid leads they had to go on, and saw him smile slightly in defeat.

'Since it doesn't look as if we're going to be allowed any more time to pursue it, the answer to that has to be no,' Clement said dryly.

'Ah. Well, in that case, we'll bid you all good afternoon. Inspector Jennings, you'll be receiving the paperwork shortly. The Edward Proctor case is now officially closed. Is that clear?'

Jennings, to his credit, flushed slightly in anger at this high-handed dictate, but he nodded stiffly. 'Of course. WPC Loveday will be reassigned, as of tomorrow.'

Both men left without another word. After the door was shut behind them, they all waited for a few seconds in an unspoken understanding that they wanted to be sure the visitors were out of earshot before speaking.

Trudy tensed, expecting to get a tongue-lashing from her superior officer. Instead, though, there was a long, thoughtful silence.

Finally, Clement lifted his Trilby hat and spun it absently around and around on his forefinger, regarding its convolutions with intense interest. Jennings watched him in silence for a while longer, then shifted in his seat. Finally, he spoke. 'I take it you know exactly what all that was about?'

Clement sighed. 'I have a good idea.'

'Care to share it?'

Clement cocked an eyebrow at him. 'Sure you want to know?' he asked.

Jennings hesitated, then nodded. Which made Trudy want to applaud, because she rather wanted to know what it was all about too!

Clement sighed. 'Very well. When we talked to Dr Oliver de Lacey at his college, I saw an old photograph of him, which reminded me of the fact that he studied at Cambridge, not Oxford. At Trinity College to be exact.'

For a moment Jennings looked puzzled. Then, slowly, a look of comprehension dawned across his face. 'Oh,' he said flatly. Then, 'But that doesn't necessarily mean *anything*, you know.'

Trudy desperately wanted to ask what they were talking about, and something of her angst must have communicated itself to her friend, for Clement glanced across at her and smiled.

'You were probably only about 10 years old or so in 1951, when Guy Burgess and Donald Maclean defected to the Soviet Union. Do you remember much about it?'

'Oh! Yes, a bit,' Trudy admitted. 'I remember there was a really big fuss about it, and how angry everyone was at the traitors. They were at Trinity in Cambridge too, weren't they? And Dr Oliver de Lacey must have been up around the same time that they were? Is that it?'

Clement shrugged. 'The moment I saw he'd gone to Trinity, I did start to wonder,' he said cagily. 'But in itself, as Inspector Jennings just pointed out, it probably means nothing,' he said. Then, turning his attention back to Jennings, he shrugged. 'After all, thousands of students will have passed through Trinity in the Forties and Fifties, and it's a bit far-fetched to think they might all be potential traitors. But added to the fact that Oliver de Lacey works in the nuclear industry, you can see why Special Branch would be keeping a close eye on *him*.'

Jennings sighed slightly. 'Just doing their job then?'

Clement shrugged. 'I did phone a few friends after I'd made the connection, asking if anything was known about him…' The older man smiled whimsically. 'I thought they could be trusted to keep it all on the old q.t., but evidently word must have got around that I'd been poking my nose into sensitive places.'

Jennings grinned sourly. 'You have a decided knack for that,' he acknowledged grimly. 'No wonder they were sent to shut you down. They can't like it when any unwanted attention is sent de Lacey's way. Not only in case it becomes public, but in case it attracts the attention of our Red friends.'

Trudy shifted a little impatiently on her feet. 'I don't quite understand, sir,' she addressed her inspector, but really she was speaking to Dr Ryder. 'Are you saying that Dr de Lacey might be a spy for the *Russians*?'

Jennings snorted. 'I think it extremely *unlikely*, Constable Loveday,' he said sardonically. 'Just that the powers that be don't particularly like it when any kind of spotlight is thrown onto people like him.'

'They tend to be a touch sensitive about it,' Clement put in with a wolfish grin. 'Burgess and his pals caused a huge scandal,

215

and caused an awful lot of red faces (pardon the atrocious pun) in Whitehall when the extent of their spying activities was uncovered. The civil service and many important men found themselves to be a laughing stock, especially in America. Heads rolled. And they didn't like it,' he finished succinctly.

'So now,' Jennings took up the running, 'whenever any chill wind blows any kind of doubt over someone like de Lacey – who was up at Trinity at the right time, and has wormed his way into a high-powered job in government... well, let's just say, they get the wind up.'

'You can't really blame them,' Clement said, a shade reluctantly. 'The Russians would be delighted to learn anything they can about our nuclear power policy and details of our nuclear reactors and such. And someone like de Lacey would be in an ideal position to tell them.'

'He'd have been watched for years, I expect?' Jennings mused.

'Almost certainly. Especially given the fact that certain, er, habits of his would leave him especially vulnerable to blackmail, should it become known,' Clement agreed flatly.

Jennings lifted an eyebrow questioningly at him.

Clement shrugged. 'He has no interest in women, Inspector.'

'Oh. One of them,' Jennings snorted.

Clement said nothing. Like most men of his background, he'd gone through the public-school system, and had a much more tolerant attitude towards homosexuals than most. His own personal opinion was that people's private lives should be just that – private. He also counted several men – and women – as friends of his, whose sexual preferences probably wouldn't stand much scrutiny by the police. Or Special Branch officers or spies recruiting for the Soviet Union, should it come to that.

'So exactly what *are* we saying then?' Trudy said, still feeling all at sea. 'Is Oliver de Lacey a spy for Russia or not?'

'Probably not,' Clement said.

'So if that's the case, why can't we continue to investigate little

216

Eddie's death?' Trudy asked stubbornly, beginning to feel angry. 'We have to give up, just like that, even though we now know that Eddie had found out about Oliver de Lacey's secret meetings with his, er… boyfriends?' She quickly filled her superior officer in on what they'd just learned from Emily. 'So it's looking more and more likely that only Oliver de Lacey had a motive for wanting the boy dead,' she persisted, beginning to get hot under the collar. 'If Eddie talked about what he'd seen, it would be bound to get all around the village sooner or later. And he must have known that his bosses would find out, and see him as a security risk. He'd be bound to be in hot water then.'

Jennings shrugged, but not without some sympathy. 'The investigation is over, Constable,' he said flatly. 'And that's that. Dr Ryder, thank you for your time.' He rose, and unexpectedly thrust his hand out.

Clement rose, too, and accepted the handshake with a wry nod. 'Inspector. I'll have to contact Mr Martin de Lacey, of course,' the coroner said, holding up a hand in a pacifying gesture as Jennings made to object. 'Just as a courtesy you understand. He *was* the one who called for a more in-depth investigation, and I owe him an explanation of our findings. If not, he might get suspicious, and make even more of a rumpus,' the coroner added cannily. 'Which will only make our Special Branch friends very unhappy.'

'What will you tell him?' Jennings demanded, conceding the older man's reasoning, but remaining highly suspicious of his true motives. Inspector Jennings might be many things, but he wasn't a complete idiot.

'Just that we've concluded our investigation, and that we have found no evidence to say that the verdict at the inquest wasn't the right one. Which is true enough,' Clement promised, looking at Trudy warningly. 'We have no evidence that Oliver de Lacey lured the boy to the well and pushed him in.'

Trudy clamped her lips together to prevent herself from saying something she might regret later. But she simply couldn't believe that Clement was just going to give up like this. DI Jennings, yes – he was a serving police officer, and had to follow orders. So she could see why he would throw in the towel.

But the coroner never let anybody tell him what he could or couldn't do!

'Perhaps Constable Loveday can come with me, just to make it official,' Clement requested mildly. 'Mr de Lacey will want to be reassured that the police have done a thorough job.'

Jennings waved a hand. 'Fine, fine, take her along with you. But bright and early tomorrow, Constable, it's back to normal duties for you,' he warned her.

'Yes, sir,' Trudy said, hoping she didn't sound as mutinous as she felt.

Jennings watched them go, then gave a grunt of dismissal. At least he could wash his hands of the whole business.

*

Outside Trudy trudged despondently after the coroner. Walter Swinburne cast her an anxious glance, but she managed to give him a brief, reassuring smile. She climbed silently into the passenger seat of the coroner's Rover and stared straight ahead.

So, back to Briar's Hall one last time to tell the squire it was all over, Trudy thought grimly. It all felt so unfinished, and so deeply unsatisfactory.

'That poor boy's parents,' she burst out, as the coroner turned the key in the ignition and slipped the car into gear. 'How can we look them in the eye ever again?'

Clement shook his head a shade helplessly. 'If you live long enough, WPC Loveday, I'm afraid you'll discover for yourself that you really *can't* win them all. At some point, life's going to slap you down hard. You just have to learn to take it, pick yourself up, dust yourself down, and get on with things.'

It was one of the hardest lessons that every youngster had to learn, Clement knew. But it was one that he'd never been able to accept with any grace. He glanced across at her and felt his heart constrict at her bafflement and helpless anger.

'Come on, let's get it over with,' he said flatly.

Chapter 36

It was just gone half past four when they drove through the village. To Trudy, who caught sight of the church clock, it felt as if hours must have passed since they'd last been here. But a quick check of her own watch showed her that it was right. Although in a farming community a nine-to-five existence wasn't really the norm, the place had the feel of slowly beginning to wind down for the day. The village shop was doing last-minute business, and the children were piling out of school. No doubt soon, weary and hungry farmworkers would start to appear for their tea.

At the Hall, they parked in the front drive, but Mrs Roper was very happy to give them the news that the squire wasn't in, but was out and about on the estate somewhere. A tree had fallen down across a stream that was the main source of water for one of the farms, and he was seeing to it.

Clement thanked her, but as usual, her only response was to slam the door quickly in their faces, her own face shuttered and grim.

'I'll bet she's always known that the old lady did something to her daughter-in-law's horse,' Trudy muttered bitterly.

'I think you'll find that's slander,' Clement rebuked her mildly. 'Which, last time I checked, is a crime. And you an officer of the law too.'

But not even his attempt at teasing could improve her mood.

Just then, they noticed the head gardener crossing the lawn towards them. He was wheeling a barrow full of something green and slimy that must have come from one of the ornamental ponds and his hands and arms were a light shade of lime green up to his elbows.

'You back again then?' Leonard Cricklade said with a smile. 'Don't know what's going on today – everything seems to be up in the air.'

'Oh?' Clement enquired mildly, but it was all the invitation the old gardener needed to stop for a gossip.

'First of all, the squire has to go and sort out something up at Danesway Farm, then Lallie goes missing, just when I need him to tie up some clematis plants. Now some big black important-looking car has arrived and taken Mr Oliver away. That'll be for some big conflab in London, I 'spect,' he added sounding proud, as if somehow the achievement was his. 'Mrs Sylvia's been tramping about all day with a face like thunder and rushing hither and yon doing who knows what, and now we get a visit from yourselves,' the old man said, with a smile to take the sting out of his final words.

'Some days are like that,' Clement said mildly. 'I don't suppose you know when the squire's due back?'

'I expect he'll be back by six,' the old man said. 'They have their supper at seven up at the Hall,' the gardener said, shaking his head slightly at such eccentricity. 'Funny time to have it, I reckon. Half-five on the dot me and the missus always eat.'

Clement looked at Trudy. 'Well, we can go back to town and try again later, or hang around. What do you want to do?'

Trudy sighed. 'Seems a waste of petrol to make two journeys,' she pointed out pragmatically. 'Do you mind if we take a walk through the gardens, Mr Cricklade?'

''Course not, that's what they're there for,' the old man pointed out with unanswerable logic. 'The tulips and forsythia are making

221

a nice show in the west garden about now. And I've just cleaned out the pond over there.'

He pointed out a section of large clipped yew. 'Head for that and follow it around, and you'll find an entrance into the knot garden. Go on past the old sundial, and you'll find another exit that'll take you straight there. There's a bench where you can sit, if you like.'

'Thank you,' Trudy said. The old man nodded happily and set out for the compost heaps, whistling an old Glen Miller tune.

Trudy and Clement set off slowly towards the yew hedge. 'So what exactly are we going to tell the squire when he comes back?' she asked listlessly.

'The truth,' Clement said flatly. 'What else.'

'Are you going to tell him that we were pulled off the case by his cousin's government minders?' she challenged.

'And give them even more reason to be at loggerheads?' Clement asked. 'I can't see the point, can you? Besides, it won't be something Eddie's father will want to hear, will it? He'll want to be reassured that we did our best.'

Trudy sighed. 'You're right. I'm just feeling mean-spirited. It's not nice,' she conceded. 'It's just that I feel so… So…'

'Hello, isn't that Lallie?' Clement said, trying to distract her. They were just about to pass through the gap in the yew into the knot garden beyond, when the coroner caught sight of the big, shambling gardener, moving among the bushes on the far side of a large herbaceous border.

'I think so. Why?' Trudy said, disinterestedly.

'Didn't the head gardener just say he'd gone AWOL?'

Trudy shrugged. 'I expect he just wanted to skive off for a while. Everybody does it now and then.'

'Come on, let's go and tell him his boss is looking for him,' Clement said, determined to find something to do to jog her out of her apathy.

'I don't expect he'll thank us,' Trudy warned, but was willing enough to forgo hanging about on a garden bench for an hour or more.

When they got to the shrubbery, however, the gardener was nowhere in sight.

'He probably went back to his gazebo,' Clement said. 'Time for tea? Come on.'

Listlessly, Trudy followed him. Soon they could see the shimmering silver line of the lake through the trees, and relying on memory, they finally found Lallie's picturesque if modest home.

But a quick tap on the door brought only silence.

Then, just as he was turning away, Clement noticed another, more ramshackle wooden building a little further in, closer to the edge of the lake, and had an idea. 'Come on, we might as well walk around the lake to pass the time. It's going to be a lovely evening.'

Trudy nodded. He was probably right. The sun was getting lower in the sky and starting to accumulate that more mellow light that presaged a lovely sunset. A few early mayflies danced their dance along the fringes of the lake, whilst a moorhen, startled by their presence, set off for the middle of the lake, screeching in panic.

But before they emerged onto the edge of the water, a noise just off to their left, made them both pause. It sounded like a door slamming against something, which was distinctly odd, given the bucolic scene around them.

'It must have come from that shed,' Clement mused.

'What shed?' Trudy demanded.

'The one over there,' Clement said, pointing. 'You know, Constable, you really should develop your observational skills more.'

'Oh, shut up,' Trudy grumbled under her breath, but followed him obediently as he set off through the laurels and rhododendrons towards a large, wooden shed.

As expected, the door was open, and even as they watched, the breeze took it and slammed it shut, only for it to ricochet open again, proving it to be the source of the sound.

Meaning only to secure it, Trudy stepped forward, but as she did so, noticed movement inside. It surprised, but didn't alarm her. She pulled open the door more slowly and looked inside, and saw Lallie standing with his back to her.

A scythe, hoe, a regular rake and a wide-pronged leaf rake hung on various nails on one wall. On some rough-hewn shelves were stacked some tins of peaches, tobacco, and a can of cocoa. Beside her by the door, a large, nearly full sack of what looked like potatoes sent their musty scent into the air. Clearly, this was part garden shed and part storeroom, which made sense. The shed was only a few steps away from the gazebo, which would make it a convenient place for Lallie to keep some things.

She opened her mouth to speak, then noticed that Lallie was intent on some activity, his large bulk bent slightly over something resting on a large wooden packing crate, which was clearly being used as a table. She took a step inside, then noticed for the first time exactly what it was that he was holding in his hands.

The sight of it made her go as still as a statue, for her subconscious mind had expected him to be doing something vaguely horticultural – like pricking out seedlings or transferring mulch into flowerpots. But nothing as incongruous as what he was actually doing.

For the gardener was holding a vast amount of money in his hands. Reams and reams of large white pound notes – a small fortune, in fact. Even as she watched, he thrust them into a large brown paper bag that was already well stuffed with pound notes. On the crate in front of him was an open battered brown leather suitcase, containing some clothes and a shaving kit, and he thrust the bag of money inside this, closed and latched it, and started to turn around.

'Lallie?' Trudy said uncertainly.

And suddenly, and completely without warning, everything changed.

Chapter 37

At the sound of her voice, the gardener swung around. He moved surprisingly fast, but then, she supposed, anyone startled moves more quickly than normal.

But the look on his face wasn't anything like normal. Gone was the placid, mild, slightly dreamy look that she associated with him, and instead she was looking at someone she'd never seen before.

His eyes were sharp, bright, and hard. His jaw was tight and clenched, and his skin was pale with fury.

Trudy tried to take a step back, but unfortunately Dr Ryder was right behind her, and his bulk brought her up short. It had taken her eyes a few precious seconds to adjust from the sunlight to the dim interior and she knew that her friend wasn't yet aware of the situation they were facing.

Trudy, herself, still wasn't really processing it fully. She'd barely had time to register the change in the normally easy-going Lallie Clark, when he began to move. She watched as his right hand reached out towards the wall, and felt a moment of total puzzlement.

She'd assumed he'd been going to reach down and pick up his suitcase, the one with all the money in it. She'd even, subconsciously, been bracing herself for him to charge her, trying to knock her out of the way before running off.

But in the next instant, she saw that no such thought was in his mind. She watched, in total and sheer disbelief, as his fingers scrabbled along the wall and found the hand of the scythe.

Trudy remembered her granddad handling a scythe. She'd only been a toddler, but she remembered him using it to cut back the grass on his allotment paths. He belonged to a generation that had no use for new-fangled lawnmowers, and she could remember watching in fascination as his old but supple body, bent at the waist, swished the curved blade backwards and forwards, in a sort of hypnotic rhythm.

She remembered too, that it had always been exciting to watch, because her granddad had insisted that she always stay several feet away.

'This 'ere blade is sharp, young'un – it could cut you and not know the difference,' he'd warned her.

Later he'd shown her how he'd kept it razor sharp by honing it on a pumice stone – both sides, so that it swept through the grass without catching. Every now and then, whilst cutting the grass he'd stop and hone it again. And when he'd finished, he always gave it a final sharpening, so that it would be ready to go next time.

And if her granddad did that, then she was fairly sure that Mr Leonard Cricklade – who was nearly of the same generation – would also insist that his own staff kept their tools in tip-top, ready-to-use shape.

She felt her mouth go dry as Lallie lifted the scythe from its wooden peg with a slight 'snick' sound.

She felt her stomach clench in sudden nausea as she watched his fingers curl around the handle, the knuckles of his hand going slightly white as they got a firm grip.

Her mind, for a terrifying amount of unfathomable time went totally blank, even as her eyes dropped to watch the gardener's feet turn to face her full on.

Then the moment of blankness went away with a cold hard

wave of complete fear, as her eyes went back up to his and saw the darkness in them.

He started to swivel at the waist and hips.

She noticed his shoulders were swinging around.

She noticed his right arm, which had been fully extended, began to bend at the elbow.

And her brain, no longer held in that weird, momentary blackness of paralysis, interpreted it all for her.

This man was getting ready to swing that scythe. He was going to bring that razor-sharp, semi-circular, strong blade right down and across the space that she was currently occupying.

And if he did that, he would kill her.

Trudy felt her mouth fall open comically.

She was going to die.

She could hear the remnants of the slight grunt Clement Ryder had given, when she'd stepped back and bumped into him. She could hear her own gasping breath, and smell the scent of the shed – a mixture of dust and potatoes and some kind of oil.

And she could feel herself moving, for without being aware of it, her subconscious mind must have been giving her right arm the order to move – to reach for her truncheon.

But she couldn't move back because her friend was still in the doorway, blocking her.

So she needed to duck down – it was the only option left open to her.

She began to drop to her knees.

At the same time, she wondered if Clement had even seen Lallie yet, or what he held and what he intended to do, and knew she had to warn him. Once Lallie had dealt with her, Clement would be next.

'Watch out!' she heard herself scream. At the same time, because she was beginning to fold in on herself, her truncheon, which had been slipping easily from her belt, caught at her waist, because her own crouching body was pinioning it, making it harder to withdraw.

She felt her knees hit the hard wooden floor of the shed with a lance of pain that she barely noticed.

She looked up, and the sunlight – feeble though it was coming in through the small, filthy window – caught the flash of the blade. In a weird sort of way, it was almost beautiful.

She heard a sound, and realised it was another sob. It was coming from her, of course, and was one of total frustration and despair, because she knew she wasn't going to be able to get her truncheon out in time.

Already Lallie's momentum was reaching its height. Soon, the trajectory of the blade, now at its zenith, would start to swing down, inevitably going faster and faster as it gained more power and momentum on its downward swing.

And even if she could get her truncheon free, would she have time to raise it over her body for protection?

But even if she did manage it, the blade of a scythe was curved. Suppose its middle section struck and was caught by the truncheon – the curved end could still… What?

Take her eye out? Slice through her cheek, disfiguring her? Or puncture her neck, where there were so many vulnerable arteries?

She heard a roaring sound behind her. She knew it was her friend, screaming out something. She knew he'd finally seen and comprehended what was happening, and in the formless roar she could hear so much – shock, denial, and a rage to match Lallie's own, murderous fury. And despair – and fear too.

And it comforted her to know that she was not going to die alone. Someone she loved would be there to witness it, and *know*. She wouldn't be going into the dark, and whatever it was that lay beyond, alone and without human company.

Some of the icy coldness that had fallen over her, almost unnoticed, melted away.

She only hoped that Clement would be able to get away from

Lallie once he turned his attentions to her friend. But somehow, she felt sure that he would. She didn't know why, but she had confidence in the old vulture. He was smarter than Lallie, and he'd be forewarned. The murderous gardener wouldn't find Dr Clement Ryder such easy prey.

The blade must be getting closer. Its arching sweep would soon be within reach of her vulnerable flesh.

But she was damned if she was going to make it easy for the bastard!

A chill ran up her spine.

Where would the tip of that scythe-shaped blade land?

She felt her flesh actually contract, as if it could already feel the cold, sharp blade slicing through it.

She closed her eyes.

She began to pray.

She was going to die.

She wasn't ready.

What could she say to God? What…

She heard Lallie shout, she heard Clement swear and grunt, and then felt the coroner's knees bang into her side, almost knocking her over.

She felt something hit her – something hard, rounded. Then again, something hit her on the back of her neck. *What the hell was that?*

She opened her eyes, not lifting her head, but looking to one side.

And suddenly, potatoes were raining down over her.

For a moment, her brain gave up. This was just too much. It had been preparing her to meet her maker, and now this.

Trudy, for some reason, found herself back in Marjorie Chandler's flat, looking at the weird surrealist paintings. And she felt, insanely, like laughing. Although she hadn't really understood Clement's lecture about surrealism, it now felt as if she was part of such a painting herself.

229

It was raining potatoes!

And then time snapped back, and she felt herself painfully knocked fully over. She could hear grunting and swearing, and sensed feet trampling perilously near to her and suddenly she realised that Clement and Lallie were grappling together, knocking against her as she crouched on the floor.

And with that, the rage came back.

Clement was an old man, and Lallie was bigger and younger – and he still had the scythe in his hand. *The bastard!* How *dare* he try to hurt her friend?

She crawled backwards, wriggling around and managing to get one hand out from under her and, groping with it, found a wall. With a grunt, she managed to squash herself against it, getting her knees back under her. Clement, finding his path now cleared, slammed his body further into the gardener. Both his hands were on Lallie's right arm, rendering the scythe useless as a weapon.

But even as Trudy, panting like a steam train with fright, shock, rage and fear, finally managed to scramble to her feet, she saw that Clement's position left him vulnerable. With both arms stretched up to pinion Lallie's arm, his abdomen was totally unguarded.

And even as she finally pulled her truncheon free of her belt, and began to step forward, Lallie – no stranger to dirty fighting – swung his free left arm down, his clenched fist connecting painfully with the coroner's ribs.

Clement let out a bellow of pain and rage and began to bend double, but even then, he didn't let go of his grip on Lallie's right hand.

The gardener swung his left arm back again, intending to land yet another bone-crunching punch, but Trudy, timing her swing with his, moved her truncheon upwards in a classic undercut as he swung his arm downwards, and the rounded top of the truncheon hit his wrist with a resounding 'whack'.

Lallie's shriek of pain and outrage filled the shed, making her jump in shock. His face, which had been looking down venomously at the coroner's lowered, white head, swung in her direction instead. And she couldn't help but flinch at the fury and murder she saw there. Luckily, in the next instant, her rage swarmed back, matching his own and making her reckless.

She took a step forward, swinging her truncheon high, intent on braining him.

But Lallie was a soldier. He'd faced combat before and was in no mood to give up his prize – the money he'd schemed and planned and killed for – or go to jail.

With a snarl, he heaved all his weight and muscle against the coroner, and Clement, still half-bent with pain from the blow to his ribs felt himself falling backwards.

Trudy neatly stepped over him, and began to pivot herself, just as she'd seen Lallie do only moments before.

With his right arm now free, Lallie began to swing the scythe again.

But Trudy wasn't thinking of the blade this time. She wasn't anticipating its sharp blade cutting into her flesh, paralysing her with fear. All she wanted to do was save her friend from dying. And she was bloody well going to do that, no matter what.

When Clement might have run and saved himself, he'd chosen to throw himself at her attacker instead. She could do no less than return that wonderful favour.

Trudy's mind began to rage, almost out of control. How *dare* this man, this *child-killer*, try to kill her and her friend and think he could get away with it? Well, she was not poor little Eddie Proctor. She was no 11-year-old child. And she was bloody well going to show him that he'd tackled the wrong person this time!

Her extended hand began to rise, but she saw the scythe was already beginning to turn to meet it as Lallie rotated his wrist. In a contest between a short truncheon and a long-handled, curved scythe, there was no question as to which of them had the greatest reach.

So she began to turn her own wrist, and the angle of the truncheon, at the same time, stepping closer to him. It felt counter-intuitive to do so, but she knew she had no other option. Paradoxically, the nearer to him she was, the less of a target she made.

From a sideswipe, she turned her weapon flat, and jabbed forward and upwards, as hard and fast as she could. And the rounded end of her weapon hit him not quite in the middle of his throat, as she'd hoped, but slightly off to the left. Nevertheless, it was enough to make him gag.

No human being likes to have their breathing cut off, even temporarily. An instinctive panic takes over, and Lallie, without thinking, dropped the scythe and raised both hands to his throat. His face began to turn red, and his eyes bulged obscenely.

It was all Trudy needed. As he bent forward, trying to draw breath, she took a step back, reversed the action of her truncheon, and brought it down hard and fast on the back of his exposed head.

It hit him with a sickening crack that seemed to go right through her.

And in an instant – again – everything changed.

Chapter 38

Lallie fell to Trudy's feet, a total dead weight.

And an appalled voice somewhere in her head said, quite clearly, 'You've killed him.'

Trudy froze. For a second, she was the one who couldn't breathe. She was the one who could see nothing, feel nothing.

And then she swallowed, hard.

She took another step back.

'You've just killed a man,' the voice said again.

She felt herself shaking her head. No she hadn't. Had she? She couldn't have. She didn't mean it…

For the second time in what felt like an eternity, she began to pray. Only this time, she wasn't asking God to be merciful and receive her soul. She was begging for forgiveness. Thou shalt not kill. A Sunday school lesson from long ago came back to her. The vicar – surprisingly young, slightly bored – drumming the Ten Commandments into her.

She had broken… Which number was it?

'Trudy!' The voice, this time, was real. It had body and human warmth, and it came from somewhere in the shed, not in her own head.

She stared down at the man at her feet, suddenly hoping…

But then she saw movement and turned her head. Clement was struggling painfully to his feet.

He took one look at her wild, white, horrified face, and took a slow, deep breath. 'It's all right now, Trudy. It's all over. You did well.'

Trudy stared at him. She'd done well? No, that made no sense. She'd just killed a man. That was the exact opposite of doing well.

Clement limped towards her, every step making his bruised ribs protest angrily. He reached her and touched her hand. It was icy. Her grip on her truncheon was vice-like.

'Trudy, you can let it go now,' he said.

Again, she stared at him. 'Let what go?' she managed to whisper. Her lips felt cracked and dry. Her heart felt the same. Her soul, likewise.

'Open your hand, Trudy,' Clement said again.

The words didn't make sense to her. Open her hand? *Open her hand?* What did that mean?

She looked at her friend, at the slightly watery grey eyes, which seemed kind and sad. Then she saw him move those eyes from her face to something else. She followed his gaze, and saw her hand, and his own hand enclosing it. And then the truncheon.

'Oh,' she said. But even so, it took her a while to make her fingers go slack. When they did, her body seemed to want to go slack as well.

'I've killed a man,' she said simply.

Clement, now that he'd got the truncheon away from her, hunkered down, giving a grunt as his ribs told him in no uncertain terms just what they thought of that particular manoeuvre. He put two fingers on the side of the gardener's thick neck.

'No, you haven't,' he said flatly. 'There's still a pulse.'

But he frowned, for it was worryingly thin and reedy. He looked up. 'Trudy, I need you to run to the house and telephone for an ambulance.'

But Trudy didn't hear the last part. She was still savouring, with sheer bliss, the other words. He had a pulse. She hadn't killed him.

'Trudy!' Clement shouted.

She flinched, and blinked. 'What?'

'Run to the house – call for an ambulance. Now.'

'Right,' she said, and looked around. The door. She stepped outside into bewildering sunlight and birdsong. She could see the lake – it was beautiful. Everything looked and felt strange. How could the world still be so beautiful?

But then her mind snapped to attention. She had a job to do. Find the house. Telephone for an ambulance. Right.

For a terrifying second, she couldn't think which way the house was. Then she remembered, and set off. At first her legs felt numb and rubbery, but after a while they began to feel as if they belonged to her once more, and she stopped staggering like a drunk, and began to run in earnest.

She had to get to the house.

By the time she reached the kitchen garden she was running like the wind. Leonard Cricklade watched her fly past, his white-bristled chin falling comically open. By the time she reached the elegant front steps, she was out of breath, but mercifully most of the fog of shock seemed to have cleared out of her mind. She ran up the steps and hammered on the door.

After what seemed an age, they opened and the housekeeper, wearing her usual grim expression confronted her, and Trudy, for a second or two, felt a bewildering sense of déjà vu.

'I already told you, the squire's not…' Mrs Roper began angrily, then squawked, a bit like an outraged parrot, as Trudy – in no mood to cope with her obstinacy – literally shoved past her.

'I need the telephone,' she panted.

'I beg your pardon…' The housekeeper began hotly, then abruptly subsided as Trudy turned savagely on her.

'There's a seriously injured man who needs an ambulance.

235

Now where is the nearest telephone?' she demanded, almost shouting in her frustration.

Mutely, the housekeeper pointed to a door, and Trudy shot through it. It was a small study, with a telephone housed on a small desk. She pounced on it, and with unsteady fingers called for the operator.

She asked first for the ambulance service and directed them to Briar's Hall. She told them someone one would be waiting for them at the main entrance to direct them. That done, she hesitated for a moment, and then asked the operator to put her through to her police station.

But she was lucky, and it was Walter Swinburne who once again answered. Right at that moment, she didn't think she could have taken a haranguing from Inspector Jennings. She gave the old PC a succinct report on what had happened, which drew a gasp from the housekeeper, who was hovering in the doorway and listening in unashamedly on the conversation.

Trudy concluded by asking for supporting officers to come to the Hall at once, and then hung up.

She turned to the housekeeper, who now looked less like a dragon guarding the de Lacey home and the family skeletons rattling around in their cupboards, and more like a scared, bewildered, middle-aged woman.

Trudy let out a long, slow breath. 'I need you to wait at the front steps and tell the ambulance men, and the police officers when they arrive, that they need to go to the lake, nearest the gazebo where Lallie Clark lives. You'll have to direct them. Can you do that?' she asked gently.

'Yes, ma'am.'

'Good.' Trudy reached out and took the housekeeper's cold hands in her own and gave them a reassuring squeeze, then she left and went back through the hall.

But she wasn't running now. In fact, she felt almost totally drained of energy. Even contemplating the walk back to the lake made her feel unbearably weary. Nevertheless, she staggered slightly down the steps and set off doggedly across the lawn.

Just as she was rounding the yew hedge, however, she had to swerve to a private spot between the laurel bushes, where she was quietly, but comprehensively sick.

After that, she felt a bit better.

By the time she made it back to the shed, she wanted nothing more than to lie down on the grass, weep uselessly, and then go to sleep. Probably in that order.

Clement was waiting by the open shed door. He was bent slightly at the waist, one hand nursing his ribs and wincing with every breath. When he saw her he straightened up, however, and managed a wan smile.

Trudy looked him squarely in the eye. Needing to know the answer, but dreading it, she asked fatalistically, 'Is he dead?'

Chapter 39

Half an hour later, Clement and Trudy, sitting exhausted and shaken on the front lawn of Briar's Hall, watched as the ambulance sped away with Lallie Clark inside. Clement watched it go with mixed feelings.

One bitter half of him almost wished that its patient would be dead on arrival. Another part of him hoped that he'd make a full recovery, but only for Trudy's sake.

DI Jennings was sitting in his car, trying to make up his mind whether to feel furious or jubilant. He'd been informed that someone from Special Branch was on their way to the Hall, and that he was to await their arrival and cooperate with them fully.

Clement had seen his arrival first, and had managed to stop him before he got to Trudy and started battering her with questions. Instead, he'd filled the inspector in on everything that had happened, emphasising the fact that they had only been trying to follow his orders, and that the totally unexpected and unprovoked attack could not possibly have been anticipated by either of them.

It had come, quite literally, out of the blue.

Jennings, perhaps sensing how close his WPC was to collapse, had allowed himself to be steered back to his car, where he now pondered and waited. Could he spin it that the investigation had been a total success? After all, it seemed clear now that the boy had indeed been murdered, and that his officer had apprehended the killer responsible. Even saving the life of the city coroner in doing so.

On the other hand, Special Branch and the people they answered to in Whitehall weren't going to be pleased. Inspectors Robinson and Brown had left his office thinking it had all been hushed up and that the case was closed.

Of course, the press hadn't yet got wind of what had happened here, and if he knew the powers that be, they would quickly slap a notice on the whole affair, meaning it couldn't be published in the press anyway. So it might not be such an unmitigated disaster!

He sighed and ran a hand through his hair, glaring out of his car window at the two people who seemed intent on making his life a misery.

Trudy, though, was unaware of her inspector's gloom.

Instead, now that she'd got her breath back, and she knew that Lallie Clark wasn't dead, she had regained some of her equilibrium.

For a while now they'd been sitting in companionable silence, too exhausted to think much, let alone talk. Trudy, for one, had simply been glad to glory in the fact that she was still alive and breathing.

Now, though, her restless mind began to demand answers.

But the first thing that popped out of her mouth took her by surprise. 'Did I imagine it, or at one point did it began to rain potatoes in that shed?'

Beside her Clement started, then grunted a short bark of laughter. 'Yes it did. When I stepped into the shed behind you, for a moment I couldn't make out anything. The first moment I knew that something was wrong was when you reached for your truncheon and began to crouch down. The next second you screamed at me to watch out.'

Trudy nodded. Funny, to Dr Ryder it had all seemed to happen more or less at once. To her, those moments had felt almost years apart.

'I saw Lallie swinging a scythe your way, and looked around for anything to use as a weapon to stop him. But all that was near me was this lumpy sack by the door,' Clement went on tiredly. 'So I hefted it up, meaning to throw it at him and knock him off balance, but it felt remarkably heavy – too heavy for me to heave it. So instead I stepped over you and held it up over you, hoping to deflect the blow.'

Trudy nodded. So that was why he was standing so close that his knees bumped into her.

'And when he swung the scythe down, it cut through the sack and potatoes poured out,' he went on to explain. 'Luckily, their bulk was enough to slow his swing, since the blade chopped through one or two potatoes and I think the tip of it even got stuck in one. Anyway, I threw myself at him and pinned him to the wall. Sorry, but I must have trampled over you at some point.'

'I didn't mind, believe me,' she said with an attempt at a laugh. And then she said quietly, 'Dr Ryder, you saved my life.'

Beside her Clement shrugged. 'And about two seconds later, you saved mine,' he pointed out just as quietly.

Trudy blinked. Had she? 'I'm not so sure about that.'

Clement sighed heavily. 'I had a grip on his arm holding the scythe, but he punched me in the side and I was going down. If you hadn't stepped in, he'd have buried that blade in my back. And I can assure you, I'd then have been quite dead. Trust me – I'm not only a coroner, but I was once a surgeon. I know about these things.'

Trudy nodded. And again managed a small laugh. 'So we're even then.'

'I'd say so.'

For a moment they were silent, contemplating this, then Trudy said, 'When I first saw him, and realised he was going to try and kill me, I saw such a look on his face… it was brutal – inhuman even. Do you think the war did that to him?'

'Almost certainly, I'd say,' Clement agreed heavily. 'I served in France, in the Red Cross tents. All I can remember is endless days of surgery – men, boys some of them, coming in with horrific injuries. We did the best we could to patch them up and save their lives… But some of them…' Clement reached up and ran a weary hand through his hair. 'Sometimes I wondered if they wouldn't have been better off dead. I know that's a rotten thing to say, but… A friend of mine worked in the psychiatric wards, and some of the things he told me about what the trauma did to them… Oh, let's not think about it,' he advised flatly.

'All right,' Trudy was happy to agree. Then, after a moment's thought, she said sadly, 'We really read him all wrong, didn't we? Lallie, I mean.'

Clement nodded. 'Yes. I think most people did.'

'He seemed so… I don't know, harmless,' Trudy said, shaking her head. 'We assumed he was kind and placid and harmless. I know we were told he was simple, when he clearly wasn't, but we just accepted it as a fact. Why did we *do* that? Was it just because he seemed to shamble everywhere? Or the fact that he hardly spoke – and when he did, in that slow, broad, country way of his?'

'Probably. It's easier to just pigeonhole people,' Clement said wearily. 'Lallie was quiet and almost invisible – it was easy to assume he was a bit soft in the head. But in fact, I don't suppose he was any less intelligent than anyone else in the village,' Clement said.

'So what exactly are we saying happened here?' Trudy asked, looking around. Briar's Hall stood with its solid, square Cotswold stone glowing mellow in the evening sunshine, and the flowerbeds growing ever more colourful and defined in the setting sun. A blackbird was singing from the top of a bush, and a yellow brimstone butterfly fluttered past them in search of nectar. It looked like a paradise on earth.

But of course, there was no such thing. 'Lallie killed Eddie, didn't he?' she said simply.

Clement nodded. 'I think that's almost certain, yes. Until he regains consciousness and tells us his side of things, it has to be speculation. But I think it probably went something like this. Eddie and Emily found out about Oliver's "wrestling lessons" and I think Eddie confided as much to Lallie. Perhaps because he saw wrestling as a man's sport, and Emily soon lost interest in the spying game, he probably turned to Lallie to talk about it. Don't forget, he was their "friend". He made them a trolley to play on, and found bird's nests for them. So why wouldn't the boy tell him all about his discovery?'

Trudy shivered, but said resolutely, 'Go on.'

'Well, I think Lallie, who'd been in the war and was no innocent child, probably guessed immediately what the "wrestling" really amounted to. And once he knew where to look, it wouldn't take him long to check out the visitors to the boathouse and see for himself how things were.'

Trudy nodded. 'And he blackmailed him, didn't he? Oliver de Lacey, I mean. That's how he came to have all that money?'

'Almost certainly, I think,' Clement said. 'And, if you look at things from his point of view, why not?' the coroner said grimly. 'He went off to fight for King and country and saw things that would turn anybody's mind. A normal country lad, he couldn't have been prepared for the slaughter of the trenches, or any of the other atrocities he must have seen. And when he finally comes home from all that horror, what does he get? A country fit for heroes? Does he hell,' he said savagely.

'He finds his old mum dead, and their cottage rented out to someone else,' Trudy said emptily.

'And the squire of the manor generously offers him a gazebo to live in. No running water, nothing,' Clement agrees. 'Oh, and a job that probably pays peanuts, working in the gardens. And he's supposed to be *grateful*? No wonder he probably felt as if the de Laceys owed him. And when he discovered that Oliver wasn't the ladies' man he pretended to be – in fact, the exact opposite – the perfect opportunity to get some revenge was dropped in his lap. Not to mention a big pay-off.'

Trudy shifted slightly on the hard grass, but was too bone-weary to do much other than shift her position a bit.

'And somehow Eddie found out about it – the cash he was accumulating, I mean,' she said. 'He must have, because at some point Emily's little brother overheard he and Emily talking about money. It even makes sense why Emily should have said that the money wasn't theirs – because it belonged to Lallie. I wonder how they found out about it?'

Clement shrugged. 'If Lallie doesn't confess, we might never know. But most likely, they were still playing spies and picked on Lallie to follow one day, and saw him either making a pick-up, or hiding his stash. I assume he left notes for Oliver to hide the money at various drop-off points around the estate. And then he'd collect it, once he was sure de Lacey had gone.'

'Do you think he kept the money hidden in the shed?' Trudy asked.

'Could be. Or perhaps he had another hiding place, and they saw him go to it and were curious, and when he'd gone, found the "treasure" that George later heard them talking about.'

'Do you think they took some of it?' Trudy wondered out loud. 'And Lallie noticed? That's why he knew they were on to him?'

'Perhaps. Or maybe Eddie just asked him about it. He was only 11 years old, remember, and he wouldn't even know what the word blackmail meant. All he'd know was that his friend, the one who let him scrump the plums without chasing him, had an exciting hidden stash of money. He'd want to know all about it, and the simplest thing to do was ask.'

Trudy shuddered at the thought, just picturing it. So much

243

innocence! The little boy, asking Lallie about the money, and perhaps wondering aloud what his friend was going to do with it. Was he going to buy a car or a boat or go somewhere special on holiday? And all the time, his excited babble was as good as signing his own death warrant. For Lallie would know that it would only be a matter of time before the boy talked. And then…

'Lallie couldn't afford to let Oliver de Lacey learn who it was who was blackmailing him, could he?' she said. 'He'd have gone out of his way to make sure that the squire's powerful brother never knew who was fleecing him.'

'Yes, I think so – because Lallie had seen for himself how things worked in this world. How it was always the officers who had the upper hand. And how easy it was for the rich and powerful to deal with the likes of himself. He'd have known that he'd be in danger if his identity were to become known. And the boy was in a position to tell.'

Trudy felt a tear trickle down her cheek. 'So he lured Lallie to the well somehow that Easter Sunday. Probably with a note – that would have appealed to his sense of adventure, wouldn't it? A secret code, asking him to meet by the well. And then… he just shoved him in?' She could barely believe she'd just said those words. They seemed so heartless and cruel – all but unthinkable.

'No,' Clement surprised her by saying. 'A soldier like Lallie would have been taught how to kill someone quickly and silently. I think he must have snapped the boy's neck first. After all, if he'd just thrown the boy into the well, there was nothing to say the fall would be enough to kill him – or that he'd be knocked out and drowned. He could have survived and called for help, and been heard.'

'Oh please, stop!' Trudy wailed.

Wordlessly, Clement reached out and put his hand over hers.

For a while, they were silent again. Then, after a few minutes, they heard someone hail them.

244

It was the squire himself – Martin de Lacey. He was walking across the lawn, clearly having spotted the police cars still on the front drive, and then detouring as he spotted them. The bottoms of his trousers were wet, and Trudy remembered something about a tree coming down in a stream.

The poor squire. He'd returned home, expecting tea and a quiet evening, and instead he was walking into all this. But right now, she had little sympathy to spare.

Trudy groaned. 'What do we tell him?'

'The truth,' Clement said flatly.

'Do you think he knows his cousin is... you know?'

'Oh yes,' Clement said flatly. 'And Oliver's mother certainly knew.'

Trudy thought back to her interview with Sylvia de Lacey, and her agitation whenever 'strange men' wandering about the estate was mentioned, and silently agreed with him.

'What's going on here?' Martin de Lacey called, but just then Jennings, of all people, came to their rescue. Hearing the voice, and guessing the man's identity, the inspector quickly got out of his car and intercepted him. After all, here was a golden opportunity for him to shine and earn the approbation of an important man.

With a sigh of relief, they watched him intercept the squire and steer him back towards the house.

'We're going to have to talk to the Proctors, sooner rather than later,' Clement said wearily. 'Already word will be spreading like wildfire around the village that something's up. The ambulance won't have gone unnoticed. Or the fact that Oliver de Lacey was swept away in a big black car.'

Trudy nodded. 'Do you think he really is a spy? Like Burgess or Maclean, I mean?'

'I doubt it. But that's not really relevant is it?' Clement sighed. 'He was paying blackmail so that he wouldn't have to go to jail or face scandal and become a social pariah. The fact that it made him vulnerable to the Soviets as well was just one more reason to make sure the truth never came out.'

Trudy nodded. 'The Proctors' house isn't far,' she said. But in truth, she felt so tired she wasn't even sure she could stand, let alone walk to the village.

The coroner looked at her, and squeezed her hand. 'We'll talk to them in the morning, shall we?' he said gently.

'You'll come with me?'

'Yes. I'll come with you.'

'Thank you, Dr Ryder.'

'You're welcome, Constable Loveday.'

Epilogue

It was a big day in the Loveday household. The man from Rediffusion was bringing the television set, and Frank Loveday was looking at the newly bought television licence with satisfaction. Four quid it had cost him – all but a week's wages! But it was going to be worth it.

He was looking forward to watching *The Arthur Askey Show*, and that *Avengers* programme that all his mates down at the pub were going on about.

Barbara was also excited. She'd rearranged the furniture countless ways until she was finally happy with where the new set would go. She suspected that her daughter would want to watch *Dixon of Dock Green*, but for herself, she would be happy to start following the doings of the people on *Coronation Street*.

*

But upstairs, lying on her bed and staring listlessly at the ceiling, television was the last thing on Trudy's mind.

It had been three weeks since Lallie Clark had tried to kill her, and she still awoke in the middle of the night, sweating, knowing that she was going to die, all coiled up and just waiting for the glinting, slicing blade to decapitate her.

The bruises on her body had healed, but her mind was a long way from feeling whole and normal.

She'd been very careful to downplay what had happened that day at Briar's Hall, telling her parents only that she'd had to arrest someone on suspicion of the boy's murder.

Lallie Clark had regained consciousness and would be tried for the murder of Eddie Proctor. But there would be no public trial – afraid of what he might say in open court about Oliver de Lacey, the Home Office had made sure the trial would be carried out away from the public eye.

Little Emily de Lacey had been sent to a boarding school in Dorset. The family thought it best to get her away from the village for a while.

Marjorie Chandler, fickle to the end, had moved back to the States, taking her fortune with her.

And the Proctors… The Proctors had buried their son.

She turned restlessly on her bed and eyed the wallpaper morosely.

They'd solved the case, but Trudy couldn't feel any sense of kudos or satisfaction, for neither she, nor Clement, had had any idea that Lallie was the killer. It wasn't as if they'd reasoned it out and been rewarded by nabbing their man. The answer had just been thrust upon them – at the point of a scythe.

It all seemed so random, Trudy thought unhappily. If she and Clement hadn't gone back to the Hall, or seen Lallie, or gone to the lake, or heard the shed door slamming – or any other number of things – then Lallie would have packed his suitcase, taken his blood money and disappeared into the evening.

But one thing was for sure. If Dr Clement Ryder hadn't been there with her, she wouldn't be here now. She wouldn't be lying on her bed, listening to her parents below playfully bickering over what television programme they were going to watch first.

248

She would be dead.

For the first time since joining the police force, she had been forced to face her own mortality.

She'd always known that she wasn't as clever as Dr Ryder. That she wasn't as strong as Sergeant O'Grady, or as experienced as DI Jennings. But all these things could be overcome. With time, she would acquire wisdom and experience.

But the one thing she couldn't do was make herself *brave*.

Somehow, she had to get over this setback and grow a backbone. Get back to her old confident self and do her job without second-guessing herself.

Otherwise her whole career would hang in the balance.

*

Desperate to know how Trudy will overcome her
run-in with Lallie? If you want to be the first to know
about the next gripping Ryder and Loveday case, sign
up to Faith Martin's email list here:
po.st/FaithMartinNewsletter

Dear Reader,

Thank you so much for taking the time to read this book – we hope you enjoyed it! If you did, we'd be so appreciative if you left a review.

Here at HQ Digital we are dedicated to publishing fiction that will keep you turning the pages into the early hours. We publish a variety of genres, from heartwarming romance, to thrilling crime and sweeping historical fiction.

To be the first to hear about new releases, competitions, 99p eBooks and promotions, sign up to our monthly email newsletter: po.st/HQSignUp

🐦 *@HQDigitalUK*

f *facebook.com/HQDigitalUK*

Are you a budding writer?
We're also looking for authors to join the HQ Digital family!
Please submit your manuscript to:

HQDigital@harpercollins.co.uk.

Hope to hear from you soon!

ONE PLACE. MANY STORIES